RULES of

Summer

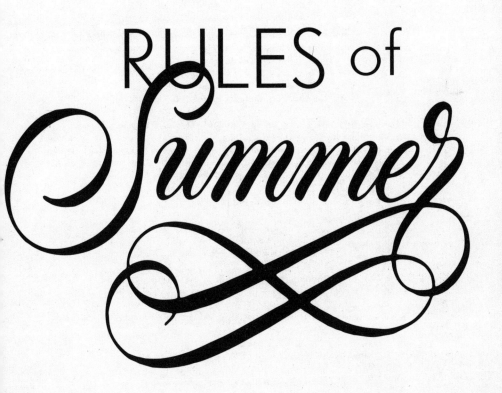

RULES of Summer

a novel by

JOANNA PHILBIN

poppy

LITTLE, BROWN AND COMPANY
New York   Boston

Copyright © 2013 by Joanna Philbin
Excerpt from *Since Last Summer* copyright © 2014 by Joanna Philbin

Poppy

Hachette Book Group
237 Park Avenue, New York, NY 10017
Visit our website at lb-teens.com

Poppy is an imprint of Little, Brown and Company.
The Poppy name and logo are trademarks of Hachette Book Group, Inc.

The publisher is not responsible for websites (or their content) that are not owned by the publisher.

First Paperback Edition: April 2014
First published in hardcover in June 2013 by Little, Brown and Company

Library of Congress Cataloging-in-Publication Data

Philbin, Joanna.
Rules of summer / Joanna Philbin. — First edition.
    pages cm
    "Poppy."
    Summary: Spending the summer working as an errand girl for the Rule family in the Hamptons, seventeen-year-old Rory befriends the family's teenaged daughter and develops feelings for their older son, but she finds that societal rules can be hard to break.
    ISBN 978-0-316-21205-2 (hc) — ISBN 978-0-316-21204-5 (pb)
    [1. Social classes—Fiction.   2. Wealth—Fiction.   3. Summer employment—Fiction.
4. Hamptons (N.Y.)—Fiction.]   I. Title.
    PZ7.P515Ru 2013
    [Fic]—dc23

                                                                2012030666

10 9 8 7 6 5 4

RRD-C

Printed in the United States of America

Book design by Tracy Shaw

Also by JOANNA PHILBIN:

The Daughters

The Daughters Break the Rules

The Daughters Take the Stage

The Daughters Join the Party

For Mom

CHAPTER ONE

She really should have just told someone. Just dropped it casually into conversation the last day of school, when people were talking about their summer plans. *Oh, really? You're going to tennis camp? You're spending a month at Wildwood? You got that internship in New York that you applied for six months ago?*

Well, that's great.

I'll be spending this summer in the Hamptons.

Rory looked up from her notebook and out the train window. She hadn't expected so many potato fields. Brown furrows lined with lush green potato plants passed by in a blur, and here and there, at the edge of the fields, a cedar shingle house stood watch. But these houses didn't look like old, decrepit farmhouses. They looked like newly built mansions. There definitely weren't mansions on the chicken and dairy farms in Stillwater, New Jersey, at least as far as she knew. And there wasn't this radiant sunlight, either, she thought, looking up at the cobalt-blue sky. It probably had to do with the ocean to the south and the bay to the north, but she'd never seen light like this before. She wished she'd known how pretty it was here when she was trying to sell her mom on the idea. But it probably wouldn't have worked.

"Errand girl?" her mom had asked when Rory had finally told her the plan. "What the hell is that?"

Her mom had stood next to her, opening a bottle of wine. Lana McShane was never home from work more than a few minutes before she had a bottle of Charles Shaw Chardonnay out of the fridge and on the counter, and a corkscrew in her manicured hand. Rory watched her mom twist in the corkscrew, then put the bottle between her knees and pull. *Thwock*, went the cork. Lana was barely a hundred pounds soaking wet, but she'd never met a wine bottle that she couldn't handle.

"I guess it means I'll be running errands," Rory said, slicing through a fat yellow onion. "Whatever they need. They weren't specific over e-mail."

"Are they going to pay you?"

"I'll be staying with them for free. In their mansion on the beach. They don't need to pay me."

Her mom shook her red hair and took a long sip.

"I don't know why you always need a glass of wine ten minutes after you get home," Rory said.

"It relaxes me. You try cutting hair for nine hours." She placed the glass down on the counter. "What about Mario? Does he know?"

"It's a pizza place. I think he'll find someone else." Rory tipped the onions into the pan and watched them sizzle. "And I have some money saved up from this past year. So you don't have to worry."

"It's not the money. It's you." Rory could hear her mom digging in her purse for her cigarettes. "You're the smartest kid in your class. If you wanted to study abroad, I'd understand. If you wanted to get a job in the city, fine. But to go off and live with some family you don't even know? So you can pick up after them like your aunt?"

"Fee's been working for them my whole life," Rory pointed out. "If they were awful, she would have left a long time ago."

"But...what are you going to do out there?" her mom continued, still digging. "Those aren't your people. You think they're going to let you in? That you're going to join their clubs and go to their parties? Oh, here they are."

Rory turned to see her mom pull a Merit out of the pack and light it with her favorite lighter, the one that said LAS VEGAS in cheery blue script.

"You're going to be a glorified servant," her mom said, taking a drag on the Merit. "Is that what you want?" She blew out the smoke and narrowed her green eyes, the ones Rory wished she'd inherited.

"I don't care about being a servant. The whole point is to get out of here," Rory said. "Widen my horizons. Don't you want me to get out of here? *Ever?*"

"Just say it," her mom said, taking her glass. "The whole point is to get away from me."

From you and *your boyfriend*, Rory thought as she turned back to the stove. Bryan, who yelled when he talked on the phone. Bryan, whose Xbox had taken up permanent residence in their living room. Bryan, who couldn't make rent at his own place, so naturally would be moving in with them, like her mom's last two disasters in tight jeans. Rory picked up the spatula and pried a burning onion slice from the pan.

"Let me know when it's ready," her mom said. Then she'd strolled out of the kitchen on her cowboy boots, trailing smoke and the smell of Paris eau de cologne. That had been the end of the discussion.

Rory checked her watch as the train rattled past a vegetable stand. She thought of Sophie and Trish, probably sunning themselves at the lake right now, taking advantage of the last free weekday before they started their jobs on Monday. Every summer she'd meet them after her shift at Mario's, and they'd hang out at the mall or in front of the frozen-yogurt place, and talk about their days. Now she was more than a hundred miles away. The farthest she'd ever been from home was New York City, and the last time had been three years ago. She'd gone in with her mom for her fourteenth birthday and seen *Mamma Mia!* Or at least, half of *Mamma Mia!*—they'd had to leave early because her mom was almost positive that Martin or Tommy or Gordon or whomever she was dating at the time was cheating on her and she wanted to catch him in the act. To nobody's shock, she did.

"East Hampton," the conductor announced over the PA. "East Hampton, next."

The train was still moving, but passengers leaped out of their seats to grab their bags off the luggage rack. Quickly, she reached into her purse and flipped open the cracked Estée Lauder compact she'd had since ninth grade. After six hours of traveling, her wavy dark brown hair had gone frizzy from the humid June afternoon, and her kohl eyeliner had bled into a raccoonlike mask around her hazel eyes. She thought about trying to fix things but decided it was a lost cause. She'd never been pretty enough—in her opinion—to care too much about looking perfect, unlike her mom, who'd been beautiful enough to be preoccupied by it for her entire life. Still, she slipped on a plastic headband and ran the last dregs of some Wet n Wild Bronze Berry gloss over her full lips. It didn't hurt to clean up a little. Rich people liked that. Actually, her aunt never used the word *rich*. *Polished* was the word she always used about the Rules. *They're a very polished family.*

The train finally screeched to a full stop. She grabbed her duffel bag, her book bag, and her favorite vintage black leather motorcycle jacket off the luggage rack and moved toward the doors. When she stepped out on the platform, the air smelled like the ocean. Squinting in the bright sunlight, she made her way past the white station house and over to the small parking lot, where a line of SUVs and convertibles waited to pick people up. Rory glanced at the people streaming over to the cars. The men wore polo shirts and khaki shorts and loafers with no socks. The women wore toothpick-thin jeans and delicate silk cardigans and flat sandals with just a sliver of beaded leather between the toes. Rory looked down at her own outfit. Her light denim miniskirt, sleeveless yellow T-shirt, and platform slides had looked stylish that morning, but now she wasn't so sure.

"Rory?"

She turned to see a guy with short brownish-blond hair and a tanned, chiseled face coming toward her in the crowd. His mirrored sunglasses gave him the air of someone paid to be athletic. Or maybe it was the matching white T-shirt and shorts.

"Hey, I'm Steve," he said. "The tennis pro for the Rules. Fee asked me to come get you."

For a moment, she felt her usual panic at coming face-to-face with a cute, athletic guy in his twenties and then willed it away. "Oh, hi," she said. "Nice to meet you."

"Here, let me take that," he said, taking her duffel and throwing it onto his shoulder. "We're over here."

Rory watched Steve walk ahead of her. Even from behind, he was good-looking, with a long, narrow back and sun-browned calves. But she put his looks out of her mind. When it came to good-looking guys, she knew her role: best buddy. It was so much easier that way, listening to their problems, making them laugh, giving them advice. And above all, staying away from drama. Because, with guys, there was always drama. And who needed more drama when she had so much of it at home already?

Steve aimed the remote at a shiny silver Mercedes convertible parked in the last spot, and the trunk popped up. "Careful, the seats might be a little hot," he said.

Rory got inside and shut the heavy door. A man walking by stared at the car with visible envy.

Steve opened the door and folded himself behind the wheel. "All right, let's get on our way," he said, turning the key in the ignition. The engine purred, quiet but strong. "Nice car, huh? The Rules just got it last week."

"*Nice* is an understatement," Rory said.

Steve laughed. "I know what you mean," he said as he backed

out of the space. "Definitely makes my Jetta seem a little lame. So how was the trip? Not too many stops?"

"It was fine," Rory said.

"That's good. Sometimes the jitney can be faster."

"Why do they call it the jitney?" she asked.

"Because people here don't like to say the word *bus*," he said with a grin.

Rory chuckled. "Got it," she said. Steve seemed funny, despite his tennis-god looks.

"So where are you from in New Jersey?" Steve asked, flipping on his turn signal.

"Sussex County. A town called Stillwater."

"*Still*water?" he asked.

"It's near the Pennsylvania border. It's really pretty, lots of farms and lakes. Very country. Where are you from? Out here?"

"Hampton Bays," he said, glancing at her. "Which is not really the Hamptons. Or at least, the *exclusive* Hamptons," Steve said, using his fingers to make quotation marks. "It's out near Westhampton, back toward the city. Went to high school out here, then went down to Florida for college. And then, after I quit playing on tour, I came back here. It's great. Lots of tennis lovers. Including Lucy and Larry."

"Lucy and Larry?" she asked.

"The Rules," he said. "They're awesome. Really down-to-earth."

They began driving along a quaint-looking main street lined with shops and cafés. American flags hung over some of the store windows, and baskets of impatiens dripped color from the tops of lampposts. A group of towheaded kids walked down the sidewalk eating ice-cream cones. It could have been any main street in any East Coast town, but there was an unmistakable sheen of money over all of it. Almost every store awning dripped luxury: James Perse. Intermix. Ralph Lauren. Tiffany. "Wow," she said, looking out the window. "This place is so . . . upscale."

"Yeah, it's gotten that way," Steve said. "It didn't used to be. There's just so much money here now."

Rory gazed at the pretty storefronts and forest-green benches. There wasn't a scrap of litter anywhere. *It's like Martha Stewart designed a town*, she thought. *High*.

"So how many kids do the Rules have?" she asked.

"Four," Steve said. "Two boys, two girls. And their youngest is about your age. You're seventeen, right?"

"Right," she said.

"So's Isabel. You'll have a lot of fun with her. She's like the queen of the Hamptons."

Fee had never mentioned Isabel, which was strange, only because adults usually thought that any two people the same age would instantly become best friends. But maybe Fee knew that anyone qualified to be called the queen of the Hamptons probably wouldn't have too much in common with someone like her. Rory had friends, but nobody would ever call her the social director of Stillwater.

They turned onto a quiet street lined with stately homes and trees that formed a canopy overhead with their branches. "Lily Pond Lane," Rory said, glancing at the sign. "That's a pretty name."

"This is a famous street," Steve said. "It's where all the millionaires built their summer homes a hundred years ago. Including Lucy Rule's great-grandfather."

"So the home's been in her family that long?"

"Yep," Steve said. As they drove down the street, the homes began to be hidden by tall manicured hedges. "And now she owns it. Her dad willed it to her when he died."

"And what about Mr. Rule?" Rory asked. "Is he also..."

"Old money?" Steve asked.

Rory had never heard that term before, but she nodded.

He turned left into a break in the hedges and pulled up to a pair of tall iron gates. "Technically, yes. But his father was found to be bankrupt after he died. So he had to go into business for himself. He works in commercial real estate." Steve lowered his window. "New money, old money—it's starting to become the same thing out here," he said with an ironic smile. He typed a code into a small security box just outside the window. With a soft clang, the gates swung open.

There was the crunch of gravel under the tires as they rounded a bend, past a stand of elm trees, and suddenly they were driving alongside the longest, widest front lawn she'd ever seen. The grass was perfectly trimmed, emerald green, and as large and flat as a football field. And perched on a slight hill at the far end of the lawn, as unreal and ephemeral-looking as something in a dream, was a sprawling shingle home.

"Over there's the tennis court," Steve said, pointing to the other side of the lawn. "And the changing cabanas, and the gym."

Through another group of trees she could see the bluish-green tennis court. A hopper full of balls stood on spiderlike legs.

"And in back, behind the house, is the pool and the beach," he added.

As they neared the house, she could see more details. The shingles had once been brown but had now faded to an elegant silvery gray. The third-floor windows were arched, with dormers, and three crumbling brick chimneys rose up from the roof. But the front door, the portico, and all the windows were covered in bright white paint, giving the house a crisp, new look despite its feeling of age.

"This is just the weekend house?" Rory asked.

"That's right," Steve said. "Most of the year, they live in the city. But their apartment in town isn't nearly this big."

She thought of her own house—a boxy bilevel with a slate roof and peeling yellowish-green paint. All her friends lived in the same kind of house, too. Could someone even call that a house after seeing this one? And did anyone *need* to live in a house this big?

Steve drove past the front of the house, where the gravel drive wound around an oval garden of boxwoods, and veered left toward a five-car garage. The row of cars parked outside ranged from a dusty black VW Jetta—Steve's car, Rory noted—to a gleaming black Porsche convertible. He slid the car between a silver Prius and the Porsche, then turned off the ignition. "We're here," he said.

"Great," she said brightly.

He turned to look at her. "Don't be intimidated. They're really cool. You'll see."

He got out of the car, and she realized that her heart was

pounding. Just before she got out, she remembered her black leather jacket lying on the floor near her feet. She picked it up, but already it felt useless and outdated, like an old party dress.

She followed Steve past a garden of pink roses and toward a side entrance. Below her she could hear the muted sound of waves. She'd almost forgotten that this house was on the beach.

Suddenly, the back door swung open, and the short, solid frame of Aunt Fee leaped onto the paving stones, her pale arms in the air. "There you are!" she cried. "My god, you're taller than I am!"

"Hi, Fee!" Rory said, giving in to her aunt's unforgiving hug. "It's been a while."

"That's because your mother has a very odd definition of *family*," she said, squeezing Rory's ribs.

Rory had always found it hard to believe that Fee and her mom were sisters. Lana was delicate and slender, while Fee, older by a few years, was compact and sturdy, with cheerful brown eyes that disappeared into squints when she smiled. The only thing the sisters shared was red hair, but Fee's was streaked with gray.

"I'm so excited to be here," Rory said, pulling away from Fee's hug. "I can hear the ocean."

"I'll take you down there in a bit." Fee plucked at the front of her forest-green polo shirt. That and a pair of pressed khaki pants seemed to comprise her uniform. "Steve, I'll take her bag."

Steve handed Rory's duffel bag to Fee. "Rory, I'll see you soon. Maybe on the tennis court?" He clapped his hand over her shoulder. "Have fun here."

"Thanks." Rory watched him walk back toward the cars. It hadn't occurred to her that she might play tennis or have fun while she was here, but hearing Steve mention both eased her nerves. Fee pulled her toward the door.

"Sorry I couldn't come get you," said Fee as she walked back into the house. "But things are a little hectic around here. We're having our first dinner party tonight and poor Eduardo is beside himself."

Rory stepped into the house, and as her eyes adjusted to the light, she noticed two things: She was standing in a long hall lined with doors, and something was scrambling around her feet. She looked down to see a tiny white dog trying to jump onto her legs. "Oh my god," she said. "Is this a puppy?"

"Puppy or dog, I'm not really sure," said Fee. "It's Mrs. Rule's. Trixie."

Rory crouched down to pet her. "She's adorable," she said as Trixie began to lick her hand. "Is she a Maltese?"

"Maltipoo. Or cockapoo. Something *poo*. Okay, Trixie!" she ordered. "Go back to your place!"

The dog jumped slightly and then trotted back to her bed at the end of the hall.

"My mom still won't let us get a dog," Rory said.

"Because she keeps dating them," Fee said, rolling her eyes. "Come on. You're down here." She began to walk toward the end of the hall. Fee walked with purpose, swinging her arms. Rory could already tell that Fee felt at home here.

"So how big is the staff here?" she asked.

"Well, there's me, Eduardo the chef, and Bianca the house manager," Fee said, as they passed a laundry room. "We're the live-ins. Then there's the help that comes in."

"Comes in?" Rory asked.

"Laura the masseuse, Siddha the yoga teacher, and Frederika, who does Mrs. Rule's hair. Steve, the tennis pro. And then there are the people they hire to come in and serve for parties. Like tonight." They finally stopped at a closed door. "So this is where you'll be staying," Fee said, opening the door.

Rory caught her breath. The room was easily three times the size of her bedroom at home and a hundred times more stylized. The king-size bed was covered with a creamy-white duvet and a pile of blue-and-white bed pillows edged in lace. A vintage nautical map of eastern Long Island hung above the latticework headboard. The nightstands, also painted cream, held a stack of the latest hardcover novels wedged beside crystal lamps. The other furniture—a curved-leg desk, a stool, and a pair of tufted club chairs—were also cream-colored, while the walls were painted the softest shade of blue. And across from the bed, nestled inside a shabby-chic white armoire, was a sleek flat-screen TV. "*This* is my room?" she asked. "Are you sure?"

"Of course," said Fee, ignoring Rory's surprise. "And the bathroom is in here."

Fee dropped Rory's duffel bag on the velvet bench at the foot of the bed and led the way into the bathroom. Rory gaped. The glass steam shower had a wide marble bench inside, big enough for her to fall asleep on if she wanted to. The sunken marble tub had a silver faucet that curved up and over like the neck of a swan.

"And there are plenty of products if you forgot anything," Fee said, opening the drawers under the sink to reveal a tidy row of shampoos and conditioners.

"This is beautiful," Rory said as they walked back into the bedroom. "Why have you never talked about how nice it is here?"

Fee shrugged. "After a while, you get used to it," she said, glancing around the room. "Some people work in an office. I work here."

Rory smiled. For years, her mom had felt sorry for Aunt Fee. "At least I'm not a housekeeper," she'd say whenever one of her checks bounced or the county cut off their heat. But here was Aunt Fee, living in the midst of all this luxury and beauty. If only her mom could see this, Rory thought. She'd never say anything like that again.

"So, let's get into it," said Fee, unzipping Rory's duffel bag. "Is she still working at that salon?"

"Most of the time, yeah."

"And the new boyfriend? Is he really twenty-one?"

"That's what he says."

"And he's moving in?"

"They always do."

Fee shook her head. "Your father must be thrilled."

"It's not like we really talk about it when I go to his house for Thanksgiving," Rory said, taking out a heap of folded T-shirts. "He and Sharon are having a third kid, by the way."

"I wonder if your mom ever regrets what she did," Fee said. "Driving away a good man like that. At least you still get to see him."

Just barely, Rory thought. No matter how hard she worked in school, no matter how diligently she returned his e-mails and phone calls, her dad seemed to see her the same way he saw her mother: a flake that was best kept at a distance.

"You know, I'm proud of you," Fee said, smoothing the wrinkles out of an unpacked dress. "You could be just like her. Chasing boys, staying out all night. She'd probably love it if you turned out like that, just so she'd have some company. But you're a hard worker." Her eyes were full of pride as she looked at Rory. "Smart. Disciplined. You're too independent to get involved with boys."

Was that the word for it? Rory wondered. Her friends said other things. *Afraid. Closed off. Too sensitive.* Sophie had the best term for it: *relationship-averse.*

"Thanks," she said, dumping the T-shirts in the middle drawer of the dresser. "So, what can I do first?"

"Yes, let's put you to work," said a voice, and Rory whirled around.

A small woman with a sharp face and piercing eyes stood in the doorway. Silver hair fell past her narrow shoulders, and she was so thin that the belt on her silk wrap dress looked like it had been pulled around her waist at least three times.

"Rory, this is the house manager," Fee said. "Bianca Vellum. Bianca, this is Rory. My niece."

"Oh," Rory said, hoping she didn't look too startled. "Hi."

Bianca stepped into the room. "Welcome," she said, approaching Rory. She shook Rory's hand slowly, regally. "I hope you had a good trip?"

"Yes. It was very easy."

"I always prefer taking the jitney rather than the train," she said, "but to each his own." She smiled faintly and patted one of the bed pillows in a proprietary way. "How do you like your room?"

"Oh, it's incredible," Rory said. "I mean, it's the nicest room I've ever seen."

Bianca smiled. "Good. And getting back to your question, about what you could do first, I'm wondering if you have any experience with serving?"

"Serving?" Rory glanced at Fee. "Like, at the table?"

"Bianca, she just got here," Fee said. "I really don't think that—"

"The person we hired for tonight just canceled," Bianca cut in, as if Fee weren't even speaking. "Can't say I'm that surprised. Things get worse every summer. So I'm wondering if you might be able to step in for them."

"But the plan was for her to run errands—" Fee attempted.

"The plan was for her to step in when we needed her," Bianca said crisply. She turned to Rory with her eyebrows raised, waiting. "So...do you have experience?"

"Well, I've waitressed," Rory said. "At a pizza place. Mario's. I'm sure I can pick it up."

"Wonderful. We can give you some pointers." She stepped closer on her ballet flats. "And you should know that this is the first time we've had family of staff here for the summer." Bianca didn't blink.

"Oh?" Rory said.

"But Mrs. Rule is a *very* generous employer. And when I told her that we could use an extra pair of hands around here, to run errands, pick people up from the train, do the shopping...well, she thought it was a terrific idea."

"And when I asked her if Rory could stay," Fee said, "she *really* thought that it was a terrific idea."

Bianca shot Fee a look. *So they don't get along*, Rory thought. *Great.*

"Why don't you unpack and Fee can get you situated?" Bianca said. "I'll have Eduardo make you a little lunch, and then I can give you a tour. Anything you don't eat?"

"No. I eat everything."

Bianca's eyes flicked up and down Rory's body. "Yes, I'm sure you do. I'll see you soon." She glided out of the room and closed the door.

"Don't pay any attention to her," Fee said before Rory could say anything. "She just likes to intimidate people."

"She doesn't want me here, does she?"

Fee put her hands on her waist. "I have seniority over her. So it doesn't matter."

Rory thought for a moment. Then she headed straight out the door. "Uh, Ms. Vellum?" she called out to the empty hall. "Ms. Vellum?"

A swinging door opened, and Bianca stepped into the hall.

"I just want you to know that you can count on me a hundred percent," Rory said. "With whatever—serving at a dinner party or running errands, anything you need. I just wanted you to know that."

"Very good," Bianca said.

"And I am very, very happy to be here," Rory went on, as Fee came to stand by her side. "I know that this is a big deal to be a guest here for the summer, and I just want you to know how much I appreciate it."

Before Bianca could reply, a girl's voice called down from upstairs. "Has anyone seen my Calypso dre-ess? The white one with the silk be-elt?"

Rory noticed Bianca and Fee look past her at a back staircase Rory hadn't noticed. A moment later, heavy footsteps pounded down the stairs.

"Anyone?" called the voice. "Fee-*eee*?"

A girl appeared on the landing, and with one glimpse of her straight blond hair, large blue eyes, and long, tan legs, Rory knew that this was the queen of the Hamptons herself. The girl stared at Rory as if she were some kind of alien species and then tossed a curtain of blond hair insouciantly over her shoulder. "Who's this?" she asked, playing with a gold charm bracelet around her right wrist.

"Isabel, this is Rory," Fee said. "My niece. The one we told you about. She's going to be staying with us for the summer."

Isabel looked at Rory blankly. "Right," she said, with a distinct lack of enthusiasm.

"Rory, this is Isabel," Fee said. "You two are the same age."

Rory wanted to cringe. "Hi," she said, and raised her hand in a slight wave.

Isabel rubbed the inside of her calf with her bare foot. She didn't smile or speak.

"And I have your dress," Fee said. "I'll bring it up when I've pressed it."

"Okay," she said, turning back to Fee. "I just couldn't find it."

"Don't you want to say hello to Rory?" Fee asked, in a voice that wavered between sweet and demanding. "I think it would be nice if you welcomed her. Seeing as you're the first she's met of the family."

Rory cringed once more. Something about this girl made her want to crawl back to her room.

"Welcome," Isabel said with a sarcastic smile. She ran a hand through her hair. "Ten bucks you're gonna wish you'd stayed at home." Then she stomped up the steps, leaving the three of them standing in silence. A door shut upstairs.

"She's just a little shy," Fee said.

Rory didn't say anything.

"I need to speak to Eduardo," Bianca said, as if nothing had happened. "We'll have lunch for you soon." She pushed through the swinging door into the kitchen, leaving Fee and Rory alone in the hall.

"She doesn't seem shy," Rory said.

"She's also spoiled," Fee said, steering Rory back to her room with an arm around her shoulders. "Someone else you shouldn't take personally."

"And Bianca?" she asked in a low voice. "What's the excuse there?"

"She worked for Oprah for six months. Now she thinks she knows everything." She stayed on the threshold as Rory walked back into her bedroom. "Really. Don't worry about anything. It's going to be wonderful."

"Okay," Rory said, looking reluctantly back at her bag.

"I need to bring up that dress," Fee said. "If you need me, just use the intercom system on the phone. And my room is downstairs, off the rec room. But I'll be back. Don't you worry. Just make yourself at home."

"All right."

Fee closed the door.

Rory looked around at the bed, at the overstuffed chairs in the corner, at the walk-in closet. For the next ten weeks, this room would be hers. She pulled out her phone and took a picture of it. My room!, she wrote in a text, then sent the photo to Sophie and Trish. She hoped that didn't seem like bragging. But there was no way she was not going to share this with them.

She sat on the bed, feeling the duvet cover collapse softly under her weight. She felt a pang for her friends. They were nothing like that girl upstairs. She'd been so cold, so snobby. Had she done the right thing, coming here? She leaned back against the pillows and closed her eyes. A soft breeze came through the open window, and in the distance, she could hear the roll of the waves. *Yes*, she thought. This place was beautiful. She'd totally done the right thing. This was going to be an adventure. She'd just stay away from Isabel Rule. Which couldn't be that hard in a house this size.

CHAPTER TWO

"Here comes Tatiana," said Thayer Quinlan, as blasé as ever, as she twirled a lock of brown hair underneath her wide-brimmed hat. "Poor thing. I hear Link's cheating on her."

"Really?" Darwin whispered, craning her head to get a view of Tatiana on the patio. Her freckles were already getting red. "With who?"

"Kearcy McBride," Thayer mouthed, just before she placed a forkful of Cobb salad into her mouth.

"With Kearcy?" Darwin gasped. "But she has back fat. And bad hair."

Thayer gave Darwin a shrug, as if this were one of the world's great mysteries.

"Well, at least Tat looks thin," Darwin grumbled, going back to her piece of lettuce topped with hearts of palm. "That's one thing she's got going for her."

Isabel watched Tatiana Gould gamely make her way across the Georgica Club patio, past the barbed-wire smiles of young moms and society matrons sitting under the green-and-white-striped umbrellas. Last summer, Tatiana Amory had been the golden girl of the Georgica. Actually, every summer, Tatiana Amory had been the golden girl of the Georgica. As the longtime girlfriend of Link Gould, who was hot and funny and always on the verge of leaving Tatiana for one of the many women who threw themselves at him, she was the subject of envy and admiration. Tatiana's power over Link was legendary. Isabel had to admit, the girl had a gift. Every time Link claimed that he was feeling "trapped," or they would "take a break," she'd make sure to show up at Crown or the Lion with a gorgeous Brazilian model from her dad's fashion line, and Link would be on his knees. But he held out forever. When he finally proposed after six years of breaking up and getting back together, the members of the Georgica rejoiced. All of the Upper East Side was in a frenzy. *Town & Country* made her its cover girl, a team of French seamstresses made the dress, and her parents threw the happy couple an engagement party at the Cosmopolitan Club.

Now, Tatiana walked bravely past the tables, aviators shielding her face. She had to know that people were talking about her. It was the Georgica patio, after all. But Isabel didn't feel that sorry for her. If she'd been the one married to Link Gould, she would have never let him get away.

"Let's talk to her," Thayer whispered.

"Oh no," said Darwin. "Don't call her over here—"

"Tatiana!" Thayer called out, waving. "Heeeyyy!"

Tatiana smiled and floated over to them. "Hey, guys," she said. "What's going on?"

"Isn't this just a gorgeous day?" Darwin asked.

22

"Yeah, it's pretty nice," Tatiana said, dismissing Darwin with one sentence. People did that to Darwin a lot. "Hey, Isabel. How was California?"

"Great," she said.

"I have some cousins in Montecito. I'll introduce you. They're wonderful."

They spoke briefly about other people they had in common, the merits of Roberta Freymann beachwear over Tory Burch, and then Tatiana moved off into the sunshine, and Isabel counted, *One...two...three...*

"So at their wedding?" Thayer said eagerly under her breath, pushing aside her plate. "Supposedly they only had sunblock and flip-flops in the welcome bags. And my mom spent, like, a thousand dollars on her airfare to Tulum."

"Are you *serious*?" asked Darwin. "That is so tacky."

"What did she want in the bag?" Isabel said, unable to stop herself. "A hundred-dollar bill?"

Thayer looked at her. "No," she said. "Where'd that come from?"

"Just kidding," Isabel said.

Thayer and Darwin exchanged a confused glance for a moment and then went back to eating.

Isabel pushed a slice of tomato around her plate. The old saying that rich people never talked about money was so wrong. Rich people talked about money *all the time*.

"So did you guys hear that the Knoxes are back?" Darwin asked. "I heard he's this huge Hollywood producer now. Maybe he'll cast me in his next blockbuster." Darwin's future stardom as

23

an actress was not a matter of if but when, at least according to Darwin. Her profile picture on Facebook, which she changed weekly, always featured her looking seductively into the camera, her reddish-gold hair falling over one eye. "Hey," she said to Isabel. "Weren't they really good friends with your family back in the day?"

"Who?" Isabel asked.

"The Knoxes. Hello." Darwin rolled her eyes.

"I guess so. I was just a baby. I barely remember." An uneasiness settled over her, but she pushed it away. "But I'm sure he'll assume you're the next Natalie Portman."

Darwin smiled wistfully at the thought.

"So what's going on tonight?" Isabel asked. "Please tell me something decent is happening."

Thayer and Darwin exchanged a knowing glance. "Aston's having a party," Thayer said. "And he wanted me to make sure to invite you."

Isabel stared back at Thayer's shrewd brown eyes. Thayer would never be a beautiful girl, but she'd gotten prettier this past year. The nose job had helped.

"I think I'll pass," Isabel said.

"Have some mercy on the guy and *go*," Darwin urged. "You're the whole reason he's throwing it. He's been waiting a year to see you again."

"The least you can do after breaking his heart is go to his stupid party to win you back," Thayer added.

"A, it's not like I wanted to break his heart," Isabel said. "And B, I don't think I owe him anything."

"Just tell us why you broke up with him," Darwin said. "I never did get it."

"Why not?" Isabel asked.

"Maybe because you were head over heels for him last year?" Thayer said.

Isabel looked down at her plate, momentarily furious. Yes, it was true, she had been into Aston last summer. Over the years he'd morphed from an overweight kid with buckteeth into a handsome lacrosse player with impeccable social connections. It also didn't hurt that he dated a string of beautiful, skinny socialites-in-training, especially Victoria Drake, who was sort of his female equivalent: good-looking, well-bred, with a father who'd donated many millions to the Metropolitan Museum of Art. All the years Isabel had known Aston, he'd never come after her, and last summer, she'd finally become a little offended. One night, at a beach party, she'd approached him with an extra cup of beer and a collection of compliments. It hadn't taken long. By the end of the night he'd left Victoria at the party to drive Isabel home. Two days later, they were officially dating.

But his appeal wore off pretty quickly. She had concrete reasons for this—he wasn't a good listener, he liked LMFAO, and he never stopped campaigning for her to lose her virginity to him, as if she were going to hand him that particular honor. But the main problem was that she'd dated him before. A hundred times, it seemed. He was just like all the other guys floating through the private-school scene. Cute, athletic, moneyed, boring. Nothing different, nothing unfamiliar, nothing she hadn't seen before.

She'd finally ended it at Madeleine Fuller's party, on the front lawn. She'd explained that she would be leaving in a few weeks for California and that long distance never worked, and that she needed to let him go so he could be happy, *blah blah blah*.

"But…but…we're so good together," he'd stammered. "Who cares about long distance if we love each other?"

She'd looked him straight in the eye and said, "Who said I loved you?"

It hadn't been her finest moment, admittedly. But he didn't seem to hold it against her. He'd e-mailed her a dozen times over the school year, sometimes just to say hi.

"Look, you guys go to his party," Isabel said. "Maybe I'll meet you."

"How are you going to get there?" Thayer asked. "Did you suddenly take another driving test in the past week?"

"Ha-ha."

"Seriously, when are you going to retake that test?" Darwin whined. "We can't be schlepping you all over town this summer."

"Don't worry. You won't be. And things are over between me and Aston. For good. So it's not like I'm gonna do him any favors if I go." She looked over her shoulder at the strip of yellow sand and, beyond it, the inky, restless water. She suddenly needed to get away from this table. "I'm gonna go get in the water."

Thayer blinked. "*That* water?" she asked. "The ocean?"

"Yeah."

"It's probably freezing."

"So what? It's good for you."

Darwin and Thayer exchanged another knowing look. *Yep, California has changed her*, it seemed to say.

"I'll be right back," Isabel said. She grabbed her towel from the back of her chair and turned onto the walkway of wooden planks that led to the sand.

"Have fun!" Darwin yelled, her voice dripping with sarcasm.

The wind met her head-on as she walked to the water, whipping the ends of her hair up past her shoulders. Nobody was on the beach. The lifeguard chair was empty—it was a given that nobody would be going in the water this early in the season. From the top of the chair, a yellow flag flapped in the wind. Hazardous, but not Stay Out at All Costs red. Hazardous, she could handle. During the past year at school in Santa Barbara, she'd become a much better ocean swimmer.

Beyond the sand, the waves swelled and broke with a thunderclap, followed by a sizzle of foam. She took a deep breath. There it was again, the sharp pain just under her lungs. Ever since she'd come back to the East Coast, it hurt to breathe, as if she were about to have a massive anxiety attack. It didn't make any sense. This was the place where she'd met most of her friends, and where she'd spent all of her summers. She knew the Georgica. It was almost like her own house. But as the ocean breeze curled around her, sending goose bumps along her bare arms, she realized why she couldn't breathe. She couldn't stand this place anymore. She pulled her cotton tunic over her head. In her bikini, she felt the cold air threaten to change her mind. Then she ran toward the waves and jumped into the water.

The cold sent shock waves over her body. She swam toward a wave just before it broke, and then bobbed back up on the surface, feeling the sting of salt in her nose and mouth. She opened her eyes and, treading water, turned around. The club looked so small and insignificant already, the green-and-white-striped umbrellas like the ones stuck in fruity drinks. Somewhere back there, Thayer and Darwin were probably talking about her. *Fine*, she thought. *Let them.*

She continued to tread water, thinking about what was ahead of her. The debutante ball where she'd come out to society. College, then internships with the Upper East Side's best interior decorators. She'd date—and marry—someone just like Aston March. Then she'd have kids and maybe, if she were lucky, a career matching silk throw pillows to someone's collection of Lilly Pulitzer dresses. Her life would be just like everyone else's she knew. Nothing fun. Nothing unique. Not a life at all.

She swam under another wave, moving her limbs through the cold water. When she broke the surface again, she was facing solid sand dunes. She twisted around, trying to find the club. And then she saw it, so far to her left that she could barely make it out. She'd already drifted at least a mile east.

She began to do the crawl back toward the club, but a wave rolled underneath her, pulling her farther out. She powered her arms through the water, swimming straight toward the beach now. Another wave came, and this time crashed over her, and she could feel the current pulling her farther down the beach. This time when she resurfaced, she faced the horizon. And a wall of water growing taller by the moment. It was a wave. Coming right at her.

She pivoted around, trying to make some headway toward the beach. The water pushed back, holding her in place. She looked over her shoulder. The wave was big, too big, and it looked like it was going to break right over her. And there was something on the wave. A guy lying on a surfboard, his arms paddling madly, cresting the top. He was about to stand up. He didn't see her.

Wave at him, she thought. *Move your arms.* Like a crazy person, she waved her arms over her head in the distress signal, or as close as she could get to it.

He was almost on his feet. She saw his wet suit, the sheen of his black hair, and the panic on his face as he noticed her, too late to reverse course. And then at the last moment, she ducked under the surface, just as the wave curled, turning in on itself, and tumbled over her, pushing her down.

This is it, she thought. *I'm going to die. Right in front of the stupid Georgica Club.*

Holding her breath, she flailed her arms underwater, trying to paddle upward, when a hand grabbed her wrist and yanked her, hard, right up to the surface.

Air. Sunlight. She opened her mouth and slammed her arm into something hard—the guy's surfboard.

"Get on the board!" she heard him yell. "Get on!"

She was so weak she could barely move, but she managed to slide onto the board. The surface of it scraped against her bare stomach.

"Hold on, here comes another wave," he said. "Paddle! Paddle!"

She forced her arms to paddle. He swam in front of her, one hand on the nose of the board, pulling her in.

"Okay, we're going to ride it in," he said, positioning himself beside her and curling an arm around her waist. "Keep going! Okay, go!"

She hung on to the sides of the board, he hung on to her, and as the wave broke underneath them, the board rose up from the water, lightly skimming the surface, like a flying carpet. A few moments later, they brushed up onto hard sand.

She crawled off the board on her elbows, coughing up water. Salt stung the back of her throat and her eyes.

"You okay?" the guy asked, on his hands and knees beside her.

She leaned down and coughed up more water.

"Hey, good job out there," he said. "You're gonna be fine."

She turned onto her back and closed her eyes. When she opened them a few minutes later, he was leaning over her, blocking out the sun. Drops of water fell from the tips of his hair, which looked like it was long enough to fall over his eyes. Although his face was cast in shadow, she made out a cleft chin, then full lips, and then large, liquid brown eyes.

"Hey," he said. His palm slid underneath her shoulder and helped her up to a seated position. "Where'd you get in the water?"

She pointed up the beach. "The club. The Geor... the Georgica."

"Okay. I'll take you. But first, you might want to fix that."

She followed his gaze downward. Her bikini top had twisted around, completely exposing her. Mortified, she pulled it back around.

He helped her up, and she took a few steps on rubbery legs. As they started walking, he slid his arm around her waist and held his board with his other arm.

"So what were you doing out there?" he asked.

"Swimming," she said.

"Did it look like a good day to go swimming?"

"Well, what were *you* doing out there?" she countered. "This beach isn't for surfing."

"So you have something against surfers."

"No. I surf."

"You do?" he asked, giving her a sidelong glance.

"I've surfed Rincon," she said. "In Santa Barbara. You've heard of it, right?"

"Yeah, I've heard of it," he said, smiling. "Surfer girl knows her spots."

A gust of wind made her shiver.

"You cold?" he asked.

"A little."

He stopped walking and stuck his board in the sand. Without a word, he unzipped the back of his wet suit and pulled it down to his waist, exposing his chest and muscled stomach.

"Come here," he said, opening his arms.

She stepped forward into his arms, and suddenly his hands were rubbing her shoulders, her arms, and her back in rapid strokes, sending heat all over her body. Her goose bumps disappeared.

This is crazy, she thought. *You don't even know this person. And he's practically feeling you up.* But standing there with her face pressed into the salty skin of his shoulder, feeling the warmth of his hands on her, she didn't want him to stop.

"There," he said, stepping back. His eyes were still concerned. "Better?"

"Yeah." She couldn't look at him. "Thanks."

31

She heard him zip the wet suit back up.

They walked the rest of the way in silence, his arm still wrapped around her shoulders, and her arm wrapped around his waist. *Just for support*, she told herself. But after their embrace, it felt more intimate than that. She could still feel the friction of his hands on her skin. *How many girls?* she thought. *How many girls are in love with this guy?*

At the lifeguard chair, she stopped. "Well, this is me," she said. "And look at this." She pointed to the empty chair. "Nice to see that the Georgica's on top of things."

"Then I wouldn't have met you," he said, looking right into her eyes. "You gonna be okay getting back from here?"

She looked over at the green-and-white-striped umbrellas on the patio. It was tempting to have him walk her back, if only to see Thayer's and Darwin's faces. But she decided that they didn't even deserve the sight of this guy. "Yeah. I'm fine. Thanks."

"No problem," he said. He took a step backward. "Hey, what's your name, surfer girl?"

"Isabel," she said. "Isabel Rule. Why?"

"Just asking," he said. "It might come in handy."

He grinned in a way that made her remember his hands on her, rubbing her skin, and then he turned around and walked away.

CHAPTER THREE

Rory stood over the Rules' butcher-block kitchen table, an unopened bottle of wine tucked under her arm like a weapon.

"When you pour, don't stand too far away," Fee advised, pulling Rory a bit closer to the table. "You need to be close. Otherwise the wine'll plop into the glass and you're liable to get drops on the table."

"Got it," Rory said, miming the act with the bottle. "Pour close to the glass."

"But not *too* close," Fee cautioned. "Then you might slip and crack the glass." Fee moved the crystal wineglass a few inches away from the place setting that she'd arranged on the table for practice. "I know, it's confusing. And no pressure, but that's a three-hundred-dollar bottle of wine."

Rory put the bottle down on the table. "So now you tell me," she said.

Ten feet away Eduardo, the chef, pirouetted between the eight-burner stove and the marble-topped kitchen island. He was a small man with a scruff of black hair and surprisingly muscular arms, and he worked with fierce concentration as he chopped, sprinkled, and diced. He wore the same forest-green polo and khaki pants as Fee, along with a stained apron that seemed to have followed him from cooking school. Looking around, Rory could see that the Rules had spared no expense with their kitchen. Four Cornish hens roasted on a spit in a glass chamber, rotisserie-style, while three miniature pizzas bubbled in the wood-burning pizza oven.

"If you don't want to do this," Fee said softly, "just tell me. We can try to find someone else. This wasn't supposed to even be something you would—"

"No, it's fine," she fibbed. "It'll be great." She smiled, and Fee seemed to buy it, though she did give Rory a sympathetic look as she put away the silverware.

The low-level panic Rory had been feeling all afternoon was getting harder to hide. It had started while she finished unpacking, and by the time Fee had brought her into the kitchen and served her a grilled cheese with a side of frilly greens, she'd barely been able to eat a bite. Later, as Bianca gave her a tour of the lower floors of the house, her anxiety had only increased. Each room had a title—the screening room, the breakfast room, the mudroom—and each was more elegantly put together than the one before. The Rules liked long white couches with rattan frames and thick, soft-looking cushions, chairs stuffed with needlepoint throw pillows, and coffee tables made out of knotty pieces of driftwood. They also liked art—expensive-looking, modern paintings in vivid colors—and other eye-catching pieces.

As they walked from room to room, Bianca would point out one of the more exquisite items on display, and combine it with a little piece of trivia. "You'll notice the Francis Bacon painting on the wall—Mrs. Rule got that at auction in London," or "You'll see the Bösendorfer piano in the corner—Mr. Rule loves to play Chopin." Outside on the spacious flagstone patio, as they stood next to a narrow lap pool built right beside the larger, rectangular pool, Bianca said, "This is for Connor, their youngest son. He's on the swim team at USC." And downstairs in the rec room, which boasted a pool table, a Ping-Pong table, a Wurlitzer jukebox, and a generous stack of board games, Bianca said, "The Rules love to play table tennis, especially before dinner."

Whenever they passed by a framed photograph on the wall or on one of the end tables, Rory caught a glimpse of one or two of the Rules, or sometimes the entire family together. They were definitely attractive, with hair that varied in blond shades from corn silk to caramel and tan, glowing complexions. But Isabel was the beauty of the family. She stood out in every picture, as much for her large, light blue eyes as for her refusal to smile.

When Rory returned to her room, her mind reeling from all the data from the tour, she grabbed one of her notebooks and jotted down as much as she could remember.

Sloane—tennis

Mr. Rule—Chopin

Mrs. Rule—Francis Bacon, art

Connor—swimming

Gregory—Harvard

The only one of the Rules whom Bianca hadn't mentioned, curiously, was Isabel. But perhaps the less she heard about Isabel Rule, Rory thought, the better.

"Let's go over the rest," Fee said, leaning against one of the kitchen's stainless steel counters. "What side do you serve from?"

"The left if I'm serving from a platter or taking around the bread basket. The right if the food is already plated."

"Good. And tonight we're doing platters, right, Eduardo?" Fee asked.

Eduardo stood bent over a knob of peeled ginger, mincing it with superhuman speed. "Hmm-hmm," he murmured, totally engrossed.

"Yes, we're doing platters," Bianca announced as she breezed into the kitchen. "But the gazpacho is coming out first."

Rory was starting to notice that Bianca had a knack for joining conversations that began before she entered a room. She'd changed into a black shift dress and a string of tiny pearls, and looked so elegant that Rory wondered if she was going to be joining the Rules for dinner. "Is it ready, Eduardo?" she asked, crossing her arms. "The gazpacho?"

"Yes," Eduardo said, finally looking up from the stove. "It's chilled."

"Good. Then it seems we're on schedule." Bianca turned to Rory and appraised her outfit. "My, we're bright tonight," she said.

Rory looked down at her white ruffled top with see-through gauzy sleeves. "Should I change?" she asked with a sinking feeling.

"It's fine," Bianca said with a tight smile. "So, everyone serves themselves from the platters except for the dinner rolls," she explained, lifting off the lid of a saucepan, "which you'll place on the bread plates, and then you'll also bring around the teriyaki sauce for the chicken and ladle it onto the plates. Understood?"

Rory nodded.

She replaced the lid. "I think that might need a bit more saffron," Bianca said to Eduardo.

Eduardo grabbed a pinch of red herbs from a small glass jar and dashed over to the saucepan.

"I think we've got it covered," Fee said. "Rory's going to do an excellent job."

"I'm sure she is," Bianca said.

A loud beep sounded through the room. Rory flinched. Both Fee and Bianca started for the intercom attached to the wall, but Bianca got there first. "Yes," she said, pressing a button.

"Can someone send down something to drink?" a woman's voice said over the intercom. "And what about Fee's niece? Can she come down, too?"

"Right away," Bianca replied. She turned to Rory. "You remember how to get to the rec room?"

"I'll take her," Fee said. She walked to a small wine refrigerator that Rory hadn't noticed and took out a bottle of pink wine.

"Who's that for?" Rory asked.

"Mrs. Rule always likes a sip before dinner." Fee poured some into a wineglass. Rory thought of her mom's disdain for rosé. "So trashy," Lana would say, shaking her head. As usual, she hadn't known what she was talking about.

37

"All right," Fee said when she'd poured a healthy amount. "Let's go."

When they were out of the kitchen and in the hall, Rory couldn't hold it in any longer. "Do I look ridiculous or something?"

"*Please* don't pay any attention to Bianca. I told you."

"But I can change—"

"Rory," Fee said with a stern look, "the last thing you should do is start kissing her butt. Then she'll *really* know that she's got you."

Good advice, Rory thought as they began to descend the back stairs. Something else she would have to remember in this house. As they neared the bottom floor, she heard the high-pitched, rapid bounce of a Ping-Pong ball.

"They're all very nice," Fee said over her shoulder, as if she'd read Rory's mind. "You'll be great."

"They're not going to ask me to play Ping-Pong, are they?" Rory asked under her breath.

"I don't think so," Fee said. She didn't sound sure.

Rory wondered if she was in for another encounter with Isabel, but when she reached the bottom of the stairs, the youngest Rule was nowhere in sight. Instead, four other blond people hovered around a table, playing Ping-Pong like maniacs.

"Come on! Get over there!"

The woman Rory assumed was Mrs. Rule—if only because of the glittering diamond ring on her left hand—leaped for the tiny ball and sent it whizzing over the net. She looked as if she might have been just a few years older than Rory. She was dressed in dark-rinse skinny jeans and a lemon-colored crochet tunic, and her bright blond hair was piled into a messy updo.

Across the net, a younger woman in a black wrap top and jeans lunged for the ball as if her very life were at stake. This had to be Sloane, Isabel's older sister. She had dark blond hair and was taller than her mother, and as she made contact with the ball, she let out a tiny grunt. She sent it bouncing over the net.

"Got it!" yelled a young man with glasses and a tall, lanky frame. He moved in front of his mother and delivered the ball back over the net. Rory guessed this was the oldest son, Gregory.

A man with the lean build of a runner and the composed, unflappable face of a CEO stepped up to the table. With one smooth movement he returned the ball without a word. It bounced, arced over the net, and sailed right past his wife.

"Larry!" Mrs. Rule snapped, freezing in her tracks. "That was on the line! That was *clearly* on the line!"

"It was in, Luce. You just took your eye off the ball." Mr. Rule smiled in a way that struck Rory as smug.

"No, I think Mom's right," Gregory said. "I think that ball was on the line."

"It was totally *in*," Sloane said testily, walking around the table to fetch the ball off the ground. "Okay, seventeen serving sixteen."

"Wait," said Mrs. Rule. She walked over to Rory, smiling warmly as if she were her long-lost daughter. "You must be Rory," she said. "We've heard so much about you. I'm Lucy."

"Hi." Rory shook her hand, aware that she might be blushing.

"What do you think, Rory?" Mrs. Rule asked. "Was the ball in or out?"

"Um. I'm not really sure."

Mrs. Rule's face softened. "Sorry. I guess I'm putting you on the spot, aren't I? It's just that I think we're going to have to install a referee around here one of these days," she said, raising an eyebrow as she glanced at her husband. "This is my husband, Lawrence," she said, gesturing to Mr. Rule. "And my two oldest—Sloane and Gregory."

"Hi," Rory said, returning Sloane's and Gregory's polite waves from across the room. "I hope I'm not interrupting the game."

"Not at all. We always like to play a little before dinner," Mrs. Rule said. "Works up an appetite." She reached hungrily for the glass in Fee's hand, took a sip of wine, and then brushed away a strand of runaway hair. "So, how's your room? Do you have enough hangers?"

"Oh, uh, yes, plenty."

"Good." She turned to Gregory and Sloane. "Rory's in the downstairs guest room."

"Oh, I love that room," Sloane said. "I'd have that be my room if I could."

"It's a great room," Gregory agreed. "You can hear the ocean from there."

"And feel free to use the beach anytime you'd like," Mr. Rule said. "We don't stand on ceremony here."

"And thank you for helping us out with the dinner party tonight," Mrs. Rule added. "The local help here...well, sometimes they come down with a severe case of flakiness."

As Sloane and Gregory put away their paddles, Rory noticed

the row of tiny Evian bottles and rolled-up minitowels on the credenza, standing at the ready in case of sweat or thirst.

"I think playing something together as a family is extremely important," Mrs. Rule went on. "When I was growing up, my father made sure that we were all very athletic. He wanted us playing tennis or taking diving lessons or riding our horses. Unfortunately, I never was good at much besides tennis. And Ping-Pong. Do you play anything?"

"Not really," Rory answered.

"What about your mother?" Mrs. Rule asked as they walked to the stairs. "Does she like to exercise?"

"Not in the traditional sense, no."

"Well, each of us is good at something," Mrs. Rule said. "Connor—he's not here yet; he's coming in a few days—he's on the swim team at USC." She gestured to a boy in one of the framed photographs in the diamond-shaped cluster on the wall. Rory caught a glimpse of a preppy-looking guy with blond hair standing beside a sailboat before Mrs. Rule motioned for her to go first up the stairs.

"And Sloane here is one of the Georgica's star doubles players."

"Really?" Rory asked.

"So what do you like to do?" Mrs. Rule asked.

"She studies," Fee put in, which made Rory blush.

"Well, that's good," Mrs. Rule said. "What do you think you want to be?"

Rory cleared her throat as they reached the landing. "I'm not really sure yet. Maybe a lawyer for children. I like making movies, but that's probably not going to lead to anything."

Mrs. Rule's expression changed suddenly, as if a wind had just blown across her face and wiped it clean. "Has anyone seen my other daughter?" she asked, moving to the bottom of the steps. "Isabel?" she yelled up the stairs. "Isabel, are you coming down? It's dinner!"

"Maybe she's still recovering," Sloane said acerbically.

Her brother nudged her. "Be nice."

Rory heard the sound of footsteps coming down the stairs.

"I hope you're dressed!" Mrs. Rule called out.

Isabel appeared on the landing in a wrinkled pink oxford and a pair of black board shorts. "I have a really bad headache," she announced with a scowl. "If it's okay with you, I'd just like to eat in my room."

"Go back upstairs and put on a dress," said Mrs. Rule.

"I almost *drowned*," Isabel said.

"But you didn't," said Mr. Rule. "So I'd like you to do what your mother says and come down here and have some dinner."

"Don't order her, Larry," Mrs. Rule murmured.

Isabel's defiant eyes traveled over the crowd until they landed on Rory in a glare so intense that Rory felt the urge to hide. "I said I'm not hungry," she said.

Rory stepped backward toward the swinging door. "I'll just see if anyone needs me in the kitchen," she said. "Excuse me." Right before she turned to leave, Isabel's eyes narrowed.

It wasn't going to be easy, living with a family and yet staying outside of it. She would have to learn the right moments to become invisible.

Especially when Isabel Rule was in the room.

*   *   *

"It's an incredible piece of land," Isabel's father said from across the table. "The whole lot's probably worth about a hundred million. Almost fifty acres he's got. I was lucky to get ten of them."

Isabel sat at the long dining table, twisting her napkin on her lap over and over as she stared at the flickering candlelight. This afternoon felt like a violent, beautiful dream. And now she couldn't stop thinking about him. His eyes and his dripping dark hair. The heat of his hands on her arms and her back. The way he'd grinned at her right before he'd turned around. Where was he right now? Was he thinking about her, too? And what was his name? And was there any way to find him?

"Who's the owner again?" asked Elisa Crawford, the painter. Isabel's mother collected her work, though Isabel had never figured out why.

"Some potato farmer," said Mr. Rule, breaking apart a roll. "Family's had the land for two hundred years. One of those old-timers who hates anyone who got there after the Civil War."

"He didn't like it that Larry was in finance," said her mother, taking a dainty sip of gazpacho.

"But he loved that I was married to a Newcomb," her dad said, looking proudly at her mom. "Lucy's maiden name still gets you somewhere with the locals."

Her mom smiled faintly into her soup.

"But get this," her father went on. "We had to promise the crotchety old guy that the house, when it's finished, would be under twelve thousand square feet."

43

"Can he ask you to do that?" asked Bill Astergard, who hosted his own talk show on PBS that nobody watched but that everyone admired.

"Unfortunately, yes," said Gregory, whom Isabel noticed liked to pipe in during their parents' dinner parties. "He's built it into the contract."

"But I've figured out a way around that," said her dad.

"And what's that?" asked Elisa Crawford.

Her father winked as he sipped some water. "My lawyers know what they're doing."

"I love Sagaponack," Sloane said, apropos of nothing. Isabel sighed softly. Her sister was so weird.

And so was the girl serving them. What was her name—Laurie? Rory? She kept shuffling into the room with the food, barely able to make eye contact as she stopped at each chair and shoved a platter in front of each person. And that white top with the Ice Capades sleeves... *Ugh.* Where'd this girl go shopping? She also didn't like the look the girl had given her in the hall before dinner, like Isabel was a spoiled brat. It wasn't her fault that her parents forced their kids to hang out with them and their friends, even after a near-death experience. She'd had no choice in the end but to go up to her room and put on a dress. It seemed a waste of a beautiful ivory Chloé shift to be wearing it here, but at least it had gotten her mom off her case.

"I'm not getting a good feeling about this, Lucy," Felipe Santo Moreno, the art critic, said in his Cuban accent. "In fact, I'm getting some very strong negative energy." Felipe, who was sitting beside Isabel, was by far the most interesting person at the table, thanks to his stories about hanging out with Andy Warhol in the eighties.

"Oh, that's right," said her mother with sudden interest. "You're psychic, aren't you, Felipe?"

"A little," Felipe said shyly. "I've been known to have a sense about things. And this doesn't feel good to me."

"And you're getting all of that through your psychic wavelengths?" asked her father with a smirk.

Isabel heard her brother snicker quietly on her other side.

Suddenly, the girl—Rory, was it?—edged up beside Isabel and shoved a platter of chicken in her face. "Chicken?" the girl whispered.

Isabel took the tongs without making eye contact and dumped a breast on her plate. The girl moved on to the next person. Hopefully that would be the extent of their contact this summer. She didn't even know where this girl was sleeping, but she hoped it wasn't anywhere near her bedroom.

"I really am psychic, you know," Felipe said to Isabel when her father and mother began discussing architects. He leaned in close to her. "Like with you. You met somebody today. I can tell."

Isabel blinked. "How can you tell?" she asked.

"He's tall, dark, and handsome," Felipe said, as a smile curled around his lips. "He's made quite an impression on you."

Isabel stared at him. "Huh. You're actually kind of right."

"Of course I am," Felipe said proudly. "And just between you and me, I think it's a good thing that your parents move. This house. It's beautiful, but..." He looked around and gave a faint shudder. "Too many secrets."

"What do you mean?" Isabel asked. In her peripheral vision, she saw the girl start to come around the table again with a small tureen and a spoon.

"Ask *them*," Felipe said, nodding toward her mother and father.

"But what kind of secrets?" Isabel asked.

Her view of Felipe was suddenly blotted out by the girl's anxious face. "Teriyaki sauce?" she offered.

"Fine." Isabel turned back to Felipe and was about to repeat the question when she felt something cool and wet. She looked down. Brown teriyaki sauce lay in a pool on her lap.

"Eeeew!" Isabel exclaimed, standing up from the table.

"What is it?" her mother asked.

"She just spilled on me!" Isabel said, pointing at the girl. "Look!" She held out the stained part of her dress.

"I'm so sorry," the girl said. Her face had gone sheet-white. "I'm so sorry."

"Isabel, please sit down." Her mom's voice struggled to stay calm.

"It's not gonna come out," Isabel said. "She ruined it!" Isabel ran to the kitchen. To her irritation, she heard the girl follow her.

"What is it?" Eduardo asked as they charged into the kitchen.

"Do we have any club soda?" Isabel asked, going to the refrigerator.

"Really, I'm so, so sorry," the girl said, hanging her head.

Isabel ignored her. "*Club soda?*" she repeated. "Anywhere?"

Eduardo opened the fridge and produced a minibottle of Seagram's.

46

"Let me have it," she said, taking it from him. She ripped off some paper towels from the roll at the sink and poured the soda over them.

"Really, I'm so, so sorry," the girl said.

"What are you doing here?" Isabel asked her as she blotted the stain.

"Excuse me?" the girl asked.

"What are you doing here?" She finally looked at the girl, who had started to wring her hands. "Why are you even here?"

The girl didn't speak.

"They shouldn't have asked you to do this, you know."

Bianca appeared in the doorway from the hall. "Isabel, what is the matter?" she asked in her usual condescending voice.

"Why did you make this girl serve us tonight?" Isabel demanded. "She had no clue what she was doing."

"The person we hired canceled on us," Bianca said. "This was the best we could do on such short notice."

"Then it should have been a buffet."

"Your mother didn't *want* a buffet," Bianca countered.

Isabel turned back to her dress. "Whatever," she snapped.

"I really am sorry," Rory said.

"*Stop* saying that," Isabel said. She threw the paper towels in the garbage. "It's done. Hopefully the cleaners can do something with it. But obviously, you don't know what you're doing." She stalked out of the kitchen, making sure to avoid Bianca's smug stare.

Rory watched her go, aware of her heart racing frantically inside her chest.

47

"That's enough," Bianca said. "I'll handle the rest."

"I really am sorry," she mumbled.

"It was an accident," Bianca said. Her voice didn't hold a shred of sympathy.

Rory placed the tureen on the counter with shaky hands. She'd been waiting tables for two years and had never dropped so much as a slice of pepperoni on someone. Why couldn't she ladle some sauce? What was wrong with her? The only thing to do was go to her room and try to recover. Rory headed for the door.

"Don't you want some dinner?" Bianca asked. "Eduardo can make you a plate."

"No, that's all right," Rory said. "I'm not that hungry."

Nobody mentioned her outburst for the rest of dinner. Instead, they talked as if she weren't even there, chewing over the usual dinnertime topics: who'd bought which house for how much, who'd been admitted to the Georgica lately, and how hard it was to find decent household help in the Hamptons these days. As soon as Bianca came out of the kitchen with bowls of lemon and blueberry gelato, Isabel pushed back from the table.

"Is it okay if I'm excused?" she asked.

Her mother flashed her a dark look. It was clear that she was still angry, but she gave a curt nod. Isabel left the room without another word and hurried upstairs.

As she left, she could feel Sloane and Gregory watching her. The two of them had ganged up on her constantly last summer, at least when they weren't tattling on her to their parents. When she'd borrowed the Range Rover to drive to a party in Sagaponack, only twenty minutes away, Sloane had been the first to tell their mom that she'd taken the car for a "joyride." When she'd stayed out all night with Aston to watch the sunrise, her brother told her in all seriousness that she was smearing the family name with her "antics." And then the way they'd both freaked out last summer with the fire, which was a total accident... The last thing she needed right now was a lecture from both of them. She couldn't wait for Connor to get home. He always defended her, and luckily, Sloane and Gregory always listened to him. Maybe it was because they knew that he was their mom's favorite.

She opened the door to her bedroom and looked at the pink walls, billowy white curtains, and the antique chandelier that hung from the ceiling. When she was fourteen, her decorating influences had been Betsey Johnson's boutiques and Sofia Coppola's *Marie Antoinette*. Now she wished that the walls were plain white and her curtains olive green, like her room at school. She walked on into her closet, which now seemed ridiculously over-the-top. It was amazing how one year away changed the way she saw things. She'd loved her closet so much when she'd first designed it, but now it just looked silly. Clothes were grouped by color, with a special section designed for stripes. Her shoe rack took up an entire wall, and in the corner, all her purses, bags, and clutches hung from fabric-covered nails. She pulled off her dress and changed into her school sweats and a T-shirt. Then she sat down on the curved chaise in the center of the room and looked at herself in the full-length mirror. Maybe she'd sort of overdone it down there with that girl, she thought. Maybe she'd acted like a jerk.

After a few minutes, the sound of footsteps in the room

outside made her sit up straight. "Isabel?" Her mother appeared on the threshold, her blue eyes stormy. "What on earth is wrong with you?"

"I thought it was pretty obvious," Isabel said. "She ruined my dress."

"So you politely excuse yourself to go to the kitchen," Lucy said. "You do not carry on like that in front of people. And you will not yell at a member of the staff. That is for me to do, not you." Her mom took a deep breath and clutched at her silk cardigan. "And I'm still waiting for you to explain today. Jumping in the ocean like that with no lifeguard, nobody around."

"I felt like swimming."

"Mrs. Dancy told me you walked onto the patio looking like a drowned rat."

"Because I did almost drown."

Her mother cocked her head, and several strands of blond hair fell out of her updo and down to her shoulder. "Don't do that, Isabel," she said. "Don't play the martyr. Things are going to be different this summer. Do you understand? No staying out all night, no borrowing the car, no lying to us. Your father has had it up to here with you, if that means anything at all—"

"It doesn't," Isabel said.

"Don't say that."

"He doesn't even talk to me," Isabel said. "Why should I care what he thinks? And this is so not about me. *She's* the one who messed up. God knows why you took her in."

"You will be nice to that girl, do you understand?" her mom

said. "She doesn't have half the advantages you do. I'm trying to do a nice thing by having her here for the summer."

"You're just terrified Fee will finally quit and leave you," Isabel muttered. "So you say yes to whatever she asks."

Her mother was quiet. "Good night, Isabel," she finally said, and walked out.

Isabel stayed on the chaise. The summer had barely started, and already she needed to get out of here. She closed her eyes. The sensation of a wave rocked her. Instantly, she saw him again. That dripping-wet hair. Those eyes. That grin.

He was here. Somewhere close by. And possibly thinking about her.

She walked out into her bedroom and over to the iPod dock on her bedside table. She turned on the playlist she'd made at school right before she'd come home and lay down on her bed. She wanted to think about him some more.

Rory lay curled on her bed in the gathering dark, unable to move or turn on a light. Pretty soon she would have to move, though, and decide what to do.

For most of her life, she'd always been cautious. Waking up an extra hour early to study before a test. Waiting until things went on sale. Saving enough money from her paycheck to make sure the electric bill got paid. So obviously it stood to reason that the one time she wasn't cautious, it would be a disaster. Her mom had been right. Coming here had been a mistake. And it had taken only eight hours to figure that out.

When she finally sat up and looked out the window, it was dark. Shadows fell on the carpet from the house lights outside. She picked up the phone on the bedside table and stared at all the buttons for the different rooms—LIBRARY, POOLHOUSE, MASTER BEDROOM. She hung up the phone. Fee had said she was downstairs off the Ping-Pong room. It would be easier just to go find her.

She stepped out into the hall. The house felt quiet. The only living creature she could see or hear was Trixie, who raised her head from her bed and regarded Rory with surprisingly soulful dark eyes. She went down the back staircase, each step creaking, and hit the dimmer switch. The light came up over the Ping-Pong table. The paddles still lay on the credenza at odd angles to each other. Just looking at them, she felt covered in shame. She couldn't even imagine what the Rules thought of her now. Though Isabel's reaction had definitely been rude. But it seemed as if the family was well used to Isabel's rudeness.

She walked down a hall until she reached a closed door with light seeping out from under it. Gently, she knocked. "Fee?" she said. "Can I come in? It's Rory."

The door opened. Fee stood in a long crew shirt that said THE GEORGICA CLUB in fancy script and a pair of pajama pants. "Well, hello, honey," she said. "Thought you'd come by. I'm just doing my crossword puzzle. Come on in."

Rory looked around the cramped room. It was just large enough to hold a twin bed, a nightstand, and a small dresser with a miniature flat-screen TV on top of it. There was no walk-in closet, no pair of overstuffed chairs. No floor-to-ceiling windows.

"This room is so small," she said. "Sorry. I mean, compared with mine. I should be in this one."

"I like it small," Fee muttered. "And nobody comes down here. Which is even better." She sat back down on her bed and picked up her crossword. "A six-letter word for 'class,'" she said, squinting at the puzzle. "Starts with *C*."

Rory thought. "Cachet?"

"Ca-*chet*," Fee said, printing the letters. "Good. Very good. You're a very smart girl."

"Yeah, except I can't ladle sauce," Rory said.

"Now, don't go feeling bad about that," Fee said, putting down the newspaper. "You did the best you could. And, by the way, they should *never* have put you in that position."

"Mrs. Rule probably thinks I'm a moron," Rory said. "And Isabel—"

"Has an attitude problem the size of Nebraska," Fee interrupted.

"I just think this might have been a mistake," Rory said, sitting on the edge of the bed.

"Because Isabel Rule threw one of her tantrums? No. Spending all summer with your mother and her latest boy toy? *That* would have been a mistake."

"I just don't really have the experience for this," Rory said. "I thought I did. But it's so confusing."

"What do you mean?" asked Fee.

"Well, the Rules. They were so friendly. They made me feel like a guest. You know, with the room, and how nice they were when I met them." Rory picked up Fee's pen, uncapped it, and capped it again. "And then all of a sudden I was serving them dinner. And not doing it well. It was just strange. I guess I just didn't expect them to be so nice. That's all."

Fee opened a drawer in her nightstand and took out a bag of M&M'S. "Well, they're not ogres, that's for sure," she said, offering the bag to Rory, who took one. "But I've never forgotten that I'm the housekeeper. Not for one moment."

"Right," Rory said, though she wasn't quite sure what Fee was saying.

"Put tonight behind you," she said. "And try to relax. Go to town, make some friends. And for God's sake, don't worry about Isabel. She's a troubled kid."

"How troubled?"

"She's never fit in," Fee said, biting into an M&M. "All the other kids, there was never any trouble. But Isabel—she's always liked to test people. And then last summer, she almost burned down this house."

Rory dropped the pen. "Are you serious?"

Fee nodded somberly. "She came home from a party three sheets to the wind and then fell asleep in the TV room with a lit cigarette in her hand. The rug caught fire and then the curtains, and she would have taken down the whole north wing of the house if her brother Connor hadn't come down to the kitchen to get something to eat."

"Yikes."

"That's when they decided to send her to school in California. She didn't come back all year. Not even during Christmas. Not until a couple of weeks ago. So it's been a bit bumpy here since she's been back. I think the family's wishing they could have kept her at school all summer, too."

Rory picked at the rope bracelet on her right wrist.

"But don't worry," Fee said, putting a hand on Rory's. "You're going to be just fine here."

Again, Fee didn't sound that convincing, but she let it pass. "What time should I be up tomorrow?"

"Eight should be safe."

"Okay. And thanks again. For everything." She leaned down to give Fee a hug. "Good night."

"G'night, dear."

She closed Fee's door. When she passed the paddles on the credenza, she no longer felt embarrassed. The Rules had to be good people if Fee had worked for them for so long. They would forgive her for one stupid mistake. She thought of them playing Ping-Pong, perfectly in sync with one another, competitive but in a friendly, supportive way. What family she knew did stuff like that? The only crack in their exterior so far was their crazy daughter.

She entered her room and kept it dark as she started to unmake the massive bed. She couldn't wait to go to sleep. Music filtered down from above her room. A familiar melody. One of her favorite songs, in fact. Florence and the Machine.

Someone else in this house liked them, too.

CHAPTER FOUR

The next morning Rory bolted awake to the sound of a lawn mower outside. She sat up on her elbow and blinked in the sunlight. She'd fallen asleep without closing the window or lowering the blinds. Chilly ocean air made the curtains rustle. She reached for the small glass clock on the nightstand and stared at the face. It was nine thirty.

She ran to the bathroom, stripping off her pajamas as she went. She got into the shower and frantically turned the lever. Nothing happened. She tried it again and again. Finally she saw the separate button to turn on the water. The lever, it seemed, was just for temperature, as if that made any sense. She got it hot enough and then stood under the needle-sharp spray, feeling it pummel her eyelids. First she'd ruined Isabel Rule's dress. Now she was the lazy oaf who slept in on her second day on the job. Next time she wouldn't use the clock as an alarm; she'd use her phone, like a normal person.

Two minutes later, she was dressed in a pair of jeans and the first top that she could unfold. As soon as she stepped out of her room, Trixie tore down the hall to greet her. "Hi, sweetie," Rory whispered. "Wish me luck today, huh?" She patted Trixie's head and let the dog lick her hand. She wondered how much attention Trixie got in this house. She guessed very little.

Just before she pushed through the kitchen door, she heard voices coming from the other side.

"Maybe if she hadn't been thrust into it her very first night, it wouldn't have happened," Fee was saying.

"She wasn't thrust into it; she *volunteered*," she heard Bianca say. "But I had no idea that she—"

Rory pushed open the door. Both Fee and Bianca had guilty expressions as they looked up from opposite sides of the marble-topped island. "Well, good morning," Bianca said crisply. "I assume you slept well?"

"I'm sorry. I thought I set the alarm."

"It's okay, Rory," Fee said. "I made you a smoothie, if you're hungry." Fee opened the refrigerator and took out a tall glass filled with what looked like a strawberry shake. "Strawberry-banana-blueberry," she said, lifting the plastic wrap off the top of the glass. "Plus some flax oil and some ground-up almonds."

"Thanks." Rory accepted the glass and looked around the room. Last night, the kitchen counters and center island had been covered with food and spices and flatware. Now every surface was bare and shiny. And something else was missing, too. "Where's Eduardo?"

"Eduardo was let go," Bianca answered coolly. "Our new chef will be joining us tonight."

"Oh." She remembered the way Eduardo had flown around

the kitchen in a blur of hyperactivity. Maybe that had been fear. She wanted to ask why Eduardo had been fired but sensed this wasn't appropriate. She took a sip of the smoothie. Part of her wanted to apologize again for last night, but then she remembered what Fee had said about not sucking up to Bianca. Better to pretend it just hadn't happened. "So, what can I do today?" she asked.

"You're going to get some things at the market," Bianca said, walking over to a laptop that she'd set up on a desk at the end of the counter. "You *do* have your license, correct?"

"Uh, yes." Rory nodded.

"Good. We'd like you to make a run over to Citarella in town. Here's a list of what to buy. Just put it on Mrs. Rule's account." Bianca swiped the printout off the printer tray under the desk and handed it to her.

Rory glanced at the list. It was alphabetized and divided into underlined categories: MEATS. SEAFOOD. CONDIMENTS.

"And please, get exactly what is on the list," Bianca said. "Mrs. Rule is very particular about her brands."

"What if they're out of something?" she asked.

"Then get the next best thing."

Rory wasn't sure what "the next best thing" meant, but she just folded the list and put it in her purse.

"And then we'd like you to pick up Isabel at Two Trees," Bianca added.

"Pick up Isabel?" she asked.

"At the stables. She has her riding lesson." Bianca scribbled the name TWO TREES on a notepad. "There. Just put that into the GPS, and it will tell you how to get there."

Rory took the piece of paper. She wondered if Bianca was doing this to her on purpose.

"You can pick her up at around eleven thirty," Bianca went on. "And you can take the Prius. The keys are in the car."

"Okay, sounds great," Rory said. "No problem."

"And whatever you do, *don't* let Isabel drive," Bianca said. Her expression was grave. "Is that understood?"

"Uh, yes. Definitely."

"I'll take you out back," Fee said, trudging over to the door.

Rory followed her out into the hall. "Why do I have to pick up Isabel?" Rory whispered. "Can't she drive?"

Fee didn't answer until the back door was shut behind them. "She failed her driver's test," she said, struggling to hide a grin. "Can't say I'm that surprised." She gestured to the shiny silver Prius. "So. You know how to work this thing?"

"I think so," Rory said.

She got into the car and pressed the engine button. The GPS switched on and a robotic woman's voice purred, "*Welcome.*"

"Just take a right, then a left, then straight into town," Fee said. "Citarella's right past Newtown off Main Street. And if you have any questions, just call the house."

"Okay," she said. Rory closed the door.

Fee knocked on the window and Rory lowered it.

"And be careful of the traffic," Fee added. "Montauk Highway can be a parking lot."

"Sure thing," Rory said.

Fee walked back into the house, and Rory looked down at the complicated dashboard, trying to get her bearings. She'd never driven a car with GPS. It always struck her as kind of unnecessary, but maybe that was because she knew every possible street and road in her hometown.

Out of the corner of her eye, she saw a black Jetta drive into the spot next to hers. Steve waved at her from behind the glass and then got out of the car, toting a bunch of tennis rackets. "How's it going?" he asked, his white teeth glinting in the sun.

Rory debated telling him the truth. Right now he was the only person in the house who didn't know how badly she'd messed up the night before. "It's going okay," she said. "Aside from the fact that I spilled teriyaki sauce last night all over Isabel."

"You did?" Steve laughed. "I wish I could have seen that."

"Everybody else did."

"Hang in there," he said, patting her shoulder through the window. "At least you've made a splash already."

"That's the worst pun I've ever heard," Rory said.

"You'll be hearing more of them—just warning you," Steve said.

Rory laughed. "See you later."

"Good luck!" Steve called out. At least she had Steve the tennis pro on her side. Maybe it was a good thing that she compulsively became buddies with cute guys.

Main Street looked sleepy this morning, and aside from a few men and women clutching takeout coffees or walking their dogs, the sidewalks were largely empty. None of the fancy boutiques seemed to be open yet. A man on a ladder changed the movie-theater marquee letter by letter using a long stick. A shopkeeper swept the sidewalk. It looked like any small town early on a Saturday morning.

But when she got to the parking lot for Citarella, she realized where all the people were. They were here. The lot was thick with cars entering and exiting. At last she found a tight spot beside a Lexus and a gleaming Bentley. As she walked to the store, an SUV almost hit her as it backed out of its spot. "Sorry!" the female driver yelled through the window, barely stopping.

Once inside the doors, she was astonished to see that the checkout line snaked through the entire store, from two steps inside the entrance, down to the far wall, and back around to the front. It reminded her of the day before Hurricane Irene, when the A&P had been full of people trying to stock up on survival supplies. But there were no gallons of water or twelve-pack cans of tuna in these people's carts. Just a lot of small, dainty packages wrapped in brown butcher paper and small jars with shiny black lids. *Yeah, this isn't the A&P*, Rory thought, grabbing a shopping cart.

Most of the items on Bianca's list were things she'd never heard of. At the cheese section, she had to elbow her way past a line of pushing and shoving people, and even then she wasn't sure if she'd snagged the right brand of *Asiago Classico*. At the pasta counter, she ordered two pounds of fresh *richetti*, which turned out to be a fancier version of penne. In the condiment aisle, she grabbed jars of harissa red pepper paste and sun-dried miso, whatever they were. She reached for a bag of granola and gasped at the price. It was eleven dollars. Eleven dollars! Rory debated putting it back on the shelf, just on principle. But she threw it in the cart.

When she was finished, she walked over to the café area and

ordered herself a hot chocolate and a croissant. She'd barely had any of that smoothie Fee had made for her.

"That'll be six seventy-five," said the man behind the counter.

"What?" she asked.

"Six seventy-five," the man repeated.

"For hot chocolate and a croissant?"

The guy didn't blink.

Rory took out her wallet and handed him the money. Maybe her mom had been right about the Rules needing to pay her, she thought.

She ate her breakfast while in line to check out. After putting the three-hundred-dollar bill on Lucy Rule's account, she loaded the two bags into the trunk and pulled out of the parking lot. At the light, she typed TWO TREES, WATER MILL into the GPS.

"*Distance, nine miles,*" said the automated voice.

Rory checked the map on the screen. Water Mill was directly west of East Hampton on Montauk Highway, and then a mile or so north. She had at least fifteen minutes until she was supposed to be there. Nine miles, fifteen minutes—plenty of time, she thought.

Twelve minutes later, she'd barely driven two miles. Fee had been right. The traffic on Montauk Highway was almost at a standstill. She fiddled with the GPS, hoping there was another way to Water Mill besides this two-lane highway. There wasn't. She gripped the wheel, picturing Isabel waiting for her at the stables, her scowl growing darker and darker. It wasn't going to be a pleasant trip home.

At a quarter to twelve she turned off the highway onto Hayground Road and sped past open fields until she reached Two

Trees Stables. Isabel stood at the end of the long gravel drive, texting on her phone. In her jodhpurs and button-down white shirt, and with an ebony riding hat dangling from a strap around her wrist, she looked even more intimidating than she had yesterday. *Don't worry*, Rory told herself. *You don't need to be best friends. You don't even need to be friends. You just need to make it through twenty minutes in a car together.*

Rory lowered the window as she approached. "Hey, sorry I'm late," she said, stopping in front of her. "There was so much traffic."

Isabel marched around to the driver-side door, opened it, and looked at Rory impatiently.

"What?" Rory asked.

"I'm driving," Isabel announced.

"Um, actually, I think it's better that I—"

Isabel lowered her chin and glared at Rory. "*I'm driving*," she repeated.

Slowly, Rory unclicked her belt and got out of the car. Isabel slid behind the wheel and slammed the door. *So much for following Bianca's orders*, Rory thought.

She'd barely closed the shotgun door when Isabel stepped on the gas and made a rough U-turn. As they careened down the drive, she picked up her phone from her lap and began to text with one hand.

"Are you sure you should be doing that?" Rory asked, holding on to the dashboard.

"Doing what?" Isabel asked as the car drifted toward the center line.

"Texting. You could get a ticket. And it's kind of dangerous."

Isabel gave her a look, then dropped the phone in her lap and turned hard onto Hayground Road.

"So, where do you go to school?" Rory asked, feeling slightly sick to her stomach from all of the hard turns.

"Santa Barbara," Isabel finally said. "It's in California."

"I've never been to California. Never been on a plane, actually."

"Huh," Isabel said. "Fascinating."

"Do you have your own horse?" Rory asked, deciding to change the subject.

"Uh-huh," Isabel said.

"I've only been on a horse a couple of times, just for trail rides. I've never really ridden a horse. They actually kind of freak me out—"

"Sorry, can I just concentrate on the road?" Isabel interrupted. She made a left onto the highway, oblivious to the car coming directly at them.

"Sure," Rory said, swallowing.

When the traffic slowed to a crawl, Isabel picked up her phone and began to text again. Rory stared out the window. They were heading toward Bridgehampton now. A few minutes later, they passed a sign that read HISTORIC BRIDGEHAMPTON SETTLED 1656. *But with horrendous traffic from 2012*, Rory thought. "There are so many vegetable stands out here," she murmured, as they passed tent after tent with signs that read SWEET SUMMER CORN and FRESH TOMATOES. "People here really love food." *And yet everyone is thin*, Rory thought. It didn't make any sense.

Suddenly Isabel veered off the congested highway and onto the shoulder.

"What are you doing?" Rory asked.

"Everyone does this here," she said calmly.

"But you're on the shoulder! This is illegal."

"You really need to chill," Isabel said. Rory gripped the door handle just as the nose of a car suddenly poked out from a hidden driveway.

"Slow down!" Rory yelled.

Isabel slammed on the brake. The Prius lurched to a stop just in time. When Rory opened her eyes, she saw that they'd stopped a few feet from the other car. The elderly woman behind the wheel stared at them, too terrified to be angry.

"Well, that was close," Isabel noted.

"Are you crazy?" Rory cried. "You could have hit her!"

Isabel backed up to let the woman edge onto the highway. As soon as she was gone, Isabel continued down the shoulder.

"What are you *doing*?" Rory yelled.

"Will you please relax?" Isabel yelled back. A moment later they'd turned off the shoulder and were driving down a quiet, paved street. "See?" Isabel said. "*Jesus.*"

Rory fidgeted in the front seat. Her knuckles ached from squeezing the door handle. *Rich people*, she thought. They never thought the rules applied to them. And when they broke the rules, everything seemed to work out for them anyway.

A few minutes later, they were back on Lily Pond Lane. Isabel turned into the break in the hedges and stopped at the gate. She opened up the glove compartment and took out a small remote. "So are you catatonic or something?" she said.

Rory watched the gates silently open. "I'm fine," she muttered, as they began to drive beside the lawn. Sprinklers whipped streams of water over the grass.

"I'm sorry, okay?"

"Fine."

Rory glanced at Isabel's hand on the steering wheel. Her gold charm bracelet shone in the sun. Among other trinkets, a gold *I* hung off the chain. "I like your bracelet," she said, trying not to sound too nice.

"Thanks." Isabel looked over at Rory's own bracelet, which was made from purple rope. Rory waited for Isabel to say that she liked her bracelet, too, simply out of politeness, but she didn't say anything. *Figures*, Rory thought, turning to look out the window. This girl was awful.

As Isabel drove past the house toward the garages, Rory noticed a weathered, dark red Nissan Xterra parked in the circular drive. A bumper sticker read AIR AND SPEED SURF SHOP, MONTAUK, NY.

"Home in one piece," Isabel said sarcastically as she parked behind the Xterra.

Rory didn't respond. She got out and went straight to the trunk. Thankfully, the dozen organic brown eggs she'd just bought were still intact.

The back door of the house opened with a creak. "Isabel?" Fee asked, coming to stand on the threshold. "There's a boy here to see you."

A guy slipped out of the door behind Fee and walked onto the flagstone steps. It was hard not to stare. He was quite possibly the sexiest guy Rory had ever seen. Thick black hair fell over his eyes, which were large and liquid and a deep chocolate brown. Stubble covered his jaw and dimpled chin, but his lips were full and almost feminine. His white Hanes T-shirt and inky-dark jeans showed off a body that was lean and muscular in all the right places. *This guy is trouble*, Rory thought. *My mom would so be into him.*

Isabel stood at the car, her hand still resting lightly on the door handle. This had to be a dream, she thought as she watched him come toward her. He looked even better in clothes than he had in his wet suit. She looked at his tanned, ropy arms and remembered the way they'd made her feel when they were wrapped around her on the beach. Safe and excited and electrified. Her mind went blank.

"Hey," he said. "I came by to check on you."

"Hi," she said. The word come out as a whisper. She needed a glass of water. "How'd you find me?"

"It wasn't hard," he said with a knowing smile.

She was aware of Rory carrying grocery bags into the house and Fee following her inside. She was alone with him now. And he was still smiling at her.

"So, you know my name," she said. "What's yours?"

"Oh," he said with a grin. "Mike. Mike Castelloni."

"Mike," she said, nodding. "So now we're even." She grinned back.

"You ride horses?" he asked.

"Uh-huh."

"*And* you surf."

"Yup."

"Which do you do better?" he asked.

"I don't know. Maybe you can tell me."

He smiled wider. "You have a wet suit in there?" he asked, tilting his head toward the house.

She shrugged. "Of course."

He glanced at the thick black watch on his wrist. "Well, what are we waiting for?"

She paused to make sure he was serious. "Wait here. I'll be right out." She headed to the house, trying hard not to break into a run when she walked through the front door.

She raced across the foyer to the stairs. Everyone was probably at the club, which was perfect—she didn't want to have to ask anyone's permission to leave. She flew up the front staircase to her room, grasping the iron banister as she took the steps two at a time. So he did like her. In her room, she changed out of her riding clothes and into her favorite tangerine-colored bikini, matching tunic, and silver leather sandals. She grabbed her beach bag, then went down the back stairs to the mudroom. The mudroom was such a stupid name—as far as she knew, nobody had ever tracked mud into this room, only sand—but her parents insisted on calling it that. She threw open the closet doors and grabbed her suit and Connor's shortboard. She knew Connor wouldn't mind.

As she darted back into the hall, Rory came out of the kitchen. "Hey. Can you tell everyone that I took off for the beach with a friend?"

Rory shook some dark curly hair out of her face. "What's his name?"

"Mike. We're friends. We're going to Montauk."

"When will you be back?"

"Why do you need to know when I'll be back?" Isabel asked, slightly annoyed.

"What if they ask me?"

"Nobody will ask you," said Isabel. "Only mention it if it comes up. Okay? Thanks." Isabel grabbed the board. "See ya."

She didn't wait for Rory to reply. She turned and ran toward the front door, the soles of her sandals slapping on the marble floor. Behind her, she could feel the girl's eyes on her back, watching her go. Thinking that she was quite possibly making a total fool of herself.

But she didn't care. She'd worry about that later.

CHAPTER FIVE

Isabel squeezed the salt water out of her hair and threw her board on the sand. The last time she'd been to Ditch Plains, all she'd seen were the pebbles and the rocks and the drainpipe that stuck out in an unsightly way from under the dunes. But today the beach looked beautiful. Surfers bobbed on the surface of the dark blue water as haze from the salt spray swirled in the air. Groups of teenagers and young people hung out on faded blankets and plastic beach chairs. An against-the-rules black Lab trotted happily down the beach with a Frisbee in its mouth. And there was Mike, coming out of the water with his board under his arm and sending a lightning-quick shiver all over her skin.

"What do you think?" he said, shaking the water out of his hair. "You up for one more?"

"Sure. One more."

"Don't take this the wrong way," he said, "but you're better than I thought."

"I told you," she replied, throwing him a smile as she set off toward the water.

She threw herself belly-down on her board and paddled out. Behind her, Mike slammed onto his board and started racing her to the lineup.

He liked her. He didn't say too much, but every chance he could get he talked to her, complimented her, gave her some advice on her form. There hadn't been much time for any personal questions yet, which was just fine with her. There was so much she wanted to know about him, though. She didn't even know how old he was. Or where he lived. Or how many girls he was currently hooking up with. *Chill out*, she thought. *You have to relax.* She hadn't had to tell herself that in years.

When they reached the lineup, they sat astride their boards waiting for a wave. He was the one to start asking questions. "So...you're in high school, right?"

"Yeah."

"What year?"

"I'll be a senior."

One of his feet kicked hers under the water.

"How old are you?" she asked.

"I'm twenty," he said. "Too old?"

"Too old for what?" she asked.

He smiled at her. "I get the feeling that you always date people safe."

"Safe? Are you about to tell me that you're an ax murderer or something?"

"I mean, guys you know. Guys you can control." He grinned. "Am I right?"

"I get the feeling that you take a lot of girls surfing," she said.

"I don't take people surfing," he said, with such a dead-serious expression that she looked away and pretended to scan the water.

When her wave came, it took everything she had to concentrate, especially because she knew that he was watching her. She got to her feet at just the right moment and stood, one foot in front of the other, her arms straight out, with her gaze on the swiftly approaching shore. Luckily she didn't fall. And as her board flew over the water, she thought, *I really don't want this day to end. I want to be riding this wave for the rest of my life.*

Back on the beach she unzipped her wet suit and dried herself off with one of the beach towels Mike had in his car. Gulls squawked overhead. It had to be after three by now. She thought of Darwin and Thayer picking at their Georgica salads, scanning the patio for her arrival. She tried to imagine either of those girls sitting here with a guy like this. At Ditch Plains, no less.

She watched Mike ride his wave in, curving the board back and forth. He was definitely good. Better than any of the guys at school.

He walked up the beach when he was done, threw his board on the sand, and sat down on the towel. "So how does a lobster roll sound?" he asked. "If you still have some time."

"I have some time," she said, trying to sound casual. "And I love lobster."

"Good." He leaned toward her. She leaned into him, expecting a kiss, but he only grabbed an extra towel he'd left next to her and dried off his hair. "Let's go then," he said.

"Uh, sure," she said, hoping he hadn't noticed.

At the car he held a towel at his waist as he changed out of

72

his wet suit. She tried not to look. But at one point, she turned her head just as the towel fell an inch or so, enough to give her a thrilling view of the skin below his navel. She got inside the car before she started to stare. Why was she being so weird around this guy? It was as if she'd never been around a member of the opposite sex.

Her phone chimed softly from within her bag. Thayer had texted her:

WHERE R U??

Isabel smiled and put the phone back in her purse.

Mike opened the car door. "So where are we going?" she asked.

"Buford's," he said, sliding in behind the wheel in a white T-shirt and shorts. He smelled like fresh laundry. "You've been there before, right?"

"Actually, I haven't."

"You're kidding," he said, leaning close to her as he shifted into reverse. "How is that possible?"

Because my mom thinks it's a dump, she wanted to say, but didn't. All she did was shrug and give him her best mysterious smile.

They drove down the highway until the faded pink walls of Buford's Lobster Shack came into view. Buford's looked like it belonged on a back road in Jamaica or some other Caribbean island, not just outside a preppy summer town. Mike pulled into the small, crowded lot, right next to two twentyish surfers getting

73

out of an old van with boards strapped to the roof. She recognized them from the water.

"Hey, Mike!" one of them yelled as they got out of the car. "Your lady can shred!" The guy had a shaved head and wore a T-shirt with the *F* word printed loudly across the chest.

"I know," Mike said proudly. "Did you guys meet Isabel? This is Brad and Matt."

"Hi," she said, suddenly shy.

Brad, the one who'd spoken, gave Mike an approving look. "See ya inside, man," Brad said.

As they walked through the lot, Mike waved to two more surfer guys, and then two more when they joined the line waiting to order.

"You must come here a lot," she murmured.

"Yeah," he said nonchalantly. "It's one of my places."

Mike stepped up to order, but instead reached out and grasped the hand of a grizzled-looking man in his fifties behind the counter. "Wassup, bro?"

"Mikey," the man said, bumping Mike's fist with his own. "How's your dad? How come he never comes by anymore?"

"He's been pretty busy this season," Mike said. "But here's someone else for you to meet. Buford, meet Isabel. Isabel, this is Buford Giles."

"Hello," Isabel said, extending her hand.

"He's a softie, this one," he said, pointing to Mike. "I know he doesn't look it, but he is."

"All right, that's enough," Mike said, unlocking Isabel's hand from Buford's grip. "We'll take two number eights with extra mayo and sweet-potato fries. And two virgin coladas," he said with a wink.

"You got it." Buford winked back and disappeared behind the counter.

"You really do come here a lot," she said.

A moment later, he handed them two foamy drinks with straws and tiny umbrellas. Isabel took a sip of hers. It was definitely not a virgin colada. The rum burned her throat.

"Thanks, man," he said to Buford, then grabbed her hand to take her around to the patio. "They'll bring us the food," he said. "Come on, let's find a place to sit."

It was only about four o'clock, but almost every table was packed with surfers or people who looked like surfers, eating from baskets of fried clams and sipping tropical drinks. The smell of Malibu rum mingled with the tang of salt and grease. Reggae played over the PA. Everybody looked older than Isabel and Mike, but Mike moved across the patio like a celebrity, exchanging bro-shakes and high fives as people yelled out his name.

"What are you, the mayor of Montauk?" Isabel asked as they sat down at the only open table.

"I grew up out here," he said, stirring the foam of his drink.

"In Montauk?"

"The North Fork." He smiled. "You've heard of it?"

"Of course I have." She'd never actually met anyone from the North Fork before. She'd only been there a few times, usually to take the ferry to Block Island to see her aunt. Lots of farmland, small shingle homes, and homey seafood places near the harbor were all she remembered of it. "How does Buford know your dad?" she asked, changing the subject.

"We have a vegetable farm and a stand near Wainscott," he said. "He keeps Buford in corn and tomatoes all summer long."

"And he keeps you in piña coladas," she said, picking up her cup.

"You could say that."

"Do you work on the farm?" she asked, hoping that this didn't sound offensive for some reason.

"In the summers I do. During the rest of the year I go to Stony Brook." Mike leaned back in his patio chair, slipped off his flip-flops, and propped his tan feet on the arms of an unused chair.

"So what are you studying?" Isabel asked. It made sense that Mike would be in college, given his age, but she couldn't quite picture him in school.

"The usual stuff," Mike said cryptically. "Nothing that interesting. Let's talk about you. What were you trying so hard to get away from? The other day, out in the water?"

"Nothing."

"Nothing?"

"I just wanted to swim."

"Far, far away from your beach club. Which most people would do anything to belong to."

"Wait. Where are you going with this?"

He laughed and leaned closer to her, so close that she could see a faint stripe of sand near his jawbone in the fading light. "I guess I just want to know why you're out right now with a guy

76

from the North Fork when you could be sunning yourself at the Georgica Club."

"Maybe I'm bored," she said.

"Maybe you are."

"And I could ask you the same question. What are you doing out with a girl who's never been to Buford's Lobster Shack?"

Without taking his eyes off her, he picked up his drink and took a long sip. She'd never seen a guy who said so little and yet communicated so much at the same time. And right now his smile seemed to say, *Because you are the sexiest girl I've ever seen, and I can't wait to kiss you.*

The pause was broken by Buford delivering their food. "Here you go," he said, setting the paper plates down on the table. "Two lobsters. Extra mayo. Enjoy."

As he walked away, Isabel looked down at the lobster roll nestled beside a mountain of salty sweet-potato fries. "This looks incredible."

"Yup. I'd say this would be my last meal."

She picked up the sandwich and took a messy bite. "Wow."

He nodded as if this was just what he'd expected to hear. "What's *your* last meal?" he asked.

"Maybe this."

"Last dessert, then?"

"Oh, that's easy. Strawberry shortcake."

He laughed.

"What?" she asked. "Why is that funny?"

"Strawberry shortcake?" he asked skeptically.

"Have you ever had it?" she asked.

"I think so."

"It's amazing," she said with conviction. "And I can make it."

"*You* can make it?" he asked.

"Yeah. My mom doesn't usually let me do stuff in the kitchen, but whenever I bake, I'm awesome."

He looked like he was trying hard not to laugh again. "Wait. Why doesn't your mom let you do stuff in the kitchen?"

"Because we have help. Why would my parents want me to cook?"

"I don't know, maybe to teach you how to take care of yourself?" he asked with a glint in his eye. He dipped a fry into the mayo. "You should make me some one day."

"Only if you're really, really nice to me." She pulled away from him and let some hair fall over one eye. "Now let me ask you something. How many girlfriends do you have?"

"Have or had?"

"*Have.* As in, right now."

The beat of the music changed and bloomed into something slow and sexy. A song she'd loved last summer.

From the very first time I rest my eyes on you, girl
My heart said follow through
But I know now that I'm way down on your line
But the waiting feel is fine

The rum was starting to make her feel dizzy. She closed her eyes and swayed a little with the beat of the music, until she felt Mike's fingers creep stealthily over her hand. She opened her eyes and saw that he was looking right at her.

"Just one. But I'm still working on it."

* * *

Rory leaned against the mountain of bed pillows and looked at the cell phone in her hand. Three missed calls, all from Lana McShane. Her mom never did like to leave voice mails. Instead, she liked to call over and over again and hang up, which always succeeded in making Rory feel both guilty *and* panicked.

At least tonight had been quiet. She'd eaten dinner with Fee, Bianca, and Erica, the new chef. Petite but strong, with a mass of light brown curls, Erica insisted on whipping up a separate dinner of pappardelle with spring vegetables and ricotta just for the four of them. The food was delicious, but Bianca barely touched it, as she was too engrossed in an episode of *Downton Abbey* to pay attention to any of them. Afterward Rory had taken a long bubble bath in the sunken marble tub, then wrapped herself in the silk and chenille bathrobe that hung on the back of her bathroom door and got into bed. It was nine forty-five and all she wanted to do was go to sleep. But if she didn't call back, her mom would probably call again. Might as well get this over with, Rory thought as she dialed.

Her mom answered after one ring. "Hullo?" It was only one word, but Rory could hear the wine in it.

"Hey, Mom, it's me. Sorry I missed your calls."

"Oh. Did I call you more than once?"

"I think so. How's it going?"

"Not so good." There was a muted sniffle. "I think Bryan and I broke up."

"Oh," Rory said, feeling a twinge of guilt. She hadn't seen that one coming—at least, not this soon. "I'm sorry."

"Honey, I need you," her mom half pleaded, half ordered. "I need you to come home. Now."

"Mom, I can't. I just got here."

"Rory, *please*. And they turned off the cable yesterday on top of everything, so I can't even watch TV—"

"I put the bill on the fridge. Didn't you see it?"

"I was just a little late with it," her mom said, annoyed. "Tell Aunt Fee you're very sorry but that I need you. She'll understand." There was another sniffle. "You're all I've got, honey."

Rory squeezed one tiny blue-and-white-speckled throw pillow. She could feel the familiar vines of guilt creeping through the phone line and wrapping themselves around her, tighter and tighter. "I can't," she finally said. "I just got here. It would be really bad for me to leave right now. Just go to bed. Everything will be better tomorrow. I promise."

There was a click and then silence.

"Hello? Mom?"

She'd hung up. Rory looked at the dark face of her cell phone. Her mom had ended their phone conversations like this before, but Rory had never felt this annoyed by it. *Screw you*, she thought. She turned off the ringer and put the phone in the top drawer of the bedside table, where she wouldn't even hear it vibrate. If her mom called back, she didn't want to know.

She pulled the covers up to her chin and sank into the plush mattress. Maybe coming to East Hampton hadn't been such a mistake after all. Nursing her mom through her latest breakup was starting to get old. And her mom was an adult, as Sophie and

Trish were always telling her. She could take care of herself. She wasn't supposed to be the mom, they would tell her over and over again.

But what if you don't know anything else? she wondered.

"Wait here," Isabel said as they pulled up in front of the iron gates. "I need to punch in the code."

Slowly she let go of Mike's hand—the one that had been holding hers all the way home from Buford's—and got out of the car. She wavered for a moment, then put her hand on the door to keep her balance. The ground teetered up and down. Buford's not-so-virgin coladas were exacting their revenge. *Focus*, she thought. She steadied herself, then walked around the front of the humming car and over to the intercom.

So far, the entire day had been perfect, except for one thing: Mike hadn't kissed her yet. She knew that he wanted to. At Buford's they'd moved their plastic patio chairs closer and closer to each other while they talked, until their faces were so close together that once or twice she'd buried her head into his shoulder and laughed. Then they'd gotten into his car in the dark, still laughing (she more than he—she'd had half of a second piña colada; he'd had a Coke), and she'd leaned her head back and looked at him and thought, *Okay, now. Now he has to do it. Now he has to kiss me.* But all he'd done was turn on the car and take her hand and say "I should probably get you home."

"Okay," she'd said, a little stunned. And it had only made her want him more.

She leaned over the intercom box, trying to remember the

81

code, when she heard Mike say, "Maybe I should just drop you off here."

She turned around. The ground teetered again. "Why?" she asked.

"Because it's a little late."

"Are you afraid of my parents?" she teased.

Mike laughed and shook some hair out of his eyes. "This just might not be the best time to meet them."

Isabel looked past the gates, at the long, softly illuminated drive. She didn't want to say good-bye to him here. She was already out of the car. How could he kiss her if she was out of the car? "Hold on," she said. "I have a better idea."

Rory bunched the pillow up under her head and grabbed the remote control from the nightstand. The night before, she'd had no problem falling asleep, but tonight she was as wide awake and alert as if she'd had two mocha lattes after dinner. This was the last time she'd call home before bed. Dealing with her mom this late at night was guaranteed insomnia.

A scratching noise sounded at the window. She looked up. Was it a raccoon? Did they have raccoons out in the Hamptons?

The noise sounded again. She sat up. This time it wasn't so much a scratching as it was a shuffling or a straining, hands grasping at the frame. Something—or someone—was trying to open the window.

Finally the window came loose and rose with a loud squeak. As Rory sat in bed, too frightened to move, she watched a guy slowly climb into her room, one leg at a time.

She screamed and turned on the light.

"Sorry!" he yelled.

It was the sexy guy she'd seen outside the house that morning. Except this time he didn't look nearly as cool. "Sorry!" he whispered, both of his hands up as if he'd just been arrested. "Sorry!"

"What the hell are you doing here?" she yelled, pulling the covers up to her neck.

The guy blinked and slowly put his hands down. "Isabel told me—"

The doorknob turned, and as the guy scrambled back through the window, Bianca Vellum charged into the room, clutching a striped silk robe to her chest. "What is going on here?" she demanded, blinking at Rory in the light.

Rory watched as Mike's right flip-flop disappeared over the windowsill and into the night. "Nothing," she said.

Bianca glanced at the window and then looked back at Rory. From the irate look on her face, Rory knew she'd seen Mike's foot, too.

"That was—it's not what it looks like—" Rory began.

"I'm only going to say this once," Bianca said, almost trembling with anger. "This is someone else's home. Not yours. Do you understand that?"

"Yes," Rory breathed.

Bianca wrapped her robe tighter around herself. "Good night," she said with palpable disgust, and closed the door.

Rory sat by herself in the empty room, feeling as if a hurricane had just swept through. This had to be Isabel's doing. She'd told him to come in this way—she was sure of it. She seemed determined to get her kicked out of here. And at this rate, it would be a miracle if she didn't.

Upstairs, Isabel lay on her bed as the floor listed to the left and right in a nauseating way. She'd just heard what sounded like a scream in the room below, then the sound of Mike tearing across the lawn, followed by Bianca chewing somebody out. Somebody had caught Mike sneaking into the downstairs guest room, and it wasn't Bianca. Who had it been?

Rory. Rory had caught him.

And by now she would have told Bianca that he was Isabel's friend, and that would be it. In the past four years that she'd been house manager, Bianca had never missed an opportunity to bust Isabel for any and every little thing. She seemed to take pleasure in updating Lucy on all of Isabel's misdeeds. By the time she woke up tomorrow, her mom would know all about her sneaking some guy into the house and she'd be lucky if she wasn't grounded for the rest of the month. Oh well, she thought, closing her eyes. Let them ground her. She had no doubt that she would see him again. And next time, no matter what it took, she'd make sure he kissed her.

The next morning, Rory woke up at dawn. Birds chirped madly in the trees as gray light filtered through the blinds. She stretched and yawned, taking her time to wake up, until the memory of last night came back to her. With a shot, she sat up in bed and clutched the sheets to her chest. This morning everyone would know some guy had tried to sneak into her room. The Rules would be furious. She had no explanation. Telling them it was Isabel's new boyfriend wasn't an option. She could handle the Rules being mad at her, but not Isabel. She was scary enough already.

She finally got out of bed and into the shower. When she stepped into the hall in her favorite pair of jeans and her prettiest cotton tank, the house was still. Apparently Sunday was the one day that the Rules slept in.

She walked down the hall and pushed open the swinging door. Thankfully, the only person in the kitchen was Fee, who was bent over the open dishwasher, unloading glasses.

"Good morning," Rory said as brightly as possible.

Fee barely glanced at her as she wiped the glasses dry with a towel. "G'morning," she said tersely. "How'd you sleep?"

She knows, Rory thought. *Of course she knows.* "Fee, last night isn't what you think," she said. "In case you heard."

"You can't be sneaking boys into your room," Fee said slowly, still not looking at her. "That's the one thing, Rory. You just can't be having romances here."

Just tell her who's really having a romance around here, she thought. But she couldn't. She reached down and pulled a heavy painted platter from the dishwasher. "Do the Rules know?"

"I begged Bianca not to say anything," Fee said, taking the platter from Rory's hands. "And she actually said she wouldn't. Of course, now I'm obligated to the stuck-up cow, which is the last thing on earth I wanted."

"I'm sorry about that. But thank you for asking her not to say anything."

"I just don't understand it," Fee said. "I didn't think you were like that."

I'm not, Rory was about to say when the kitchen door swung open. Rory turned around, expecting to see Bianca's disapproving face, but instead Isabel staggered into the room, looking like she'd hardly slept. Her eyes were bloodshot, her skin looked sallow, and her hair hung in messy clumps around her face. *Hangover*, Rory thought. *Big-time*.

"Is there any more of that green juice that Eduardo used to make?" she asked in a raspy voice.

"I think some's in here," Fee said, opening the refrigerator and rummaging around. She seemed not to notice Isabel's hangover. Or she was used to it.

Rory took the opportunity to shoot Isabel a look, but Isabel staunchly avoided her eyes.

"Here you go," Fee said, handing an unmarked plastic bottle of green sludge to her. "You feeling okay?"

"I think I might have the flu," Isabel said.

Flu? Rory thought, glaring at her. *Puh-leeze*.

"Oh, well, in that case you better get right back to bed," said Fee.

"Thanks." Isabel shuffled out, pushing the door with the tips of her fingers.

"Something must be going around," Fee murmured as she turned back to the dishwasher.

"I'll be right back," Rory said. She pushed through the swinging door. She couldn't let Isabel get away with this.

"Hey, can I talk to you for a sec?" she asked as soon as she and Isabel were alone in the hall.

Isabel turned and gave Rory an annoyed look.

"So, can we talk about the guy who snuck into my room last night?" Rory began. "The one I took the blame for?"

Isabel's expression betrayed nothing.

"I was just curious if you have a reaction," she said.

"Thanks," Isabel said in a toneless voice. "Is that what you want me to say? Thank you so, so much for covering for me? And just so you know, I had no idea you were staying there. And I wouldn't call it 'your room.' It's the guest room. And *you* are a guest." She turned back to the stairs.

"I'm sure you wouldn't mind if I got kicked out of here, but I need to be here," Rory said. "I'm sorry if you have a problem with that."

"I don't have a problem," Isabel said over her shoulder. She stomped up the staircase, out of sight. A door closed upstairs.

Rory took a deep breath, clenching her hands into fists. For the first time she understood the impulse to punch something. This girl was terrible. She was a snob. She was spoiled. And she had absolutely no scruples, whatsoever. From now on Rory would do whatever she could to avoid her. She'd also try to convince Bianca and Fee that she wasn't clueless, reckless, or immature enough to ask guys to sneak into her room, though she doubted that was possible now.

When she walked back into the kitchen, Fee was gone. She looked around at the shiny counters and glistening appliances and felt the sudden urge to flee. She needed some fresh air. And then she remembered the beach. She still hadn't even seen it. *We don't stand on ceremony,* Mr. Rule had said. And yet, she got the distinct impression that the staff at this house didn't spend too much time sunning themselves on the Rules' private strip of sand.

She walked out of the house, through the rose garden, and out onto the flagstone patio. At the far end, past the two pools and the line of chaise longues with spotless white cushions, an American flag snapped in the breeze. She walked toward the flag until the grayish-blue ocean came into view. Feeling excited, she followed a pathway of wooden planks that led over some grassy dunes, down to the sand. She slid off her flip-flops. She couldn't believe how clean it was down here. No beer cans or empty suntan-lotion bottles or even footprints. And there was nobody in sight on either side. It truly felt like her own private island.

It was low tide. Tiny birds waddled in the wet, suedelike sand. A wave gathered momentum and crashed. She walked to the edge, and an icy span of water covered her feet. She turned and looked at the chimneys and dormer windows of the mansion next door, just visible over the dunes. Did that family ever come down to the beach? Did any of them ever get outside their own heads to notice any of this? Why did the Rules belong to a country club when they had this all to themselves? Someone like Isabel Rule obviously didn't appreciate this house, but she wondered if any of the Rules did.

After countless minutes of staring at the ocean, she turned back. Bianca was probably looking for her. She climbed up the sun-warmed planks, feeling the burn in her hamstrings and a strong sense of defeat. No doubt Bianca was still going to be a little disgusted with her. She'd have to brace herself for another lecture.

When she arrived at the patio, she saw that it was no longer deserted. A swimmer cut through the surface of the lap pool, doing a perfect crawl.

It was a guy—that much she could see. *Connor Rule*, she thought. The swimmer. Had to be. She slipped on her flip-flops and set off across the flagstones, hoping to walk right by him. Then she heard the chime of a cell phone. She spied the iPhone lying on one of the cushioned chaises, right next to a fluffy towel and a burgundy sweatshirt. She looked back at the swimmer, still doing his crawl. Before she really knew what she was doing, she'd picked up the phone and walked back to the pool.

"Um, excuse me?" she called out. "Your phone! It's ringing!"

The swimmer darted his head up from the water. Goggles looked back at her. "What?"

"Your phone!" she said.

He swam to the side of the pool, and she leaned over to hand it to him. But their hands didn't quite meet. A moment later, there was a soft *plunk*. She watched his phone sink straight to the bottom of the pool.

"Oh my god," she said.

Without a word, he dove down, retrieved the phone, and swam back to the surface.

"Oh my god...I'm so...I'm so sorry," she said.

He didn't hear her. With a splash of water and a ripple of

triceps, the guy hoisted himself out of the pool and got to his feet. For a moment, Rory thought he was naked, but then she saw his navy Speedo. His very tiny navy Speedo.

"No worries," he said, whipping off his goggles. "I was getting sick of it anyway."

"I'm so sorry," she repeated. "That was so clumsy of—"

"Really, don't worry about it," he said, running a hand over his wet hair. "I'm Connor, by the way. And you are—"

"Rory."

"Right," he said. He put out his hand, and she shook it, trying not to be too taken by his greenish-blue eyes. "My mom said you're staying with us for the summer." He tossed the phone on the chaise as if it was already forgotten and grabbed a towel. "How's it going so far?"

The same nerves she'd felt in front of Steve were amplified a thousand times by the sight of blond, tan Connor Rule in his very tiny Speedo. "Good. Except for all the phones I've thrown in the pool," she joked.

"Well, like I said," he said, drying his shoulders, "you've just done me a big favor."

"Oh yeah? Why?"

"It's just nice to get a little break once in a while," he said. "I don't always like being reachable."

"Yeah, I know what you mean," she said.

"Oh yeah?" he asked. "Is there someone you'd like to avoid?"

"Sometimes, yeah."

"So who's that?" he asked, and he actually sounded as if he really wanted to know.

She thought about telling him the truth and then decided against it. "Nobody you know," she said.

He smiled as he dropped the towel on the chaise. "My mom drives me nuts, too," he said.

Rory laughed.

"So I was right, huh?" he asked.

"Absolutely," she said. She felt the flutter of something electric and unsaid pass between them, a type of connection being made. This guy wasn't just cute. He was funny and nice and easy to talk to. Almost on instinct, she stepped back toward the house. "Thanks for being so cool about the phone. I'm sorry again."

"No problem," he said, snapping on his goggles. "Next time I'll make sure everything's nailed down out here."

She laughed again and then hurried back to the house, feeling like she was being watched. Turned out, she was.

"We need you to go to Dreesen's," Bianca said in a sour voice when Rory walked back into the house.

"Sure thing," Rory said. "I'll just get my bag."

"And another thing," Bianca said. "Staff aren't supposed to be down at the beach after nine. *Or* on the patio."

Before Rory could respond, Bianca turned and walked back to the kitchen.

CHAPTER SIX

There were only so many times that you could read a text before you went crazy, Isabel thought as she looked down at her phone under the table.

Hey Beautiful. Had to bolt. Maybe we hang this week?

She scrolled down to her reply, which she'd sent a strategic seventy-five minutes later:

Definitely. ☺

That had been yesterday morning, and she still hadn't heard from him. Had it been the word *definitely*? The smiley face? It was probably the smiley face, she thought. She'd have to dial it down next time. Mike could probably tell how much she liked him.

Just two nights ago, she'd been sitting next to him in the car, laughing and listening to music, and holding his hand as if their mutual attraction was an assured, understood thing. He'd wanted to kiss her. She was positive of that. And she'd been *so* close to it. And now, she had no idea if she was ever going to see him again, let alone kiss him.

"Put the phone away," her father said from across the breakfast table. "You're going to see everyone at the club in a couple of hours."

"It's not someone from the club," she said.

"Isabel," he said in a warning voice, and she put the phone facedown on the table with a sigh. Family breakfast on Monday morning was one of her family's more torturous summer rituals. Her dad had started it as a way to spend more time with them before he drove into the city for the week, but all it did was make everyone edgy and tense with its feeling of forced togetherness. Isabel would have much preferred sleeping in.

"Good morning!" said her mom as she and Sloane walked into the breakfast room. Her mom liked to stay in her yoga clothes for as long as possible after a lesson, the better to show off her toned figure. Sloane, on the other hand, always changed into one of her shapeless tunics and Capri pants immediately. Sloane had been in a battle with the same ten pounds ever since seventh grade, and all these years later, she seemed no closer to victory. Most of the time, Isabel wished her sister would just accept her body shape and find something more interesting to do with her time than diet.

"We had a fantastic class," her mom said, taking her usual seat. A copy of the *New York Times* had been left on her place mat as always, along with a glass of thick green vegetable juice. "What a beautiful day," she said, taking a sip from her glass.

"They said it's going to be almost ninety," Sloane said, digging into a sectioned grapefruit, which she ate every morning. "First heat wave of the summer."

Isabel rolled her eyes. Her sister was so lame.

"I think we'll stop by the Sagaponack place on our way into the city," her father said. "Can't hurt to just show our faces."

"If you want to," her mother said.

"Plus the old guy likes Gregory," her father said.

"He's just not scared of me the way he is of you," Gregory said.

"Well, that sounds wonderful." Her mom opened her newspaper and began to read as if they weren't even there.

"You know, a little enthusiasm wouldn't hurt," her father said. "Especially for sixteen million."

"But I don't want to sell this house," her mother replied, her eyes on the paper. "I've told you that. A hundred times."

"Right," her father said. "You want to worry about the old plumbing and the beach erosion and the historical-preservation people on our backs all the time—"

"Yes, I do," her mother said.

"Why are you so attached to this house? It's a money pit. All the renovations, all the landscaping—"

"It's *mine*," her mother said, with a finality that made her father push his chair back from the table with a loud screech.

"Greg? You ready?"

Isabel studied the untouched stack of pancakes on her plate. She hadn't missed any of her parents' bickering. Now she had three more months of it to endure.

Gregory put down his fork and stood up, like the dutiful son he'd been since birth. "No problem," he said.

Gregory started working for their dad's company the day after he graduated from Harvard, and a year later, he seemed right on track to turn into Lawrence Rule in every way, shape, and form. Isabel could just picture him in twenty years: married to a wife who couldn't stand him and the father of four kids he desperately wanted to be friends with but didn't know how to be.

Sloane was slightly better-looking than Gregory, but she wasn't the type to go into the family business (or any kind of business, for that matter), and therefore got much less of their dad's attention. But their father, Gregory, and Sloane seemed to form a little triad, and their common bond and purpose was Isabel—what to do with her, how to control her, how to punish her. She'd noticed this for the first time last summer, after all that business with the fire. Sloane had suggested they send Isabel away to a school in Denver where they put kids in solitary for a night if they broke any rules. Gregory had suggested one of those places that kidnap kids in the middle of the night to take them to a wilderness survival camp. And her dad had gone ahead and paid tuition for her first year at school in California before her mom had even agreed to it. Most of the time, Isabel couldn't believe that she was related to the three of them in the slightest. At least she had Connor, but for some reason he didn't feel the same utter dislike she felt toward their oldest siblings. But then again, Connor got along with everybody. She would have to teach him how to be much more of a jerk. Girls were always walking all over him.

"Have a good week," her mother said languidly as her father exited the room.

Gregory walked over and leaned down to give her a kiss on the cheek. "See you Friday, Mom."

"Good-bye, honey," she said. "Work hard."

As they walked out, Isabel felt the urge to leave, too. She always felt like this after her parents had a fight. Maybe she could just borrow the car and go find Mike's farm stand near Wainscott. It wouldn't exactly be stalking, because it was probably right on the highway.

"So, what are we all going to do today?" her mom asked brightly. "Go to the club? Or go shopping?"

"I heard there's a sale at Lilly Pulitzer," Sloane said.

"Sounds fascinating," Isabel muttered.

A curly-haired brunette with a perky smile came into the room carrying a bowl of wild blueberries. Isabel assumed that this was the new chef. She never bothered to learn their names— they never stayed very long. "How does everything taste out here?" she asked as she placed the bowl in front of Mrs. Rule.

"Everything's wonderful, Erica," her mom said, barely meeting her eye. "Could you send Bianca out here, please?"

"Sure," she said. Isabel could see the worry creeping into Erica's smile.

She left, and Bianca entered the room. "Yes?" she asked.

"Bianca, would you please let Erica know that from now on, I will speak to her about the food *after* we've finished eating?"

"Of course," Bianca demurred.

"And did FedEx come yet?"

"Yes, I'll have them brought out," Bianca said, and slipped out again.

"Mom, can I borrow the Prius?" Isabel asked. "Just for, like, an hour. I'll bring it right back."

"No," her mom said, sounding annoyed, spooning some Greek yogurt into her bowl of blueberries.

"Why not?"

"Because you don't have your license."

"But I know how to drive," Isabel assured her.

"Um, no, you don't," Sloane put in. "You almost drove us right off a cliff in Vail over spring break."

"Because someone gave me wrong directions," Isabel countered. "Plus, I need to practice for my next test."

"Not by yourself," her mom said.

Isabel glanced at Connor.

"No way, Iz," Connor said, holding up his hands. "I tried. You won't listen to me."

"That's not true."

"Sorry, but I'm not gonna do it anymore," Connor said.

"Well, if nobody's going to give me lessons," Isabel said, "then how am I going to pass the stupid test?"

Rory entered, FedEx envelopes in her hands. She still looked terrified, or at least robotic, and she avoided all eye contact with Isabel as she carried the letters over to Mrs. Rule. "Here you go," Rory said, handing her the FedEx letters.

"Thank you, Rory," Isabel's mother said. "How's everything going? Is everything all right?"

"It's great," Rory said, her eyes on the floor.

Isabel saw her steal a glance at Connor—or was it at her?—and then look away.

"Tell me, you have your driver's license, right?"

Rory looked up. "Uh, yes."

"Then maybe *you* could give Isabel some driving lessons."

Isabel almost bolted out of her seat. "That's a really bad idea."

"Why?" Her mom turned back to Rory. "You passed your driver's test on the first try, right?"

"Right," Rory said, swallowing hard.

"Well, there you go, she's obviously good at this—"

"But she *just* got her license. She's not even allowed to teach *me* how to drive," Isabel said. "Legally."

"I seriously doubt that's going to be a problem," her mom said, ripping open one of the envelopes. "As long as she knows what to do. Rory will give you lessons in the car a few times a week until you're ready to take your driver's test. That's fine with you, isn't it, Rory?"

Rory's face was so pale by now that Isabel thought she might be sick. "Uh, sure," she said.

"What if it's not fine with *me*?" Isabel asked.

Her mom glowered at Isabel.

"Whatever," Isabel muttered. She looked back at Rory's pale face. She'd be at Mike's farm stand in no time.

After breakfast, Rory sat in the passenger seat of the Prius, trying not to let her palms get sweaty as Isabel sped down the center of Lily Pond Lane. The two girls still hadn't spoken. It had been obvious how Isabel felt about this arrangement, and Rory didn't blame her. But she needed to say something before Isabel managed to get them on the highway again.

"So, how about we try a three-point turn?" she asked nicely.

"You're not a driving teacher," Isabel said. "Just thought I should remind you."

"I know," Rory said. "Your mom asked me to do this."

Isabel threw her a disdainful look and then suddenly turned hard to the left and braked. They were inches away from the curb.

"Great," Rory said, swallowing. "Now, put the car in reverse."

Isabel yanked the gearshift up to reverse, revved the gas, and the car lurched backward.

"That's good," Rory said, trying to sound encouraging. "Now shift back into drive."

Isabel yanked the gearshift back down and slammed her foot on the gas again. The car leaped forward, narrowly missing a child on a bike.

"*Slowly!*" Rory cried.

"I am going slowly!" Isabel yelled. "See?" She touched the brake slightly. "Everything's fine. What's the problem?"

Rory took a deep breath. No wonder nobody in Isabel's family wanted to do this. "Okay, how about we practice parking?" she asked.

"Why don't we just drive for a while?" Isabel said, turning off Lily Pond and onto the road that led to the highway.

"Maybe we should stay in the neighborhood," Rory said. "While we're still getting the basics down."

"Nah. I think we should go to Wainscott."

"What's in Wainscott?" Rory asked.

Isabel unsnapped the beaded clutch bag at her hip. "Want some gum?"

"What? Uh, no. No, thanks."

Isabel pulled out a pink pack of bubble gum and unwrapped a piece as the car swerved to the left.

"Watch it!" Rory yelled.

Isabel grabbed the steering wheel.

"Just...pull over!" Rory said.

Isabel pulled over to the side of the road and then calmly popped the gum in her mouth.

"You really are kind of bad at this," Rory marveled.

Isabel narrowed her eyes.

"I mean, no offense."

Isabel chewed her gum for a moment in silence. "I'm sorry about the other night. About Mike sneaking into your room. That was really cool of you to take the blame."

"That's okay," Rory said, a little stunned.

Isabel pulled some blond hair behind her ear. She slid her iPhone out from her bag and clicked it on. "I wonder if I should just text him."

"Who?"

"The guy who tried to sneak into your room. Here, look." She held up her phone so that Rory could read the text on her screen. "What do you think that means?"

Rory read the three lines. "I guess it means he wants to hang this week."

"Uh-huh," Isabel said. "Then why hasn't he written back?"

"Wasn't that just yesterday?"

"Yeah, but normally he would have written again by now."

"What do you mean, normally?" Rory asked.

"I mean, when I've been with other guys. You know."

"So in the past, guys have texted you back right away, every time you text them?"

"Pretty much."

Rory looked out the windshield. *Another thing we don't have in common*, she thought. *Among thousands.*

"What about you?" Isabel asked. "Do you have a boyfriend?"

"No."

"Well, how many guys would you say you've gone out with?"

Rory turned to look at her. "Why?"

"I'm just curious."

"I don't know," she muttered.

"Ballpark."

"I'm not really sure."

"Two? Three? Six, seven?"

"I don't know," Rory said, dusting the dashboard with her fingers. "Not that many."

Isabel gave Rory a searching look, as if she were trying to count the number of pores on her face. "You've never had a boyfriend, have you?" she finally said.

Rory looked back in front of her and sat up straighter in her seat. "Um...well...if you mean, like in the actual sense of dating someone? Uh...no."

Isabel sat up straighter. "Oh my god." She put her hand on the steering wheel to brace herself. "*Seriously?*"

Rory felt the telltale burning behind her eyes. She was turning beet red. "Yes."

"Are you a lesbian?" Isabel asked. "Because, if you are, that's perfectly fine—"

"No, I'm not a *lesbian*," Rory said. "I'm *busy*. I work every day after school. I pay all the bills, I do the grocery shopping, I make sure my mom goes to work and doesn't drink herself into a coma every night.... I have more important stuff going on, okay?"

Isabel seemed to consider this for a moment. "We need to find you a boyfriend."

For a second, Connor's face flashed across Rory's mind.

"Or at least a fling," Isabel added. "Have you even been kissed?"

"Of course."

"And other stuff?"

"Oh my god," Rory said, starting to fidget. "This is so none of your business."

"Good," Isabel said, undeterred. "So, we're gonna find you a guy. It's summer. You're supposed to be having fun right now. And trust me, *you* really need to have fun."

"But guys are never just fun," Rory said.

"What? Of course they are."

"With my friends, it always starts out really fun, and then it can become really *un*-fun. They're just waiting for him to call, or they don't know how to read him, and then they get all insecure, and then they start to obsess—"

"Because those girls don't know what they're doing," Isabel

said, folding her tan arms. "You just need to keep the upper hand."

"The upper hand?" Rory asked. "How do you do that?"

"Every girl can have the upper hand," Isabel said, rolling her eyes with the obviousness of it. "If you stay mysterious and you don't give away too much information and you always keep a guy guessing and never let them know how you really feel, then you'll be the one in control. And if you're the one in control, then you'll never get hurt."

Rory paused to take this in. "So you've never been hurt by a guy?"

Isabel looked out the windshield, chewing her bottom lip as she mulled this over. "Nope," she finally said. "Uh-uh."

"Well, my experience has been a little bit different."

"So you *have* had a boyfriend?"

"There was one guy, but he wasn't really my boyfriend."

"What happened?"

Rory scratched a mosquito bite on her leg. She couldn't believe that she was having this conversation with Isabel Rule, for one, and now she couldn't believe that she was about to tell her about Jason Merrick, who'd flirted with her for most of last fall. He'd finally asked her out to see a Ben Stiller movie, then made out with her in his car, only to get back together the next Monday with his ex-girlfriend. "I'd rather not get into it."

"Fine." Isabel took out her gum and stuck it in the wrapper she still had in her hand. Then she tossed it out the open window behind her. "But whatever happened, it doesn't have to be like that next time."

"But what if you're not that kind of person?" Rory asked. "What if you just want to be honest with someone? Why does it have to be a game?"

"It's always a game," Isabel said, turning the key in the ignition. An earsplitting screech followed.

"The engine's still on," Rory sighed.

"And it works," Isabel said, oblivious to her mistake. "Any girl can have a guy wrapped around her finger. You just need to know how to do it." She checked her watch. "I guess I should head over to the Georgica. Can you drop me?"

"I'll drive," Rory said, opening the car door.

Isabel gave up her seat quietly and walked around the front of the car to the shotgun side. Once behind the wheel, Rory adjusted the mirrors—Isabel had twisted them into all kinds of unusable angles—and pulled back onto the road. Beside her Isabel began to tap out a text on her phone. "Um, where am I going?" Rory asked.

"Oh, just take a right here, then take it all the way down, then make a left," she said, not looking up from her phone.

Rory drove as Isabel texted. As they glided down the winding back roads, past homes set back behind long sloping front lawns, Rory thought about dating. Isabel was right—for some girls, it *was* just a game. There were the three or four girls in her class who took turns dating all the good-looking guys in school, trading them with as little emotion as if they were bottles of nail polish. There was her mom, who'd certainly broken her share of hearts. There were the girls at summer camp who practically seduced a few of the male counselors and laughed about it. And there was Isabel Rule, who could say with utter certainty that she'd never been hurt by a guy. So what was wrong with Rory? Why couldn't she be one of those girls?

Rory drove past an ancient-looking cemetery, with its rows of sun-bleached tombstones sinking into the grass, and then down Main Street, past a cluster of girls walking out of Blue & Cream with shopping bags. Maybe it really was just about knowing how to play the game, and maybe she could learn to do it here, in East Hampton, where nobody knew anything about her. But if all guys were so easily played, then how could you ever fall in love with one of them? Like Connor—he didn't seem like the kind of person who would fall for all of that.

Connor, she thought, sighing inwardly. Ever since their talk by the pool, she couldn't stop thinking about him. Knowing that he was under the same roof made it impossible to concentrate. She'd had to ask Bianca to repeat the names of the morning newspapers she was supposed to get at Dreesen's, just because she thought she heard his voice outside the kitchen. In the breakfast room today, she'd almost broken out into a sweat when she had to deliver the FedEx envelopes. And when Mrs. Rule had asked her to give Isabel driving lessons, she'd barely been able to focus because Connor had been at the breakfast table, watching the entire interaction.

But maybe the chemistry she'd felt between them was really just wishful thinking. He was so good-looking, and so smart, and so friendly, that of course she was going to think that there had been some kind of connection when they met. And, really, even if he didn't have a girlfriend, which seemed impossible, what could a guy like Connor Rule ever see in her? She didn't know a thing about college or growing up in New York City or living on your own private beach. Not to mention that he was, technically, her employer. Which meant that they couldn't date anyway.

"Just take this street all the way," Isabel said.

Rory headed straight for the shingle mansion that lay at the end of the road. The Georgica Club was only slightly bigger than Isabel's house, and the approach to it was just as grand and intimidating, with a series of empty roads that wound around a pond that sat directly in front of the club like a moat. As they neared the building, Rory noticed a small sign that said PRIVATE PROPERTY MEMBERS ONLY NO TRESPASSING. *Well, this place looks friendly,* Rory thought, as she drove over the bridge across the pond.

"So, there's a beach party tonight in Bridgehampton," Isabel said, reading her phone. "Wanna come?"

"Tonight?"

"Yeah. What, are you busy?"

"Um, no," Rory said. "But is this just because you need a ride or you're actually inviting me to go with you?"

Isabel smiled. She seemed impressed with Rory's honesty. "Yes, I need a ride, but I thought it might be good for you to meet some people. Unless you don't want to."

"No, that'd be great," Rory said. "Thanks."

"Cool," Isabel said.

The valet opened her door and offered Isabel a hand as she stepped out of the car. "Bye!" she called over her shoulder.

Before Rory could respond, the valet slammed the door shut.

Then I'll just be on my way, Rory thought, as she drove off.

CHAPTER SEVEN

Rory slipped on the top she'd bought at Hot Topic a week ago
and stepped back from the mirror. The bright electric blue
brought out her eyes. The shape showed off her narrow waist,
which was just about the only body part of hers she liked to show
off. And the lacy cap sleeves and deep V-neck seemed cute and on
trend. But now she wasn't sure. Would she just get the same look
she'd gotten from Bianca the other night, like she was one of
those fashion disasters on *What Not to Wear*? She added a stretch
belt that made her waist look even smaller and her favorite pair of
white jeans. She'd also gone for her fanciest dangly gold earrings.
Hopefully she was inching her way closer to Hamptons style; she
needed a second opinion. She looked out her window and saw
Steve loading tennis rackets into his Jetta.

"Hey," she called to him through the open window. "Can I
ask you a question?"

"Be there in a minute," he called back.

A moment later, there was a knock on her door. She opened it
to see Steve on the threshold, his wraparound glasses on a string

around his neck. His cuteness was starting to wear off, thank goodness.

"Okay," she said. "I need an honest opinion. Am I too dressed up for a beach party?"

Steve looked her up and down. "I have no idea," he said. "Why are you asking me?"

"Because you're the only one I can ask," she said. "What do girls wear to beach parties out here?"

"I don't know. Jeans. A shirt. I think you look fine."

"But fine isn't great. Is it?"

"You always look great," Steve said. "Every guy's gonna want to talk to you. And I did see you talking to someone yesterday morning. Out by the pool. And both of you seemed pretty happy."

"Connor?" she blurted. "I mean, we were just talking. I dropped his phone into the pool by mistake."

"He didn't seem too broken up about it," said Steve.

"What does that mean?" she asked.

"Nothing. Have fun tonight. And seriously, you look great."

"Thanks, Steve."

He left, and Rory slipped on a pair of dark blue Keds. As she passed by a mirror she caught a glimpse of herself. She was blushing. So maybe the chemistry she'd felt between her and Connor hadn't just been in her head. If Steve had felt it, too, from across the lawn . . .

"Are you ready?" Isabel entered Rory's room in a cloud of amber-scented perfume. She looked like she was on her way to a red-carpet event. She wore an ivory crochet dress, silver gladiator sandals, and a cocktail ring that looked like one large pearl set in gold. So much for feeling overdressed, Rory thought. Next to Isabel, she looked like she was about to do laundry.

"You look nice," Rory said. "Great dress."

"Oh, this? I've had it for forever. That's a nice top."

"You think?"

"Uh... sure," Isabel said, less confidently. "Hey, I just need to get one thing. Come with me."

Rory followed her down the hall and out toward the dining room and study.

Isabel darted into a room, which turned out to be a bar, and crouched down in front of a small refrigerator and opened the glass door.

"What are you doing?" Rory asked.

"Just getting something for the party," Isabel said, pulling out a bottle of champagne.

"We can't drive with that in the car."

"Why not?" Isabel asked. "It's not open."

"Because we're *underage*."

Isabel smiled as if Rory were an adorable toddler. "You have *got* to relax. Come on." She stood up and walked out of the room swinging the golden bottle.

"Do your parents just let you take champagne?" Rory asked.

"This isn't just champagne," Isabel replied. "This is Cristal."

Rory didn't say anything as they walked out to the car.

"So, where are we going?" she asked when they got in the Prius.

"Sagg Main Beach. You just take the highway past Wainscott and make a left on Sagg Main. And I'm gonna think of some guys who are probably going to be there." Isabel opened another clutch—this one raffia—and took out her phone as Rory drove down the gravel driveway.

"You know, I was thinking that tonight I'd just focus on trying to make some friends here," Rory said. "Like maybe with some of the girls."

"Have fun with that," Isabel muttered in a cryptic way.

Rory made a left onto Lily Pond. Did Isabel mean that Rory wouldn't be able to make friends? Or that Isabel's own friends weren't worth knowing?

"So, tell me some cool stuff about you," Isabel said, putting away her phone. "Do you play sports? An instrument? What do you do?"

"Why?"

"Because we need to make you sound amazing," Isabel said. "And it's better not to lie."

"Well, they showed some of my photos at the Farm and Horse Show last summer," Rory said.

"The *what*?"

"The Farm and Horse Show. It's, like, a huge, three-day fair. It's a really big deal where I live."

Isabel was quiet. "What else?" she asked.

"I'm the president of the science club."

"Uh, *no*."

"What's wrong with that? I can't let him know I'm smart?"

"You can't let him know you're a *dork*," Isabel said, and then turned on the radio. "I mean . . . you know what I mean."

"I like making documentaries," she offered. "I won a special prize in my film class last semester."

"Okay, that might be cool. What was your documentary about?"

"This woman who lives in my neighborhood. She's collected, like, a hundred of those black velvet paintings of Elvis. And all sorts of other stuff about him. She's sort of like a walking Graceland."

"That's who you made a documentary about?" Isabel asked.

"Yeah."

"Why?" Isabel asked.

"I don't know. Because she's passionate about something. I think that's cool. To be so into something that you don't care how it looks or if it's weird or if people are going to make fun of you."

Isabel changed the radio station. "I guess," she said listlessly.

A song started playing. It was one of her mom's favorites, from the seventies. Rory opened her mouth to sing along, but Isabel beat her to it.

"*Rhiannon rings like a bell through the night and wouldn't you love to love her...*" she sang in a surprisingly throaty voice.

"You like Fleetwood Mac?" Rory asked in disbelief.

"Sure," Isabel said. "So?"

"So I just think that's weird that we both like Fleetwood Mac. I mean, how many people like Fleetwood Mac to begin with?"

Isabel yawned. "I don't know."

Rory drove in silence, feeling a little stupid for bringing that up.

After a few minutes, Isabel said, "Oh, here's the turn."

Rory swerved off the highway. "Thanks for the notice," she muttered.

"The beach is just straight down this road," Isabel said. "You'll see the parking lot."

"Is it safe to park the car here?"

"Oh my god, of course," Isabel said, reaching down to grab the bottle of Cristal.

They found a spot at the far end of the lot, or at least Rory thought it was a spot. There were no streetlamps—there obviously wasn't supposed to be a lot of action here at night. She locked the car and followed Isabel toward the sand. Up ahead she could see people gathered around a giant bonfire that spat out sparks into the darkness. A chilly gust of wind rose up from the water, and she pulled her sweater around her shoulders. In her light dress, Isabel barely shivered. Like most beautiful girls, she seemed immune to the cold.

"Hey," she called out to two girls standing by themselves, red plastic cups in hand.

"This tastes like dog pee," the taller girl said. "You'd think that Niccolo could spring for some decent beer. Here." She held up her cup and stared at Rory.

"That's okay, I got backup," Isabel said, brandishing the bottle.

"Oooh, my favorite," said the other girl, who had thick hair that looked to be reddish gold in the firelight. She dumped the contents of her plastic cup onto the sand and held out her cup. "Just a little. It has a lot of sugar."

Rory stayed quiet. Neither girl had even talked to her yet. The taller girl with the dark brown hair and the ultrablasé manner also wore a dress and delicate leather flip-flops with a Navajo pattern between the toes. The other girl wore toothpick-slim jeans that still managed to look roomy around the thighs. Neither of them wore anything resembling Keds or a stretch fabric belt.

"You guys, this is my friend Rory," Isabel said. "Rory, this is Thayer," she said, gesturing to the taller girl, "and this is Darwin. We've all known each other since, like, kindergarten."

"Hi," Rory said, waving.

Thayer and Darwin didn't wave, but their eyes did a quick head-to-toe sweep of her outfit. "Hey," Thayer finally said. Darwin murmured something, but Rory couldn't make it out.

"Rory's staying with us for the summer," Isabel continued, unwrapping the foil from the cork. "Remember? I told you guys."

"Oh," Darwin said, nodding. "Where are you from again?"

"New Jersey," Rory replied.

"So, is this, like, the Fresh Air Fund or something?" Darwin asked.

Thayer nudged Darwin hard, and they both giggled.

"Um, I don't know," Rory said. She knew that Darwin had just insulted her, but she wasn't sure how.

"Where in New Jersey are you from?" Thayer asked. Her voice had a funny drawl to it, as if her mouth couldn't completely open and the words took extralong to pronounce.

"Sussex County. It's right near the border of Pennsylvania."

"Huh," she said, and didn't say anything else.

Finally Isabel pushed out the cork with her thumb. A jet stream of fizz shot out of the bottle and all over Darwin's pants.

"Oh my god!" Darwin shrieked, stepping backward. "Iz! What the hell?"

"Oops," Isabel said, as champagne sizzled down the sides of the bottle. "My bad."

"These are my Rag and Bones!" Darwin cried. "Now I'm going to have to wash them!"

"I'm sorry." Rory knew that Isabel wasn't the most naturally apologetic person in the world, and there was just the smallest hint of a smirk on her lips as she looked at Rory. "Wait a minute, you and I don't have cups," Isabel said.

Rory looked over at the keg sunk into the sand and the sleeve of cups on top of it. "I'll get them," she said, eager to escape. She could feel Darwin seething.

As Rory set off across the sand, Isabel tried to squelch her anger. Her friends were such snobs. At least she'd managed to spray Darwin with the champagne, though. That had been pretty awesome.

"Why'd you guys have to say that?" she said to her friends. "About the Fresh Air Fund?"

"She didn't even get it," Thayer said.

"So what? Would it kill you guys to be friendly once in a while?"

"Why do you care?" Thayer asked. "She's the housekeeper's kid."

"*Niece*," Isabel corrected. "And I'm trying to introduce her to people."

"Why?" Darwin asked. "She doesn't fit in here. I mean, look at what she's wearing, for God's sake."

"Don't be such a snob," Isabel muttered.

"*I'm* a snob?" Darwin said. "You're the one who acts like you're too good to hang out with us anymore. You were supposed to go with us to the Talkhouse on Saturday night, and you totally flaked."

"I told you guys, I was sick," Isabel said, wincing a little at the lie. She'd been at Buford's with Mike.

Thayer looked off in the distance and then stepped closer to Isabel. "Oh my god. Andrew Mayman just looked at me. I think he's into me. What should I do?"

"I have to pee," Isabel said, and handed the champagne bottle to Thayer. "Here," she said. "Enjoy."

She walked toward the water. She couldn't pretend to care one iota about Thayer and her stupid love life right now. How long had she been here? Five minutes? Already she wanted to jump in the car and leave. Standing around the bonfire clutching red cups were all the same people she saw every summer, at every single beach party: Tripp Pressley, whose father worked at Goldman and traveled to Southampton by helicopter; Anna Lucia Kent, with her Brazilian blowout, bright white veneers, and flair for social climbing; and Whit Breckinridge, whose parties in the city were so popular that his doorman needed a list and a lacrosse stick to keep things in line. There had been a time when she would have moved through this crowd kissing and hugging every single one of these people, spilling over with things to say. But tonight she saw them through Mike's eyes. He wouldn't have thought these people were so interesting. In any case, not nearly as interesting as they thought themselves to be.

Rory was almost at the keg when a stream of smoke from the bonfire wafted straight into her face. She began to cough.

"You okay?" someone asked.

Through her watering eyes, she could see a guy watching her with concern.

"I think...I think...I think I'm okay," she sputtered between coughs.

"You want some?" He took a cup from the sleeve and pumped it with beer.

She tried to shake her head while she was coughing, but he didn't understand. "Here," he said.

Rory brought the cup to her lips and took a sip. She didn't like the taste of beer, but it felt good to drink something.

"That should do it," said the guy. "Though it's really bad beer."

She took another sip. "Thanks," she said.

Her eyes stopped watering, and she could see that he had curly light brown hair and wore a navy-blue Patagonia fleece. Cute but not too cute, she noted gratefully.

"I'm Landon," he said.

"Rory," she said.

"Wait," he said, squinting. "Do you go to Nightingale?"

"I'm sorry, what?" she asked.

"Do you go to Nightingale?" he repeated. "In the city?"

"I live in New Jersey," she said.

"Oh," he said, looking confused.

"I'm here with Isabel," she said. "Isabel Rule?"

"Oh, cool," Landon said. "How do you know her if you live in New Jersey?"

Rory thought about how to respond to this. "I'm staying with her. Well, with her family. For the summer."

"What, is your family friends with hers or something?" he asked.

As if on cue, Rory heard a keening voice call out, "Hey, Landon!" and turned to see Isabel walking over to them with outstretched arms. "What is *up*? Long time no see, *mio amico*."

"Hey, Isabel," he said, going over to her.

Rory watched Landon and Isabel embrace like old, long-separated friends.

"Oh my god, it's so good to see you," Isabel said, keeping her hands on his shoulders. "How's your sister? She's at Vanderbilt, right?"

"Yep. She's loving it. And she's already met your friend Haven. How's California?"

"Awesome. And have you met Rory?" Isabel said, glancing approvingly at the cup of beer in Rory's hand.

"Yeah, she was just telling me she's staying with you for the summer."

"That's right," Isabel said. "She's our houseguest."

"Yeah, my aunt is her—" Rory began.

"Landon and my brother Connor went to St. Bernard's together," Isabel said, cutting her off. Whether this was deliberate, Rory couldn't tell. "Connor was like his big brother at school.

Anyway, Rory is supercool. And she's never been out here before, so I want everyone to show her a really good time," Isabel said, putting special emphasis on the last three words.

"Uh, sounds good," Landon said.

"Could you excuse us for a second?" Isabel asked.

Rory felt herself pulled aside by the elbow into the darkness.

"Okay, this is perfect," Isabel said. "Landon is nice, cute, smart, and not too in love with himself. But if you're gonna seal the deal, you have to *do* something. Not just stand there."

"O...kay," Rory said. "What are you talking about, exactly?"

"You have to *flirt*," Isabel said. "Smile, laugh, say something funny. Act mysterious. And don't tell him about being the housekeeper's niece."

"Why not?"

"Just don't, okay?" Her eyes darted over Rory's shoulder. "Okay, he's looking over at you right now."

"He is?" Rory started to look over her shoulder.

"Don't look!" Isabel ordered. "He likes you. Trust me."

Rory wasn't sure she could believe this, but coming from the queen of the Hamptons, it was probably true. "Are you sure?"

"Totally sure," she said. "Now all you have to do is encourage him. Laugh at what he says, smile, stand close to him, touch him on the arm, et cetera. You ready?"

"Okay."

Rory walked back to Landon and took a quick, shallow sip from her cup to bolster her confidence. Sand sloshed inside her Keds, but she tried to have an elegant gait just the same. "Sorry about that," she said when she joined him. "I didn't mean to leave you alone."

It was an unbearably corny line, and one that she would never have said before, but Landon perked right up. "That's okay," he said. "Just nursing my cup of truly awful beer."

She dissolved into laughter, then smiled more brilliantly at him than she'd ever smiled at anyone in her life. "So where do you go to school?" she asked, batting her eyes. *I can't believe I'm doing this*, she thought. Maybe Isabel was right. Maybe guys weren't as smart as she'd thought.

Isabel headed back to her friends. She felt a little weird telling Rory not to say anything about Fee or being the housekeeper's niece. But Rory needed to have some fun, and she knew how snotty most of these people were. Rory would just go back to New Jersey at the end of the summer and never have to really hang out with these people again. She, on the other hand, would be stuck with them for life.

"Isabel," said a voice from behind her.

She turned around. Aston March walked toward her out of the shadows, like a ghost. His hair was shorter than she remembered it, and his face looked fuller, his body thicker. He looked like he'd been drinking a lot this past year. She wondered if she was the reason.

"Hey, Aston," she said, feeling her stomach begin a slow slide to her ankles.

"Hey, Iz." He sipped from the red plastic cup in his hand. "We missed you at my party last weekend."

"Yeah, sorry. I was sick."

He looked past her as he took another swallow of beer. "How's California?"

"Amazing," she said. "Just what I said in my e-mails."

"Right," Aston said. He shuffled his feet in the sand. "I'm going to Yale in the fall."

"I heard. Congrats." She looked beyond his shoulder to see if there was anyone who might be able to rescue her. She'd been hoping to put this off for at least a couple more days.

"I think we should hang out again this summer," he announced, stepping closer. "You know? I mean, why not?"

"Aston—"

"I thought things were pretty good," he said. "You just got scared."

"Aston, no. It's over. Really, really over."

His eyes stayed riveted on her, as if he expected her to suddenly laugh this off. When she didn't, something hardened in his face. "You know, I was totally there for you last summer," he said. "When you got kicked out of school, when you got into all that shit with your parents about the fire, I stuck up for you. I said that none of it was your fault, that you were just the victim. But maybe it's right what people say about you. Maybe you are just a mess."

A gust of wind blew across her face. "Go to hell," she said, and walked away.

She waded through the sand, shivering from the cold air seeping in through her dress. Mike. She needed Mike. She unsnapped her clutch. Maybe she would text him right now.

Screw her rules about waiting. She didn't care anymore. She pulled out her iPhone and almost dropped it when she saw the lit-up screen.

Hey Beautiful. When can I see you?

She read the text over and over. Her heart raced. She felt dizzy.

Tomorrow, she typed, and then hit send.

Normally she would have waited a good twelve hours to text him back, or maybe even a day. But that seemed petty right now. If he texted back right away, that meant he really liked her. Maybe almost as much as she liked him, too.

Her phone chimed again.

Cool. See you soon.

She smiled. Of course he liked her. Of course he did.

CHAPTER EIGHT

"Come on, girl! Come on, Trixie! Run!"

Rory threw the stick high and long, and Trixie raced toward it. Clumps of wet sand spattered her back legs and rump. She'd have to make sure to give Trixie a bath when they were done, but it would be worth it. She'd never seen a dog so excited to be let out of the house.

"Get it, Trixie!" she yelled. "Go!"

As soon as the stick hit the sand with a thud, Trixie clamped it in her jaws and ferried it back, letting one end of it drag along the sand as she went.

"Good girl!" Rory yelled. Trixie ran to Rory's feet and dropped the stick on the sand. "Very good girl!"

It was early, and the beach was deserted. A thick layer of clouds hid the morning sun. Rory felt the cool sand between her toes and breathed in the fresh air. She'd never played fetch with a dog on a beach. She'd also never given her number to a guy she'd just met at a party. She was changing here. Already she felt lighter, happier, freer. Different. Maybe Isabel had been right about her needing to relax. She'd also been right about something else: Guys liked to be flirted with.

It was incredible. Every time she thought that she was over-doing it, and that Landon might burst out laughing at the way she was batting her lashes, or that he might get tired of her questions, or that he might ask why, exactly, she was so interested in his brief experiences on the wrestling team, he responded with another joke, or another story that wasn't really funny, but that she knew *he* wanted to be funny, or something else that was designed to get her attention. Apparently, he didn't think she was acting weird at all. He was *flattered*.

They talked for what seemed like hours, until she finally allowed there to be a long pause. And then he said, "You want to hang out sometime?"

"Sure," she said.

He took out his phone, and she gave him her number. And that was that. She'd walked back to the car, almost feeling a little guilty for her fantastic performance. She wasn't sure that she even really liked Landon. But when they'd gotten in the car to go home, and Rory had shared the good news, Isabel had exclaimed, "Thank the Lord!" with so much relief that Rory felt like she'd done them both an enormous favor.

Of course, if it had been Connor Rule who'd asked for her number, she'd be walking on air right now. But she doubted that she'd ever be able to pull off that kind of behavior with Connor. He probably would have wondered what on earth she was doing acting that way. And she would have liked him even more for it.

Trixie dropped the stick at Rory's feet. Rory glanced at her watch. It was almost eight thirty. If she stayed down here any longer, Bianca would be wondering where she was, and she didn't feel like another lecture on staying away from the beach. If the Rules weren't going to use it, then why couldn't she?

"Okay, let's go back," she said, looking at the crust of brown sand on Trixie's legs. She slipped on the flip-flops she'd left at the bottom of the wooden walkway and started the climb up the dunes. Suddenly, Trixie raced past her up the path, barking and wagging her tail.

"Trixie, wait!" she yelled. "What's the big rush?"

At the top of the dunes, she found her answer. Connor Rule crouched down over Trixie, who was intent on licking his long, tan shin.

"Hey," he said, looking up at her. "I just stopped by your room to see if you wanted to go for a run."

She stood for a moment, thinking about her hair, which had probably gone frizzy, and the damp spots under her arms, and the shininess of her nose that she couldn't see but that she absolutely knew was there. "W-what?" she sputtered.

"A run? You know, on the beach?" He stood up.

"Oh," she said. "Yeah. I just took Trixie for a run. But I don't run. I'm not much of a runner."

"I'm not, either," he said. "My coach thinks there's something wrong with me."

"Your swim coach?"

"Yeah."

"Why does your swim coach care about running?" she asked.

"Because it's part of my training?" he replied. "You know, cardio?"

She brushed a curl off her face. Her newfound flirting skills seemed to have disappeared. "So, uh... no swimming today?"

"Nah, I need a break. Actually, I'm thinking of quitting."

"You are?"

"I've been doing it for years," he said. "I think I'm ready for something else. But it's not really up to me."

"Why not?" she asked.

He smiled and looked down the beach. "I guess it is up to me, but my parents would be pretty pissed off. My dad ran track when he was in college. All-American. He's kind of reliving his glory days through me." He shook some blond hair off his forehead. "What about you? What do your parents make you do?"

"My parents?" Rory said. "Well, that would be just my mom. And she makes me do everything."

"What do you mean? Sports?"

"No." She laughed. "Like, pay the bills. Do the shopping. Figure out the car insurance. That kind of stuff."

Connor's smile disappeared. He obviously thought she was a freak.

"But when I'm not doing that," she said, "I like to make films. Documentaries."

"Yeah?" he asked. "What about?"

"This past year at school, I did this piece about people who collect bizarre stuff in my town. One woman was really into Elvis memorabilia. And another woman, she collected vintage diner stuff. Like, place mats from when Denny's first opened, and napkins with the old Waffle House logo on them. Stuff like that."

Connor just looked at her. Wind ruffled his hair. *I'm dying here*, she thought. *Help.*

"Anyway, it's sort of my dream to go to USC film school. Though I'll probably just end up going to Rutgers and studying econ or something else that's useful."

"Yeah," he finally said after a pause. "I know what you mean." He looked down at the beach again. The clouds were starting to lighten, and she was aware that she needed her sunglasses.

"Well...I guess I should get going," Connor said. "I have to get to work soon. I'm teaching sailing at Devon in Amagansett. I did it last year. You sail?"

"Uh, no," she said. "Not really. But that sounds cool."

"Sure you don't want to keep me company?" he asked with a smile that made her heart speed up.

"It's tempting," she said, "but I think Bianca's probably looking for me. Have fun."

"Yeah. Have a good day, Rory."

"You, too."

She turned and left right away, even though she longed to watch him disappear down the wooden planks toward the sand for as long as possible. This time, she knew that she hadn't made it up. Something was there between them. Something that made her smile so hard that her cheeks ached as she walked into the house.

As soon as she stepped inside the hall, she heard the familiar sound of her Katy Perry ringtone. She ran into the bedroom and fumbled around in her purse. It was about time she spoke to Sophie and Trish. They'd all been playing serious phone tag since she'd arrived.

But it wasn't Sophie or Trish. An unfamiliar 631 number was on the screen.

"Hello?" she asked, picking up.

"Hey, Rory," said a slightly familiar voice. "It's Landon. How are you?"

She sat on the edge of the bed. Her conversation with Connor had given her a bit of a buzz, and now hearing Landon's voice on her phone made her struggle to focus. "I'm great," she said, her heart beating fast. "How are you?"

"Good. You want to do something tonight?"

She shot to her feet. "Sure," she said, a little more quickly than she'd meant to.

"Cool. *Mission: Impossible Five* is playing," he said. "We could see that. Then get some pizza afterward."

She thought about waiting to see if Bianca would need her before she gave him an answer, but she didn't know how to tell this to Landon. "Sounds great."

"Okay," Landon said. "I'll pick you up at seven. And yes, I do have a very cool car."

She laughed. "I look forward to experiencing it."

"Oh, and you will," Landon joked. "See you at seven."

She hung up and jauntily tossed her phone back in her purse. She had a date tonight. A *date*.

She smiled at Trixie, who waited patiently beside the bed, still panting from the excitement on the beach.

If only it were with Connor, she thought. But she refused to think about that too much. Isabel was right—Landon was cool, funny, and not too in love with himself. The perfect candidate for her first real boyfriend. Or at least an East Hampton fling.

CHAPTER NINE

At exactly three forty-five, Isabel rode her bike through the open gates and turned east on the smooth, sun-baked asphalt, pedaling toward Main Beach. The wind blew her hair off her bare shoulders, and the sun beat down on her back. For the past twenty hours, ever since she'd texted him at the party, she'd barely thought about anything else besides seeing Mike. So it seemed almost incomprehensible that she was about to be face-to-face with him again. She'd agonized over what to wear. Mike hadn't told her where they were going, so she'd settled on jeans, an off-the-shoulder ivory peasant blouse, and platform espadrilles that could work just about anywhere. She hoped that he'd take her to another place like Buford's. Though this time she'd take it easy on the rum.

At Ocean, she hooked a right and headed straight for the parking lot at the end of the street. She slid off the bike, wheeled it over to the rack by the snack bar, and locked it. It was warm, which accounted for the smattering of young mothers on plastic chairs and striped towels, watching as their babies and children dug and played in the sand. She looked at one blond woman in particular, trying to talk to her friend while at the same time keeping an eye on her toddler, who was busy flinging sand with a shovel. *That could be me one day*, she thought. She shrugged it away. It was too weird to think about that right now.

And then, from far down the street, she saw a dark red Xterra glide into view. She felt her stomach rise and fall. He was here. She pulled a lipstick out of her pocket and ran it over her lips, then felt the crazy urge to run. But the SUV was too fast, and before she knew it, Mike made a sweeping turn right in front of her, sand hissing under the wheels. The window came down. Mike leaned his head out, and she saw those liquid brown eyes and full lips and that smile that said *I know everything that you don't want to tell me.*

"Hey," she called out. "Nice turn."

"Glad you liked it," he said, grinning.

She walked to the car and got into the passenger seat. "So, what's the plan?" she asked, trying not to think about how hot he looked in his plain white T-shirt.

He examined her shoes. "Are those comfortable?"

"Yeah. Why?"

"Just checking," he said, putting the car in gear and heading out of the parking lot.

"Um, you still haven't told me where we're going," she pointed out.

"I know," he said, covering her hand with his own.

Rory pushed through the swinging door. "Have you seen Bianca anywhere? She just called me on the intercom, but I don't know from where."

Erica looked up from the egg whites she was whipping into fluffy peaks with an electric mixer. "I think she's down in the screening room." She gave Rory a closer look with her kind brown eyes. "Are you okay, Rory? You look all flushed."

"Oh, I just got a little too much sun today, that's all. Thanks!"

Rory stepped back into the hall and patted her damp hands on the front of her shorts. If Erica was already onto her, then no doubt Bianca would be, too. She was going to have to figure out a nonchalant opening line. *Someone just invited me to the movies* was all she needed to say. She didn't need to get into who and how and why—and the fact that she'd already said yes. And being out of the house for two nights in a row couldn't be that big a deal. Could it?

"Oh my god, don't even worry about it," Isabel had said in the car while Rory drove her home from Two Trees that morning. "It's not like you're a prisoner here. You're supposed to make friends. You're supposed to meet people. It's no big deal."

"Except Bianca thinks I'm some partying freak. Remember? *Mike?* In my room?"

"Oh, yeah," Isabel said, looking out of the window and smiling at the memory. "I'm sure she's forgotten all about that."

"I highly doubt it," Rory said.

"But that's great that he called you," Isabel said. "What are you guys gonna do?"

"We're seeing *Mission: Impossible Five*. Then maybe we'll get some pizza."

"Not the most imaginative first date," Isabel said, "but okay. Did you tell him yes right away or did you make him wait a little bit?"

Rory glanced at Isabel. "How was I supposed to make him wait? We were on the phone, he asked me, and I said yes."

Isabel pulled some hair behind her ear. "Okay," she said. "But for the next one, make him wait a *little*."

"Fine," Rory said. "What about you? What are you and Mike gonna do?"

"I don't know," Isabel said. "He's being kind of mysterious. But I'm sure it'll be fun."

"Just be careful," Rory said. "He's older, right?"

"What does that have to do with anything?"

Rory had been about to say that it had a lot to do with everything, but she decided not to say anything. After all, she knew that she wasn't an authority on relationships.

She crossed the marble floor of the foyer and descended another set of stairs, which she was fairly sure led to the screening room. She'd seen the screening room only once, on her tour with Bianca, but she remembered it being extremely, almost ludicrously, luxurious. It had Art Deco–style sconces that dimmed to the lowest lights, oversize suede easy chairs with matching ottomans, and thick red-and-black-patterned carpeting that looked just like what she imagined movie theaters used to have, back before multiplexes and stadium seating. "Why do they have a screening room?" Rory had asked Bianca as they stood on the threshold. "And such a nice one?"

Bianca had looked at her strangely. "For entertaining," she'd said, as if it were the most obvious answer in the world.

Rory had felt stupid at the time, but now she was getting used to the over-the-top touches in this house. Things were all about plenty on Lily Pond Lane. It wasn't enough to have a Ping-Pong table; you had to place a pyramid of rolled-up towels nearby just in case someone worked up a sweat. It wasn't enough to have a Blu-ray player; you needed real movie-theater seats and carpeting so that you could feel like a Hollywood mogul.

She knocked softly on the double doors and entered. Bianca and Fee were dusting the mahogany tables between the easy chairs.

"There you are," Bianca said as she pounded an orange throw pillow with her fist. "We're going to need you to make a run over to Amagansett. Mrs. Rule is having some people over to watch *The Geisha's Lament.*"

"So then why do I have to go to Amagansett?" Rory asked.

"Because Billy Withers is going to lend it to her," Bianca said, as if Rory were already supposed to know this.

"He's a publicist," Fee said, guessing Rory's next question. "He gets all the first-run movies and sometimes loans them out."

"The guests should be getting here around six," Bianca said. "After you pick up the movie, you'll help me pass out some drinks and hors d'oeuvres. We'll see if Mrs. Rule wants to serve a full dinner after the film."

"Um, okay."

Bianca put down another pillow and folded her arms. "Do you have other plans?" she asked, her voice dripping with sarcasm.

"Well, actually," she said, forcing herself to look Bianca right in the eye, "someone asked me to go to the movies tonight." She noticed Fee break into a smile, but Bianca had no expression.

"Didn't you go out last night?"

"Yes, but I just thought in case you didn't need me—"

"Here everyone is!" Mrs. Rule said, bouncing into the room on white tennis shoes. Her face glowed from a lesson, and in her pleated tennis skirt and damp ponytail, she looked younger than Isabel. "I'm so excited to see this movie. *Nobody* has seen it yet. Not even Birdie, and she sees everything."

"Rory's going to go over to Billy's now," Bianca reported.

"Oh, good!" Mrs. Rule beamed. "And I hope you can help out tonight," she said to Rory. "My friends will be so interested to meet you."

"Actually, she's asking if she can go out," Bianca said.

"I've just been invited out—by a *friend*," Rory said quickly, looking at Bianca. "But I don't need to go if it's going to be a problem."

"Oh, of course you can go out," said Mrs. Rule. "Bianca and I can manage."

"She still needs to get the movie," Bianca said.

"Then she can get the movie," Mrs. Rule said blithely. "Fee, have you seen my black James Perse dress? I just can't find it anywhere, and it would be so perfect for tonight. Can you come upstairs with me?"

"Of course," Fee said.

As Fee and Mrs. Rule left, Rory realized that she was blessedly in the clear. Mrs. Rule didn't care at all if she had a date tonight or not. But Bianca gave Rory a searing look anyway. "You'll find Billy's information in the book in your room. And I don't think I have to remind you not to bring anyone back with you tonight."

Rory didn't blink. "No, you really don't," she said. "But thanks anyway." She walked out of the room. She wasn't going to let Bianca keep intimidating her all summer long.

"Okay. I guessed it. We're obviously going to your house."

"Nope."

"But this is the North Fork," Isabel said, looking out the window at sweeping cornfields and vineyards, and beyond them, the still blue waters of Peconic Bay. They'd been driving for almost an hour, talking nonstop as Mike headed west past Bridgehampton, Water Mill, and Southampton. When he'd gone north at Riverhead, she hadn't been surprised. She just hoped that he wasn't taking her home to meet his parents.

"I know, but we're not going to my house," Mike said as the sun slanted in through his car window and threw golden light across the dash.

"It's really pretty here," she said. "I read once that it's all the water around here that makes the light so beautiful. You know, the bay on one side, the ocean on the other. It makes everything really specular."

"Specular?" Mike asked.

"It's the opposite of diffuse," she said. "The surface of water is smooth, so light gets bounced back all in one piece. That's specular." *God, what's wrong with me?* she thought. *I sound like Rory.*

Mike glanced over at her. "Do you get straight A's or something?"

"No. I just remember a lot of things." She looked out the window, a little elated that Mike had just asked her that. "So where are we going?"

"I told you. It's a surprise."

Suddenly, Mike made a left off the highway, away from the bay, and they were traveling down a long gravel drive shaded by oak trees. "Okay, I'm completely at a loss," she said. "Are we at some kind of farm?"

"You said you liked strawberries, right?" said Mike.

"Yeah. So?"

He rounded a bend, and acres of strawberry fields came into view.

"Wait," she said. "You brought me to a *strawberry* farm?"

"It's my friend's," he said. "He said we can pick as much as we can carry. And these are amazing. All organic. He sells them down on Montauk Highway for six bucks a pound. Now you can make me that strawberry shortcake you were telling me about."

Aston March would never have remembered that, she thought. Not in a million years. He parked, and she unbuckled her seat belt. "You have a good memory, too."

"Are you kidding? I can't wait to have some."

Mike walked around to the trunk, opened it, and took out an empty fruit crate. "You spend any time around farms?" he asked.

"My dad just bought some property near a potato field in Sagaponack," Isabel said.

"What's gonna happen to the other house?" Mike asked, carrying the fruit crate as they walked toward the field.

"I don't know. Someone'll buy it," she said. "I'll miss it, though. I think the next house will be even bigger. If my dad has anything to say about it."

"Bigger?" Mike asked.

"Believe it or not, there are bigger homes out here than mine." Dirt flew up into the heels of her shoes as she walked, but she didn't care.

When they opened the gate that led out to the field, Mike put down the crate and reached into the green leaves. She could see the dangling strawberry stems, with the berries hanging at the ends like rubies.

"Okay, try this," he said, picking one off. "This looks good. The redder, the better. If it has any green, it still needs to ripen." He placed the crimson berry in her hand. "Go ahead, try it."

She popped it into her mouth and took a bite. "Oh my god." Strawberry juice, ripe and sweet, seeped onto her tongue. "It's so sweet. It's amazing."

"I told you, right?" he said. "You also want to make sure you pick them with some of the stem on. It keeps them fresh."

She watched him start picking and tossing berries into the box with the brisk pace of an expert.

"You rock at this," she said.

"Just so you know," he said, looking back at her, "I prefer real whipped cream. No Cool Whip."

She laughed out loud. "I'll remember that."

Rory pulled up to the Rules' garage, parked, and picked up the DVD from where it lay in its plastic case on the shotgun seat. Reaching Billy Withers's home at the end of a twisting, barely paved road had taken some time, but once she was there, the entire transaction had taken less than a minute. A tall man answered the door dressed in khakis and a polo shirt, just like the Rules' staff wore.

"This needs to be back by nine AM tomorrow," he said, waving the disc in front of her as if she didn't quite deserve it yet. "Nine AM."

"Okay," she'd said.

Then he'd placed the disc in her hand with a flourish and closed the door in her face.

Still holding the disc, Rory ran to her room. She changed into a stretchy black top from Aéropostale and a pair of white jeans, then pulled her hair back into a ponytail. It wasn't exactly the grooming routine she would have liked for her first real Hamptons date, but it would have to do. She left her purse by the door and went looking for Bianca. Hopefully this would be quick.

She found Bianca in the kitchen, taking trays with mother-of-pearl handles out of a cabinet. "I got it. His butler or manservant or whomever it was says that we need to get it back by nine AM tomorrow." She held up the disc. "Now what should I do?"

"Get it set up," Bianca said sharply.

"But I don't know how to work the projector."

Bianca gave a long, irritated sigh and walked over to the intercom pad in the wall. "Connor?" she said, pressing a button. "Can you meet Rory in the screening room and help her with the projector?"

Rory felt the DVD almost slip out of her hand.

"Connor?" she repeated.

"I'll be right down," said the voice, which Rory couldn't help but notice sounded a little grouchy.

"He'll show you," Bianca said. "Now go. You're blocking that cabinet."

Rory moved into the dining room, too giddy to focus on anything. Connor was going to help her? Connor and her, alone in the screening room? She was so distracted that she walked right into the edge of the dining table.

"Ow!" She patted her aching hip as she heard Connor come down the front steps.

"Hey," he said, walking into the dining room. "You need some help with the projector?"

"Yeah, I just have no idea how to use it. Sorry you got dragged down here."

"No problem," he said, smiling. "At least now I won't be the only one who knows how to work it."

Several minutes later, they stood side by side in the narrow projection room, in front of a tall media cabinet. She scratched her ankle with the opposite heel and redid her ponytail while he slid the DVD into the player. Standing this close to him made it hard for her to stand still. She looked at his hands as he fiddled with some buttons, and noticed that his arms were almost completely hairless. "Do you have to shave your entire body for swim meets?" she blurted out.

"What?" he asked.

"Sorry," she said, catching herself. "I don't know why I just asked that. Forget it."

"No, that's okay. Yeah. We have to shave." He touched another button. "Okay, is something coming up?"

She looked out at the screen. "It looks like something's on, but the screen is still black."

He sighed and muttered, "Only my parents would get a system that nobody but Stephen Hawking can figure out. Okay, what about now?"

"Still nothing. Wait." A picture flashed on the screen—the Universal Pictures logo—and then cut out. "Something *almost* worked."

"Okay, what about now?" he said, turning around so abruptly that his right arm grazed her own.

She watched as the opening credits began and then turned into blackness. "It happened again."

"I think it might be the disc," he finally said, ejecting it. "Let's try this one." He slid another DVD into the slot, and a title came up on the screen. PHISH LIVE IN UTICA. Trey Anastasio stood with his hands outspread as he leaned into a mike, an acoustic guitar slung over his shoulders.

"So when are you gonna show me that documentary you did?" he asked. He stepped closer, blocking the tiny source of light in the projection room.

"Oh, right," she said, as if she'd forgotten their conversation. "I'll show it to you anytime."

"We could screen it in here."

"Actually, it's more of a low-fi kind of thing." The roar of a crowd made her jump, and up on the screen, she saw Phish launch into a song.

"Okay, looks like it's the disc that's the problem," Connor said. "I think you got a lemon."

"Great," she muttered.

"It's not your fault. They'll understand."

"No, it's just that I'm probably going to have to return it and find something else. And I'm supposed to go out tonight."

"Oh." He sounded surprised. "I can go for you, then."

"That's sweet. But you don't have to do that."

"It's no problem. I know how it is when my mom is planning to have people over. Anything I can do to keep the peace, you know what I mean?"

He stepped toward her and she suddenly froze. He was going to kiss her, right now, and she wasn't ready for it.

He cocked his head and gave her a strained smile. "Are you okay?"

"Yeah," she said. "I'm great. Uh, let's go up and tell them it's not working."

She turned abruptly on her heels. Of course he wasn't going to kiss her. And why couldn't she come up with some witty things to say? Or at the very least, follow the thread of conversation? Why was she acting like a complete idiot?

She led the way up the stairs and through the dining room,

where she managed to avoid the sharp edge of the table. So far, he was still following. "Thanks again for your help," she said, just before they went into the kitchen. "I can take it from here."

"I'll go with you," he offered.

"You sure?"

"I'm not gonna feed you to the wolves," he said with a smile.

She turned around, biting her lip, and pushed through the swinging door. *He doesn't want to leave me*, she thought.

Erica and Fee stood in an assembly line at the kitchen island, arranging pieces of bruschetta on a platter as Bianca supervised. "Good, you're back," Bianca said brusquely. "Is it all set?"

"Not really," she said. "We couldn't get the movie to work."

"Something's wrong with the disc," Connor said. "I got something else to play down there, so I know it's the disc that's the problem."

Lucy Rule breezed into the kitchen through the opposite door, pinning up her hair. She'd changed into a floor-skimming black tank dress and an elaborate gold-and-tiger-eye necklace. "I think I just heard the doorbell," she said. "Did you all hear the doorbell?"

"I'll get it," Fee said, patting her hands on the half apron around her waist. She glanced at Rory, and her eyes seemed to warn of something.

"How are we doing in here?" Mrs. Rule asked, lifting one of the bruschetta pieces and inspecting the pieces of tomato. "Hmph," she said, sounding less than impressed. "Maybe a little less topping on each, Erica."

"Of course," she mumbled.

"Something's wrong with the movie, Mom," Connor said. "We can't get it to play. You're going to have to use something else."

Mrs. Rule looked up from the bruschetta. Rory remembered her expression that first day she met her, when all her features had gone slack as if they'd been wiped clean. "Are you sure?"

"Yeah, I'm sure," he said. "Rory and I tried everything."

Mrs. Rule's eyes fell on her for the first time. "*Both* of you tried it?"

"Basically," Connor said.

Rory nodded.

"Well, everyone is coming over here, expecting to see *The Geisha's Lament*," Mrs. Rule said in an irritated voice. "What am I going to do?"

"Maybe you guys can watch something from on demand?" Connor asked.

"I don't want to watch something from on demand," Mrs. Rule said. "People can watch on demand at home. I want to watch *The Geisha's Lament*."

"Well, it doesn't work," Connor said calmly. "Is there another copy you can borrow?"

Rory recognized something in Connor's voice: the same careful, measured tone that she took when her own mom was being unreasonable.

"Bianca?" Lucy Rule said. "Please call Billy right now and tell him that his disc is defective and I would like the next best thing he has, immediately."

"Of course," Bianca said, reaching for the cordless.

"And Rory will just go back to Billy's and get something

else." Mrs. Rule smoothed her hair and shook her head, as if this was all getting too trivial for words. "And Connor, can you help Bianca get the guests something to drink?"

Rory saw Connor almost say something, but the sound of laughter out in the hall sent Mrs. Rule to the door. "I have to go," she said warmly, and waved over her shoulder.

Rory glanced at the clock. It was six fifteen. If she raced back to Billy's, she might just be able to be ready in time. She started toward the door.

"Hey!"

Connor rushed after her with the DVD. "Don't forget this," he said, giving it back to her.

For just a moment, that old feeling came over her again, that electric sense that something more was going on here between them than just friendly conversation.

"Thanks," she said. "And thanks for everything."

"Have fun tonight," he said. Then he pushed his way back into the kitchen and disappeared.

It was already twilight when they pulled off the highway and bumped along a winding gravel road that seemed to head toward Lake Montauk. Isabel looked down at her fingers, which were stained with strawberry juice. She'd eaten so many strawberries she probably wouldn't even be hungry enough for dinner. Finally, they drove up in front of a house so small and lonely-looking that it could have passed for an abandoned shack.

"So it's a little bit smaller than your place," Mike said as he parked, "but it has just as much character."

"You live here with how many people?" Isabel asked, eyeing the crooked screen door and the strand of Christmas lights that ran haphazardly along the porch.

"It's me and my friends Pete and Esteban. But they're in Quogue for the night."

Isabel got out of the car and followed Mike up the cracked concrete driveway. There was no yard to speak of, just bare dirt with some grass making a cameo appearance here and there. Beer cans lined the arms of two Adirondack chairs on the porch, and sat along the porch railing, and surrounded a pile of supermarket circulars and mailers that had fallen out of an overstuffed mail slot in the front door. "What's that sound?" she asked.

"Frogs," he said, carrying his box of strawberries in front of him. "From the lake. It's just on the other side." She watched him climb the peeling porch steps, balance the box on one arm, and grab a beer can from the porch railing. "I'll just put the berries in the kitchen, and then we can get out of here," he said.

"Or we can stay."

He looked at her over his shoulder with surprise. "Yeah?"

"Sure," she said. He still hadn't kissed her. And hopefully this place didn't look as bad on the inside.

"I can make some pasta," he said. "You like spaghetti?"

"I love it," she said with a smile.

He unlocked the front door and she felt herself get nervous again. Did she even remember how to kiss someone she really, really liked?

He opened the front door. Bright lights switched on and blinded her.

"*Surprise!*" screamed a crowd of voices.

She looked over Mike's shoulder. A group of twenty people stood elbow-to-elbow under a sign that said HAPPY BIRTHDAY in accordion letters.

"Is it your birthday?" she asked him.

Mike didn't seem to hear her in the din of people. He put down the strawberries and waded into the crowd, giving high fives and yelling, "No *way*! No *way*!" over and over.

Perfect, Isabel thought. *Just perfect.*

Someone started singing "Happy Birthday," and soon the entire room was belting it out as Mike gave more high fives. She recognized some of the faces in the room from Buford's, but almost everyone was a stranger. As for the house, it was definitely shabby, but not quite chic. All the furniture—a gray sofa with large pink flowers, a scratched cherry-wood oval coffee table, a La-Z-Boy with a long rip in the pleather seat—looked like it came from Goodwill. The TV was large but an antique— definitely from ten years ago. The orange shag carpet had a mysterious dark stain in the corner. It wasn't dirty, though, and there were little touches that she liked: a black-and-white poster of surfers that said MONTAUK, 1965, and a vase of yellow flowers on the round kitchen table.

Mike walked back to her and grabbed her hand. "Hey, meet my roommates," he said, leading her over to a guy with sun-bleached blond dreads and a tattoo creeping out of his shirtsleeves on both arms. "This is Pete," he said. "Pete, this is Isabel."

"Hey," said Pete, shaking her hand. "Hope we didn't ruin

your romantic night. It's just we really wanted to bring in Mikey's first legal birthday in style, seeing as he's always getting carded."

"Dude," Mike warned, playfully giving him a jab on the arm. "And this," he said, steering her by the shoulders, "is Esteban. Esteban, this is Isabel."

A shorter guy with piecey black hair and a scar on his cheek leaned in to give Isabel a hug. "Don't listen to a word this guy says," he said with a smile. "He's a complete liar."

"Hey—" Mike warned.

Esteban clapped him over his ear and laughed. "You guys want something to drink?"

Mike looked at her. "Anything?"

"I'll take some champagne," she said.

"How 'bout a beer?" Mike asked her.

"Fine," she said.

Esteban headed into the kitchen, and Mike pulled her in close. "Sorry about this. I had no idea. These guys can't even pay the rent. I'd never think they'd be able to pull this together—"

"Maybe I should call a cab and let you have your party," she said.

"No," he said. "Don't go. Please."

Suddenly, a girl with brown hair and a tight purple tank top stepped between them and gave Mike a kiss on the cheek. "Hey, stranger!" she said.

"Leelee, what's up?" he asked, with a bit more enthusiasm than Isabel would have liked.

"I heard you were finally legal, and I figured I had to be

there," she said in a saucy voice. She reached up and patted him on the shoulder.

"Hey, Leelee, meet Isabel."

"Hey," Isabel said.

The girl gave her only the briefest smile and wave before turning back to Mike. "Come by the Ripcurl sometime. I'm working there now. And there are some really cool bands next week."

"Where's the bathroom?" Isabel asked.

"It's right through there, first door on the left," Mike said. "You okay?"

"Yeah, I'm fine," she said, forcing herself to smile. "I'll be right back." She gave Leelee as fake a smile as she could muster. "Nice meeting you."

Leelee barely looked at her. "Yeah."

She pushed her way through the crowd and into the hall, and located the first door on the left. She flipped on the light. The bathroom was a mess. Razor stubble coated the sink, while razors, tubes of toothpaste, and bottles of shaving cream crusted with dried foam competed for space on the counters. A wet suit hung from the showerhead, dripping sandy water onto the bathtub floor. And there wasn't a scrap left on the toilet-paper roll.

She lowered the fuzzy-covered toilet lid and sat down. Copies of *Maxim* and *Surfer* were jammed into a magazine rack on the floor. God, this place was dirty. Her mom wouldn't have stood for this for one minute. But that was probably the point. This was Mike's house. There weren't parents around to tell him what to do. There weren't even parents at this party. This was his very own place. She couldn't even imagine having that kind of free-

148

dom. She'd never dated a guy before who didn't live at home or live in a dorm. It was exciting but also slightly disorienting, like leaving a department store through a side exit. Suddenly, she realized why she felt so off her game out there in the living room, and during most of the date. She was feeling something she'd never felt before. She felt young. That girl outside talking to Mike—and frankly, hitting on him—was more appropriate for him than she was. Leelee probably also had her own tiny, messy shack with a few friends, her own kitchen, and her own unsupervised bedroom. And a car. That she was legally able to drive.

Isabel stared straight ahead at the wrinkled and stained towels on the rack, feeling herself begin to get depressed. She needed to vent. She unsnapped her clutch and took out her phone.

Date total disaster, she typed. How's yours?

Hopefully Rory was having a better time than she was.

Rory gunned the Prius up to forty-five as she drove past the hedges and vast front lawns of Further Lane. Somewhere in her purse, her phone chimed with a text, but she ignored it. The replacement DVD slid along the leather seat beside her and slammed into the door. She still wasn't even sure which movie this was. Billy Withers's butler had placed it in her hand with only a stormy look on his face, as if she'd ruined his night, and uttered, "Here." This time, she didn't wait for the front door to slam in her face. She ran straight to the car.

When she drove through the Rules' iron gates, she glanced at the clock on the dash. Six forty-five. She zoomed up the long gravel drive, parked the car, then picked up her phone and tried Landon.

It went straight to voice mail. She pictured him driving toward the house, music too loud for him to hear his phone, oblivious to the small drama happening here on Lily Pond Lane. She hung up and threw the phone back in her bag.

Downstairs in the projection room, she slid the disc into the machine and pressed the same buttons she'd seen Connor press. She paced the floor, one eye on the screen through the box-shaped hole in the wall. *Please work*, she thought. Otherwise she'd be sent back to Amagansett for yet another movie, and her date with Landon would definitely be canceled. Upstairs, she could hear Mrs. Rule's guests in the living room. One woman was laughing noisily and stomping her foot on the carpet.

The screen went black, and then credits came up on the screen. Whichever movie he'd given her, it was working.

As if on cue, the door to the screening room opened, and the guests trickled in. They were all well-kept women around Mrs. Rule's age, but like her, each of them looked much younger, with long hair highlighted some shade of sandy blond and faces devoid of wrinkles. Their martini glasses were half full, and one woman sloshed some liquid onto the carpet. There was no sign of Connor, but Mrs. Rule brought up the rear of the group, chatting with a petite, dark-eyed woman swathed in black whom Rory recognized as a world-famous fashion designer.

"Rory!" Mrs. Rule called out, a bright, hectic look in her eye. She seemed to be having a really good time. "Is everything set?"

"It's working," Rory said. "I'm not sure what this is, but it's working."

"Oooh," Mrs. Rule cooed as she looked at the screen. "It's *The Geisha's Lament*."

"I hear that this is just fabulous," said the woman next to her.

"Okay, well, have a good time," Rory said.

"Oh, would you mind staying down here?" Mrs. Rule asked. "Just to make sure that we don't have any problems? And if you can also bring down some of the snacks from upstairs, that would be wonderful."

Before Rory could answer, Mrs. Rule picked up her conversation with the designer and sat down in one of the deep suede chairs. Rory tried to think of a way to remind Mrs. Rule that she had plans tonight. After all, she'd been totally fine with her going out just a little while ago. But then Rory realized something. Mrs. Rule hadn't forgotten that she had plans. She was just going to act like she had.

She stood and watched the women whisper and giggle and slosh more martinis onto the floor until Mrs. Rule gestured for her to go upstairs. "More drinks, please!" she called out cheerily.

So much for the date, Rory thought as she left the room.

"Hey, Isabel." A soft knock came from the other side of the bathroom door. "Isabel?"

She put down the copy of *Surfer* and stuck it back in the magazine rack. She'd lost track of time reading about the winter swells at Mavericks in Northern California, and now Mike probably thought she had some kind of intestinal disorder. She stood up and turned on the faucet, then splashed some water on her face. She looked at herself in the mirror. She looked about twelve. The idea of going back out there and trying to talk to his friends gave her a hopeless feeling inside.

"Hey," she said, opening the door.

"Hey." Mike stood with a Corona in his hand. Loud music and laughter drifted in from the living room. It sounded like the party had picked up while she'd been in the bathroom. "Here's your beer. It's probably a little warm by now."

"Thanks," she said. She took it but didn't have the least interest in drinking it.

"Are you all right?" he asked. "You've been in here a long time."

"Oh yeah," she said. "I was just reading."

He stepped into the bathroom and closed the door. "So you'd rather read in the bathroom than meet my friends?"

"Sort of. I mean, this was all kind of a surprise."

"You're telling me," he said, grinning.

He was still so hot, she thought. Especially when he grinned at her like he already knew everything that was going through her mind. It made this awkward feeling even worse. "You know what? You enjoy your party. I'm just gonna call a cab."

"That's ridiculous," he said.

"No, it's not."

"Yes, it is. You can't be mad because my friends threw me some surprise party that I didn't know about."

"I'm not mad. Who said I was mad?"

He leaned against the door. "You get your way a lot, don't you?"

"That's rude," she said.

"It's an observation," he said. "But hey, if you want to bolt, fine." He folded his arms and looked down at her as a smile curled around his lips. "We'll just hang out another time."

His stare was so intense that she had to look away from him. "You know, you really need to clean this," she said, pointing to the sink.

"Okay," he said, without taking his eyes off her.

"And you know, fuzzy toilet-seat covers aren't really in style these days," she added.

He reached out and encircled her waist with his arm, bringing her in closer. "Okay," he said.

"And you really need to organize that magazine rack," she added, almost unable to breathe. Standing this close to him, she could feel his chest through his thin T-shirt. He smoothed her hair with the flat palm of his hand, all the way down her back.

"I'll remember that." He moved his hand to the back of her head and leaned down.

She closed her eyes.

His lips touched hers, softly, hesitantly, feather light. She allowed them to linger on hers, daring him to kiss her deeper. He did. His hand on the middle of her back pressed her close. By the time she let her arms reach up around his shoulders, she knew that she no longer wanted to leave.

Rory sat hunched over the butcher-block table in the kitchen, poking her fork at a plate of fried chicken. Mrs. Rule had finally released her from duty, but she wasn't even hungry. She'd made at least twenty trips up and down the stairs to fetch drinks and appetizers and, finally, individually plated dinners of Erica's miso black cod, fried chicken, and Caesar salad for Mrs. Rule and her guests to eat on their laps. Now they were having coffee and blueberry cobbler downstairs and pretending to watch the movie, which Rory had been asked to start from the beginning several times. It was nine o'clock. Rory yawned. Erica stood at the island, wrapping up pieces of leftover cod and fried chicken and carefully storing them in glass containers.

"Weren't you supposed to go out?" Erica asked, snapping the plastic lid onto one of the glass bowls.

"Yup," Rory said. "I had to cancel."

"Was it important?"

"Not really." She ate a morsel of coleslaw. "My friend didn't take it too well, though."

"Was it a date?" Erica asked.

"Sort of," she said. "But that's okay. I wasn't really that into him anyway." Rory watched Erica stack the bowls in the refrigerator and then start cleaning the counters. "How long have you been a chef?" she asked.

"About ten years," she said. "But I've only been a private chef for about five."

"It seems stressful," Rory said.

"Oh, it is," Erica sighed. "These people want what they want when they want it. And it's the nice ones that you really have to watch out for." Erica gestured downstairs to the screening room, and Rory knew that Erica was referring to Mrs. Rule. "Just a little piece of advice. You didn't hear it from me."

Rory nodded. It had been hard to name the feeling that she'd been having in her gut all night about Mrs. Rule. It felt a little like the time her mom had promised to take her to Great Adventure for her eleventh birthday, just the two of them, but at the last minute had brought along her boyfriend—some guy with shaggy hair and a bad smoking habit—whom she made out with at every opportunity in public. *Manipulated* was probably the word. From now on, she'd be more careful about Mrs. Rule.

The swinging door creaked open, and Connor peeked his head into the kitchen. "How'd it go?" he asked.

Rory put down her fork and tried not to blush. "Fine. Crisis averted."

"But you didn't go out tonight."

She smiled. "No. That didn't happen."

"Well, can I make it up to you?" he asked. "I'm just hanging in the TV room if you feel like being social."

Rory could see Erica watching this entire interaction very, very closely.

"Great," she said as casually as possible.

"Bring your food," Connor said. "You need to keep your strength up around here," he said with a smile.

She looked at Erica, who nodded and mouthed "*Go!*" Rory grabbed her plate. She felt giddy and vulnerable. After what had happened tonight, she wasn't sure if she could trust anyone in this family.

"So I know that my mom can be kind of high-maintenance," Connor said as they walked down the hall. "Sorry she ruined your night."

"Oh, it's fine," she said. "She really didn't. It wasn't that big a deal."

"It's not the point," Connor said. "She's just used to getting what she wants. Same thing with Isabel. Is my sister being nice to you, by the way?"

"Yeah," Rory said, smiling. "She is being nice to me. She took me out last night to a party."

They walked into the TV room and sat down next to each other on the couch. Rory balanced the plate on her lap and prayed that she wouldn't drop any food anywhere.

"Well, in that case, be careful," Connor said. "My sister can be kind of crazy. Don't get sucked into the vortex. Take it from me. It's not pretty." He aimed the remote at a hidden cabinet, and soon Van Morrison was playing through hidden speakers.

"But is Isabel that crazy? I haven't really seen that. Except behind the wheel, of course."

Connor put down the remote and chuckled. "Yeah, driving with her can be a little intense. But the rest of it…" He looked off into the distance. "I don't know. She's always acted out a little. She's always been hard to control. And I think it's because she's always felt like an outsider."

"Really?" Rory asked. "Why?"

"No clue. But she does. She hates Gregory and Sloane." He looked at her, catching himself. "Sorry. I shouldn't be telling you this."

"I'm not going to tell anyone," she said.

For a moment, there was just silence as they looked at each other, and then the sound of women's voices and the *click-clack* of heels wafted into the room.

"Con-nor!" Mrs. Rule yelled. "Connor, are you still down here? Mrs. Van der Cliff has something to ask you!"

Connor looked at Rory hesitantly.

"I guess you need to go," she said.

He nodded and got to his feet. "I'll create a diversion. So you can get back to the kitchen."

"Thanks."

"I've had lots of practice," he said wryly.

He walked into the hall, and soon she was listening to him talk to the women. She waited until she heard them move to the front door, and then she slipped out of the room with her plate.

Tap-tap-tap. Rory lifted her head off the pillow. She'd been dreaming about someone knocking on her wall, and now she realized that she wasn't dreaming at all.

Tap-tap-tap.

Someone was at the window, again.

She sat up and turned on the light. After her eyes adjusted to the brightness, she could see blond hair and big blue eyes peering in through the window. "Hey!" Isabel tapped her knuckles on the glass. "Can you open this?"

Luckily, she appeared to be alone.

Rory threw off the covers and padded to the window. "Isabel?"

She raised the window and was hit with the overpowering smell of beer.

"Hey!" Isabel clambered through the window and fell right onto the floor.

"Are you okay?" Rory crouched down and helped Isabel sit up.

"I'm fine," Isabel said, but Rory could tell that she was slightly drunk.

"How'd you get home?"

"I got a ride with some really nice people," Isabel said. "Nice, *sober* people."

"Okay, we need to get you back to your room." Rory slung an arm around Isabel's narrow shoulders and helped her to her feet. She weighed almost nothing. "So I guess you had a good time?"

"Wait! How was Landon? Did you guys make out?"

"No, we didn't go out," she said, dragging Isabel by the arm to the door.

"What do you mean, you didn't go out?"

"I mean, the date was canceled," Rory said. "But that's okay, it's so not a big deal."

"Did you chicken out?" she asked.

"No, I didn't chicken out. Your mom had stuff for me to do."

"I'll totally yell at her for you," Isabel said, weaving unsteadily on her platform espadrilles.

"Thanks, but that's okay," she said.

They walked past Bianca's room as quietly as possible, though Isabel did manage to bump into the wall. Being caught helping a tipsy Isabel might actually be worse than having a guy sneak into her room, Rory thought. When they reached the second floor, Rory looked down the dark, slumbering hall. "Which one's your room?"

"I can take it from here," Isabel said. "But you—*you*," she said, pointing to Rory as she tripped backward, "are awesome. You know that?"

Rory nodded. "He kissed you tonight, huh?"

Even in the dark, Isabel's smile was blinding. "Yes, he did."

"Good. Well, good night."

She released Isabel, who flew out of her arms, twirled down the hall, and then crashed into a wall. "Uh, you okay?" Rory asked, not sure if she should laugh or gasp.

"Oh yeah," Isabel said, righting herself. "Definitely. G'night."

Rory waited until Isabel opened a door and disappeared behind it. Then she padded down the stairs, smiling to herself. Someone had finally gotten to the ice princess. Isabel was totally whipped.

CHAPTER TEN

"So I'm thinking, next weekend, when my parents go out of town to visit my sister in London, I should just say to hell with it and have a party," Thayer said as they walked out of the dining building with their trays. "What do you think? It would be cool, right? People would come."

"Yeah," Isabel said, trying to keep her tray stable as she reached for some napkin-wrapped utensils by the door. Her head was pounding, and she thought she might throw up right onto her sandals. She also hadn't heard a word Thayer had said while they'd been standing in line, waiting to order, but it didn't really matter. Thayer liked to have a captive—and quiet—audience.

"Because I'm thinking then I can just invite Andrew over and that way we're sort of just hanging out already and then maybe something can happen. Instead of waiting for him to get it together and ask me out."

"Uh-huh," Isabel said, as she almost tripped over a small child in front of her.

"Are you okay?" Thayer asked. "You seem a little out of it."

"I'm just tired."

Thayer cocked her head and stared at her. "And maybe a little hungover?"

Isabel looked at her.

"Did you go out last night?" Thayer asked with an uneasy smile. They'd talked about going out to see a movie, but Isabel had said she couldn't.

"No," she said. "I would have told you."

"Maybe you wouldn't have," Thayer said, as they walked over to Darwin sitting at a table, reading *The House of Mirth*. "Hey, D," Thayer said as they placed their trays on the table. "Check it out. Isabel's hungover."

"Yeah?" Darwin looked up briefly from her book and then returned to it. "Sorry, I'm just really into this right now."

"I hate summer reading," Thayer said, digging into her Cobb salad. "So boring. Anyway, where were you getting hungover, and with who?"

Isabel picked up her fork, and a memory slammed into her brain, taking her breath away: she and Mike kissing in the bathroom, her hands in his hair, feeling his hands on her, holding her, lifting her onto the sink so she could sit with her legs wrapped around his waist as they kissed, then later, on his bed, underneath him, feeling his hands travel up her shirt, her hands feeling the hair on his chest...She shook it away. "Nobody you know," she said softly.

"Huh. The plot thickens."

"Just someone I met."

"*Someone?*" Thayer asked, her eyes on her plate. "That's a vague pronoun—"

"You don't know him. Okay?"

Thayer was quiet as she ate her salad, but Isabel knew that she'd just broken the first commandment of being Thayer Quinlan's best friend: Thou shalt not keep anything to yourself.

"His name is Mike," Isabel offered.

"What school?"

"I told you, you won't know him."

"So he doesn't go to school?" Darwin asked, putting down her book.

"I think he goes to Stony Brook."

"He goes to *college?*" Thayer asked. She and Darwin looked at each other. "Where's he from?"

Isabel started to feel a swell of anger build. "He's from here. The North Fork."

"*What?*" Darwin said, amusement and shock mingling on her face.

Isabel looked down at her salad.

"Wow, that's a first," said Darwin. "He must be really hot."

"So, let me get this straight," Thayer said. "You're hanging out with some Jersey girl who's working for you and now you're dating some local? What happened to you?"

"That is so gross that you just said that," Isabel said.

"Oh, please, don't tell me that I'm being horrible here," Thayer said. "I'm just trying to figure out what's going on. Is this to get back at your parents or something?"

"What?"

"Sorry, but it just sounds like another one of your crazy stunts," Thayer went on. "You do have a thing about giving everyone the finger."

"Thanks for your support, T," Isabel said. She stood up and grabbed her bag, sending her chair screeching across the concrete.

"Where are you going?" Darwin asked.

"I suddenly lost my appetite," Isabel said.

"Oh god, Iz," Thayer groaned. "Fine, throw a fit. Whatever."

Isabel wove her way through the tables, feeling her face flush. The exquisite pounding in her head had settled right above her eyebrows and was fast turning into a migraine. She hated that these girls had embarrassed her. She needed to go home. She took out her phone and texted Rory, not even caring about the no-cellphone policy down at the patio.

Can you pick me up? At the GC.

She headed for the family cabana, which was the only real spot to hide at the club. The Georgica changing cabanas were a relic from the club's earliest days, when members needed a fully private place to change into their bathing costumes. Now owning one of these narrow shingle closets meant that you were one of the club's elite. They actually weren't good for much, besides a few memorable make-out sessions whenever there was a good party.

She headed for the plaque that said LAWRENCE RULE and was almost inside when she heard a man call her name.

"Isabel? Is that Isabel Rule?"

She turned around and saw a couple coming toward her. They looked to be her parents' age. The last thing she felt like doing right now was talking to her parents' friends.

"Peter and Michelle Knox," the man said, a smile on his face. "Friends of your parents. We had the house on James Lane."

With one hand shading her eyes from the sun, she was able to see them more clearly. She recognized them. The man was handsome, with youthful blue eyes, a sharp nose, and close-cropped brown hair that had gone gray at the temples. Mrs. Knox had black hair, luminous skin, and, hands down, the perkiest breasts Isabel had ever seen, at least on a woman in her late forties. "Oh. Hi," she said. "It's good to see you again."

"We just decided to come back for the summer from LA. We moved there a while ago," he said. "How long has it been?" he asked his wife. "Ten years?"

"Almost twelve," Mrs. Knox said. She slipped her arm through her husband's.

"Wow," Isabel said, unsure of what else to say. "That's a long time."

"It sure is. But it's good to be back," he said. "The place looks terrific. I love what they did to the pool."

"Are you still members?" Isabel asked, before she realized that this might be a little rude.

"Oh yeah," Mr. Knox said. "As long as you keep paying the dues, the Georgica lets you hang on as long as you want."

"Honey, you're going to be late for your tee time," Mrs. Knox advised.

"Oh, right, right," Mr. Knox said, but Isabel could hear in his voice that he didn't really care. "Anyway, it's great to see you, Isabel. Krista and Holly—our daughters—they'll be out in a few weeks. You should meet them."

"Yeah, sure," she said. "And I'm sure my parents will be having you guys over soon."

The Knoxes traded an uncomfortable glance, and Isabel sensed that she'd said the wrong thing.

"Sure," Mr. Knox said uneasily. "Well, you take care, Isabel. Bye-bye."

Mrs. Knox gave Isabel an artificial smile, and she and Mr. Knox walked across the patio toward the main house.

She wondered why they'd even come back. If she were able to escape this place for good, she'd never come back, ever. But some people just couldn't stay away, she guessed. There was something about the iciness of the Georgica scene that was like an addiction— some people couldn't get enough of feeling like they were somehow falling short.

She walked into the cabana and shut the door, breathing in the smell of coconut-scented sunblock and mildewed towels. She took out her iPhone and clicked it on. Rory hadn't texted yet, but someone else had. Mike.

When can I see you?

One line, five words. All of her questions answered.

JULY

CHAPTER ELEVEN

Traffic—avoiding it, driving around it, anticipating it—had become her job. Or, it would have been her job, had she been getting paid. But she wasn't. And ever since the fiasco of movie night, there was no doubt in Rory's mind that not asking for minimum wage had been a big mistake.

The traffic was there in the mornings, it was there in the afternoons, and it was there in the evenings. It was there when she went to Southampton to pick up another pair of needlepoint Stubbs & Wootton slippers for Mrs. Rule (size seven; style: Crest Techno), and it was there in the afternoons when she went to get heirloom tomatoes for five dollars a pound at the stand on Scuttle Hole Road. All day long she crawled east and west on Montauk Highway, and by the end of June she knew every fruit and vegetable stand, every bagel and coffee place, and every Pilates studio and beauty salon, on both sides of the highway. She also began to know the back roads. The Rules had a dog-eared copy of *Jodi's Shortcuts* that she kept in the car at all times, and soon she knew to take Ocean Road and then a left on Sagaponack if the traffic was really terrible. A few minutes later, she'd be driving past open fields golden with fading light and the wind blowing through the open window.

Sometimes she'd pass groups of teenage girls walking down the street in Bridgehampton or coming out of the Candy Kitchen, laughing and talking and swinging shopping bags in their hands, and she'd think of Sophie and Trish. At first, the three of them had traded e-mails every day, but now the messages had tapered off to once a week. She could tell that they already had a million private jokes from working together at the campgrounds, jokes that she'd never get. But she couldn't really explain this place to her friends, either. It was clear from their e-mails that they still didn't understand her job or why she wasn't getting paid. She wondered how things would be when she got home. She'd never spent a summer apart from her friends, and already it felt like this break might have lasting repercussions.

But little by little, she was getting to know Isabel Rule.

"So what do you and Mike have planned for the Fourth?" Rory asked one day, as Isabel drove them along the back roads of Sagaponack. After a couple of weeks of driving lessons she now stuck to the right side of the road, but every once in a while, the car would drift to the center.

"I don't know," Isabel said, fiddling with the iPod plugged into the dash. "There's always a huge party at the Georgica, but that's not really an option. At least, not with Mike."

"Why can't you bring him?"

Isabel gave her an incredulous glance. "You think I should take Mike to the Georgica?"

"Maybe if those girls met him, they'd see how cool he is." Isabel had told her about the fight she'd had with Thayer and Darwin about Mike. Having seen their snarky side in person, Rory believed every word of it.

"Uh, *no*," Isabel said as she turned on the wipers instead of her blinker. "You've met those girls."

"Then what about bringing him over to the house so you can be at your own place for a change?" Rory asked, pulling down the visor against the setting sun. "He's got to meet your friends and your parents sometime."

"Are you high?" Isabel asked. "Do you want me to tell my parents that I'm dating a guy who works at a fruit and vegetable stand?"

"Well, yeah," Rory said.

"The last thing I want is my parents involved in my love life," Isabel said, accelerating. "They'd start making rules about that, too. And they'd never approve of him. Ever."

"Really?"

"Never," Isabel said emphatically. "Everyone belongs in their place, you know what I mean?"

Rory had suspected as much about the Rules, but hearing it directly from Isabel only confirmed it. They'd probably hate the idea of their son dating someone like her. Not that it was even an option, Rory reminded herself. "Well, doesn't *he* want to meet your friends and family?" she asked.

Isabel shrugged. "I don't know. We don't talk about it."

"You don't?"

"No. I like the way things are right now. Everyone thinks I'm going over to Thayer's, I go out with Mike, I come back, you let me into your room—it's perfect." She smiled and made a sudden left before they hit the beach. "What about Landon? Has he called?"

"No."

"What the hell is wrong with him?" Isabel asked. "Just because you had to cancel? You should just call him."

"Okay, *no*," Rory said.

"Why not?"

"Because I really don't care about going out with him," Rory said.

"You *have* to get over this fear of guys," Isabel said. "It's not healthy."

"I'm not afraid of guys."

"*Please*," Isabel said. "You so are."

"Maybe I like someone else," Rory heard herself say.

Isabel whipped her head around. "Who?" she demanded, just as Rory realized what she'd said.

"Nobody. Nobody you know."

"I know everybody," Isabel said. "Who is it? Where'd you meet him?"

"It's nobody," Rory said, praying that she wasn't blushing.

She hadn't been alone with Connor since movie night. Once in a while, he'd come into the kitchen and ask Erica for something, and Rory would allow herself just the barest glance at him, especially if Steve was in the room. But they hadn't run into each other. He was usually out of the house by the time she got up, and after work he'd be in the pool, doing his laps. Sometimes at night she'd hear his Audi pull into the gravel drive, and it would take everything she had not to run to the window and watch him walk into the house. She wondered if he was avoiding her. By now she was almost positive that the flirtation between them had just been in her head.

"Why are you being so weird?" Isabel asked. "Just tell me."

"It's nobody, seriously. I just said that to get you off my back. That's all. There's nobody."

Isabel narrowed her eyes as if she still didn't quite believe her.

"Stay on the right side!" Rory yelled.

Isabel swerved back on the other side of the yellow line. "Oh, wait," she said, gazing out of Rory's window. "This is where our new house is gonna be."

Rory reluctantly turned to look out the window. She saw acres of flat brown potato fields laid out under a pink and gold sky.

"*All* of this?" Rory asked.

"A piece of it," Isabel explained. "Can you believe one guy owns all this, and he doesn't want to sell to anyone?"

"Some people don't care about money." Rory shrugged.

"So if you were sitting on something that was worth twenty million bucks, you wouldn't sell it?"

"Maybe not."

"Oh, come on," Isabel said. "Seriously?"

"Some things are more important than millions and millions of dollars."

"Wow," Isabel said, rolling her eyes. "I'll make sure to tell my dad that." Her phone chimed, and she looked down.

"No texting while driving," Rory said by rote.

Isabel swerved over to the side of the road and read her phone. "That's my mom. Connor's at the Audi dealership in Southampton. We need to pick him up."

Rory felt as if a bolt of electricity had just zapped her through the car seat.

"We should probably switch," Isabel said, unclicking her seat belt. "He'll freak if he sees me driving on the highway."

Rory got back behind the wheel and tried to focus on the road. She wasn't sure what made her more nervous—the idea of Connor sitting next to her in the shotgun seat, or Isabel figuring out Rory's feelings for him.

When they pulled into the dealership, Connor was standing outside the front doors with his hands in the pockets of his jeans. Sunlight glinted off his blond hair. *God, he's cute*, Rory thought. *So, so cute.* She watched him head toward the car, her heart beating. *Get in the front*, she thought, staring at Isabel, hoping she might get out. *Please please please get in the front.*

Connor opened the backseat door. "I'll get in back," he offered.

Rory watched him slide into the backseat in the rearview mirror, trying to hide her disappointment.

"What's wrong with your car?" Isabel asked.

"Everything," he said. "Need to change the tires and replace the brakes. Guy says it'll take at least a day."

"Sucks for you," Isabel said.

Rory pulled back onto the road, trying to concentrate on driving. She could feel Connor looking at her.

"Hey, Rory," he said. "How's it going?"

"Great," she chirped, making eye contact with him in the rearview mirror. "How's teaching?"

"Cool," he said.

"We're trying to find Rory a boyfriend out here," Isabel said out of nowhere.

Rory gripped the steering wheel so hard that she almost forgot to turn onto the highway.

"Oh?" Connor asked.

Isabel nudged Rory in the arm. "I keep telling her that she needs to have a summer fling. But she won't listen to me."

Rory's heart pounded. *Shut up, Isabel*, she thought. *Shut the hell up.*

"Yeah, well, sure," Connor said wanly. "What about you, Iz? When are you going to admit that you have a new boyfriend?"

"His name is Mike," Isabel said quickly. "He lives in Montauk."

"How old?" Connor asked.

"Twenty-one."

"That's too old for you," Connor said.

"Oh, please."

"No, it is. Dad would not be psyched."

"Well, Dad's not going to know about it," Isabel said testily. "And you better not tell him." She twisted around in her seat. "I mean it. *Don't* tell him."

"I don't think you need to say that," Connor said.

"What about you?" Isabel asked in a teasing voice. "Are you still—"

"Iz, when there's an update, you'll hear about it," he said, cutting her off.

Rory glanced in the rearview mirror. Connor looked the most irritated she'd ever seen him. *So Isabel gets on his nerves, too,* she thought. *Another thing he and I have in common.*

"So, Mom wants to throw Dad a surprise party. Have you heard about that?" Connor said.

"Ugh," Isabel said. "Dad hates surprises."

"That's what I told her, but you know Mom, anything for a party."

Rory drove quietly, trying to recover from one of the most awkward and embarrassing moments she could remember. But she wondered what Isabel had been talking about when she'd asked Connor for an update.

"Oh, I ran into the Knoxes a few days ago," Isabel said. "They're back from California."

"I don't think Mom and Dad talk to them anymore."

Rory made eye contact with Connor in the rearview mirror once more.

"Then that's why they looked so weird when I asked if they'd be coming over," Isabel said as she gazed out the window. "My bad."

When they reached the house, Rory took a long time turning off the ignition, just to give Connor plenty of time to get out of the car and make his way to the house. But when she stepped out of the car, he and Isabel were still standing and chatting on the gravel, and he gave her an expectant look as she slammed the car door closed. Almost as if he was waiting to talk to her. She walked toward them, listening as Isabel and Connor talked about their parents' old friends.

"See you, guys," she said when they entered the hall.

"What are you doing now?" Isabel asked her. "Do you want to watch TV with us?"

"I think I'm actually pretty tired." She couldn't look at Connor.

"Well, thanks for the driving lesson," Isabel said.

"No problem," Rory said.

She glanced at Connor, who seemed almost about to say something, but she turned and hurried to her room before he could.

She buried her face in the pile of pillows on her bed.

He thinks I'm some boy-crazy freak.

He thinks that I need help getting guys.

He thinks that I like someone else besides him.

So many worries, and each one of them made her gulp and press her face further into the bed linens. Maybe the right thing to do was tell Isabel the truth, so if the three of them were ever together again, at least she wouldn't have to deal with this.

But something told her that would be much, much worse. The only thing she could do was avoid Connor Rule for the next few days. And pray that he would forget the entire conversation.

CHAPTER TWELVE

That night, Rory woke to a gentle but firm tapping on her window. She yawned and switched on the light. Isabel waved to her excitedly from behind the glass, and any lingering irritation at what she'd said in the car disappeared. Rory slid out of bed and padded over to the window.

Isabel climbed in, carrying with her the scent of beer and Axe body spray. "Did I wake you up?" she asked. "Sorry!"

"That's okay," Rory said, shutting the window.

Isabel kicked off her shoes and lay down on the floor to chat, as she did whenever she snuck in now. "So how was your night?" she asked, yawning loudly into her fist.

"The usual. Pretty quiet. I played Trivial Pursuit with Erica and Fee."

"Sounds horrible," Isabel groaned, folding her hands under her head. "You should come out with Mike and me sometime. You'd have fun."

Rory got back into bed and slipped under the covers. "Did he sneak you into a bar again?"

"No. We just grilled out with some friends of his at his house. It was fun."

"Good. So it's going well."

"Oh god, no," she sighed. "It's not going well. I like him too much."

"And that's a bad thing?" Rory asked.

"It sucks," Isabel said, sitting up on her forearms. "I try to play it cool, I try to be mysterious. I try to be the way I used to be. But it's useless. I'm too into him. And then I think about him just never texting me back, or just *disappearing*, you know? Like, vanishing one day, never hearing from him again, and I almost have a heart attack."

"Do you think he might do that?" Rory thought of Mike walking out of the house that first day, all slow and sexy and dangerous. She hoped for Isabel's sake that her first impression of him had been wrong.

"No," Isabel said carefully. "But I worry about it sometimes. It's like I'm so scared of losing him I can't even have a good time with him. And when we hook up," she went on, "it's like this thing comes over me and I have no control. I can't stop myself." She looked Rory straight in the eye. "Don't worry. I haven't slept with him."

"I'm not thinking that," Rory said.

"I'm not trying to stay a virgin the rest of my life. It's just that I've never liked anyone enough to do that with them. But this guy, I have to literally stop myself, you know? I *want* to do it with him. Does that sound slutty?"

"No. Of course not."

"But you're, like, Miss Haven't Done Anything," Isabel said.

"It doesn't sound slutty," Rory said. "It sounds normal. You're attracted to him."

"So much," Isabel said, lying back down on the floor. "But the weird thing is, I don't really know that much about him. I mean, I know his last name, and I know that he works for his dad, and I know that he goes to Stony Brook, and I know little things, like that he really likes reggae and that he hates mushrooms, and stuff like that, but I don't really know him. And here I am thinking about sleeping with him, which is something I wouldn't even think of doing with a guy who I know everything about. That's weird, right?"

"Not necessarily."

Isabel sighed. "Sometimes you sound like a shrink."

"Ha-ha," Rory said.

Isabel yawned again. "I guess I'm falling in love."

Rory lay her head on the pillow. She couldn't even imagine how it felt to actually be in love. At least, with someone who might possibly love you back.

"What about you?" Isabel asked. "There has to be someone for you to go out with around here. Let me think."

Connor, Rory thought, willing the name to come out of Isabel's mouth. *Think of Connor.*

"Wait, I've got it!" Isabel exclaimed, sitting up. "What about one of Mike's friends? He has all these surfing buddies. And they're totally single!"

"That's okay," Rory said. "And we should probably get to sleep."

Isabel sat up and got to her feet. "Thanks for listening. I can't really talk to my friends about this. In case you couldn't tell," she said, smiling.

"No problem."

Isabel nodded. "Well, g'night."

"G'night."

Rory watched her tiptoe down the hall, then closed the door and got back into bed. It would have been hard to believe only a few weeks ago, but it seemed as if she and Isabel Rule were actually becoming friends. Except, if they really were friends, wouldn't Rory have been able to tell her that she liked her brother? Was that always going to be weird with a friend? And did it even make sense to tell her? Rory turned out the light and let the questions vanish as she closed her eyes.

The next morning, she woke with an antsiness in her legs, like she needed to run or do sprints. The morning was gray and chilly, and there was the scent of recent rain in the air. Not exactly Fourth of July weather, she thought. If she were home, she'd be going to Trish's family's house for a barbecue today and then fireworks at Lake Hopatcong. She'd call Sophie or Trish today and say hi. She missed them. Maybe this time she'd reach them on the phone.

She got up and changed into sweatpants and sneakers in her dark bedroom, then threw on a jacket. She was pretty sure that she'd have the beach to herself this morning.

But when she opened the door, Trixie was waiting there, head cocked and eyes imploring. "Okay, let's go," she whispered.

They slipped out the back door, Trixie trotting at her heels. Steam rose from both of the pools as they walked across the

181

patio, toward the American flag. From the dunes, the ocean looked greenish gray and bearded with foam. She bent down to pick up a small stick. Trixie bounded down the walkway toward the sand, too excited to wait.

Down on the empty beach, Rory began to run. "Come on, girl, get it!" she yelled, tossing the stick of driftwood toward the water.

Trixie raced up the beach as fast as her little legs could carry her, then clamped the stick between her teeth as she plucked it out of the wet sand. Rory ran alongside the water, faking left and going right, letting Trixie chase her with the stick in her mouth.

Then she saw the jogger with his dog. The two of them were still far away, half the distance to Main Beach, but she could see that the dog was large and muscular and dark, and not on a leash. It had something in its jaws that the man kept trying to wrench away, and every time the man got close enough, the dog ran ahead, taunting him.

Trixie dropped the stick at Rory's feet, eager for more. Rory threw the stick a few more times, letting Trixie get sandy and wet as she ran up and down the length of the beach. Her lungs burned, and sweat lined her brow. At one point, she felt cool water rush over her sneaker and seep in all over her foot.

"Come on, girl," she yelled to Trixie, who was searching for her stick in the shallow water. "Time to go home!"

Trixie stood in the shallow water, hunting for her stick.

"Come on, Trixie!" she said.

Trixie looked up with the stick in her mouth, but the faintest sound of a jingling collar grabbed her attention. She saw the other dog. Almost instantly, she dropped the stick and took off down the beach, straight toward the jogger and his dog.

"Trixie!" she yelled. "Trixie, come!"

Trixie only ran faster, so fast that Rory couldn't hope to catch up with her. The black dog began to run toward Trixie, leaving his owner far behind. *Maybe this isn't a big deal*, Rory thought. *Maybe this is nothing to worry about.* But the adrenaline coursing through her body said otherwise. She started to run.

"Trixie! Come back here, now!" she yelled again, willing her legs to run faster.

But it was too late. As soon as the big dog was near enough, it lunged forward and snapped its jaws, just missing Trixie as she jumped back. Trixie danced around in front of it, trying to play, but Rory could tell that the other dog had no intention of playing. The dog lunged again.

"Trixie!" She reached down and grabbed her, just as the other dog lunged forward and snapped its jaws.

"Ow!" she yelled, feeling a stab of pain. She saw the bite marks on the back of her hand.

The dog lunged for her again, baring its teeth, just as someone ran up from behind her and stepped in front of her, shielding her with his body.

"Hey!" Connor yelled. "Off! *Off!*"

The dog reached up to bite him, but Connor pushed it away with one hand on its chest. "Off!" he yelled firmly. Then he let out a startling, bloodcurdling growl.

The dog lowered its head and forelegs to the sand.

"Stay!" Connor yelled.

The dog stayed in its crouch for a moment, then trotted back to its owner, who jogged up to them, panting.

"Don't you have a leash?" Connor asked.

The jogger reached for the dog's collar and held on to it. He was a stocky man, and his hoodie framed a face with large, startled green eyes. "I thought he'd be okay without one."

"Dogs are supposed to be on leashes here, man. It's the law." Connor turned to Rory. "Are you okay? Are you hurt?"

She looked down and saw some blood oozing from the bite marks. "It's just a little nip."

"Hey, your dog bit her!" Connor said to the jogger. "I could call the police. I *should* call the police."

"He got his rabies shot a few months ago," the jogger said, showing the tag on the dog's collar. "Sorry, man. I guess he's just a little protective."

"Whatever, just don't come back here with it not on a leash."

It was jarring to hear Connor speak so firmly to someone, but it was also exciting.

Connor let go of his protective grip around her waist and stepped beside her. "Let's go clean this up, okay?"

He looked down at Trixie. "You okay?"

Trixie licked Connor's hand happily, as if nothing had happened.

At the poolhouse, Connor rinsed her hand with cold water from the hose, then wrapped it in a fluffy white towel.

"But it's white," Rory protested. "I'll get blood all over it."

"Don't worry about it," he said gently. Then he dried Trixie with another towel, scraping off the sand and sending her curls up all over the place. "I think there's a first aid kit in here somewhere," he said. "Hold on." He disappeared into the poolhouse for a moment and then reappeared with a small box.

"That was pretty impressive," she said as he sat beside her on the chaise. "I've never heard anyone growl like that. Cesar Millan would have been proud."

"It's not that hard," he said, opening the box and unwrapping a gauze pad. "You just have to say it like you mean it. Dogs can understand when you mean business."

"Well, *I* almost rolled over," she joked.

"Good to know." He squeezed some clear liquid onto the gauze and began to dab at the bite. "So I'm starting to worry about something."

"What's that?"

"That between my mom and her craziness, and my sister and *her* craziness, and this, you're going to want to get on the first jitney home." He stopped dabbing at her wound and looked warily into her eyes. "Do you?"

"No. Of course not."

"So, you're having fun here?" he asked.

"Absolutely. I love getting bitten by dogs—it's one of my hobbies."

He smiled as he taped a piece of gauze over the bite. "Well, as long as you're not gonna leave or anything."

Rory felt her heart do a somersault.

"I mean, as long as you're still having a good time," he said quickly. "And tonight should be fun. You know, the fireworks and everything."

"Where do you guys go to watch them?"

"The club. But there's just as good a view from the beach right here. It's almost better."

"Really? Then who knows? Maybe I'll stay here." She became aware of his hand still holding her own, not in any hurry to let go, and his eyes looking into hers. He liked her. She could feel it now with certainty. And then a creak sounded and the back door opened, and Steve walked out onto the patio. Rory dropped Connor's hand. "Well, thanks for that," she said awkwardly.

"Yeah, feel better, Rory," he said. He reached out and touched her bandaged hand, sending a shock all the way up her arm. "Have a good day."

"You, too," she said. "Come on, Trixie!"

She turned to walk back to the house, unable to stop smiling. But when she saw that Steve was waiting for her, she made sure to look as nonchalant as possible. "Hey," she said as she approached him.

"What happened to your hand?" he asked. His voice sounded flatter, more toneless than she'd ever heard it before. His wraparound shades hid his eyes.

"I got bitten by a dog on the beach," she said. "Connor helped clean it out for me."

"Be careful," Steve said. "I don't want to see you get hurt."

"Well, I think it's a little late for that."

"I don't mean about the dog bite," Steve said, taking off his sunglasses. His expression was serious. "I'm talking about you and Connor. I know it's none of my business, but it's a weird situation."

"It is?"

"Not for you guys, but for everyone else. And you are working here, you know."

"I know that," she said, starting to get irritated.

"Take it from me. I've gotten involved with people before. Maybe it's different for a guy, but—"

"Nothing has happened," Rory said.

"I know," Steve said. "Which is why I'm telling you now. Don't do anything that you might regret. You're in the vulnerable spot here, not him. This is *his* house. Not yours."

Rory stepped backward, away from Steve's stern eyes. "Wow. Thanks for the support, Steve."

"Rory—"

"Whatever," she said. She walked away from him, feeling like she'd just been slapped in the face. Steve had teased her about Connor. He'd seemed excited about it. He'd been on her side. Now he was telling her that she was going to get hurt. It didn't seem fair. And somewhere inside her, she wanted Steve to think that she was good enough for Connor Rule. Someone had to.

CHAPTER THIRTEEN

"Hi, there," she murmured, feeling the stubble on his jaw scrape against her nose. Her fingers played with the wet hair on the back of his head. "You smell good," she said, lightly kissing his cheek.

"You smell better," he whispered.

Her lips traveled down the side of his face, breathing in his salty smell, until he raised his chin and his soft, pillowy lips were finally on hers—

The car behind them honked.

"Move!" yelled the driver, sticking his head out the window. "You gonna sit here all day?"

"Fourth of July," Mike said. "It brings out the best in everybody." He put the car in drive and turned out of the Main Beach parking lot. "Stupid weekend people." Then he grinned at her. "No offense."

"Uh, don't worry about it," she said wryly, taking his hand and squeezing it.

She was starting to love the drive from East Hampton to Montauk. Mike would plug in his iPod and put on Jane's Addiction, and she'd look out the window at the quaint shops and farm stands of Amagansett, then the roadside seafood shacks painted bright colors with their 1950s era signs, then the lush state parks on either side of the road. With each mile east, the Georgica and her parents and Thayer and Darwin faded farther and farther away.

Except it was becoming harder to lie. So far, her mom had been too busy with paddle tennis to notice when Isabel wasn't at the club during the day. But this morning, she'd had to make up a story to get out of going to the Georgica for the fireworks.

"The Bayliffs," she'd said, looking at her mom across the breakfast table. "You know Melissa Bayliff, her parents have a place out in Montauk? They're having a party."

"I thought you didn't see her anymore," said her mom, stirring her coffee.

"We've sort of been in touch. She just invited me."

Beside her, Connor was quiet as he ate his scrambled eggs.

"Will there be supervision?" her father asked.

Isabel nodded. "Well, it'll be at their house."

"That's not the same thing," he said.

"Yes, there'll be supervision. Her parents are the ones throwing it."

"What's their number?" her father asked.

Isabel almost laughed. "Seriously? You're going to call them? How old do you think I am?"

"Larry, I don't think that's necessary," said her mother.

"Fine," he said, getting to his feet. "Whatever you think is best." He left the table, whistling loudly.

"He's in a good mood," Connor said.

Her mom twisted open one of her bottles of supplements. "He's just mad at me because I don't want to sell this house. Go to the party," she said to Isabel. "Just be safe getting home. There'll be lots of drunk drivers on the road. Maybe Rory can go with you and take the Prius?"

"Or maybe Rory can come with us to the Georgica," Connor ventured.

Mrs. Rule tipped some vitamins into her hand and froze. "Why would she do that?"

"Well, because we're all going tonight and I just thought it would be the nice thing to do," Connor said.

Isabel realized that this was her cue to leave. She didn't want to wind up having to ask Rory to a party that didn't exist. "Can I be excused, please?" she asked, standing up from the table.

"Fine," her mother said. "You're excused."

She left just as her mother began to explain to Connor that Rory would be much happier going out with the staff tonight to Sag Harbor. As Isabel headed back to her room, she rolled her eyes to herself—deep down inside, her mom was such a hypocrite. She didn't mind having a girl around the house to get her dry cleaning, but she would never actually let her be part of the family.

Now it felt like a lucky escape to be sitting next to Mike in heavy traffic, headed to the very farthest tip of Long Island.

"What do you want to do when we get out there?" he asked. "Hit the waves or hang out?"

She knew what he meant by hang out. They'd been doing a

lot of that lately. Possibly too much, she thought. She was going to have to slow it down, even though it never worked. Somehow they always ended up at his place, to have a soda or grab a snack, and then somehow they would wander down the hall to his bedroom. She'd lie down on the creaky bed with its thin burgundy bedspread and he'd turn on the oscillating fan that did nothing to cut the humidity that swept in from the lake. And soon things would get passionately, deliriously out of control, until hours had passed and the light outside had dimmed, and her hair and skin were damp with sweat and she'd know that she'd have to leave.

"Let's go to the beach," she said. That was safer. She'd still need to go to his house to pick up her wet suit, but she knew he'd stay in the car.

"Cool," he said. "And then after, we could meet Gordy and those guys. They're going to the Ripcurl to see the fireworks."

She'd met Gordy a few days earlier at a party at Mike's house. He'd gone to high school with Mike. He was loud, abrasive, and weathered-looking. Isabel had instantly disliked him. "Okay. Will I be able to get in?"

"Leelee works there. She'll make sure you don't get carded."

She still remembered the way Leelee had looked at Mike that first night a few weeks back—like he was number one on her list of prey. "Are you sure?" she asked. "I thought you hated places like that."

"If it's lame, we don't have to stay," said Mike. "It's either we go there or we do the lighthouse, which is even more of a scene." He looked over at her from behind the wheel. "You are so beautiful."

"Liar," she said, and then leaned over and kissed him.

The waves were almost blown out by the time they got to Ditch Plains, but there was just enough curl for them to paddle out. She was getting more confident on the board in front of Mike, though it was still hard to keep her mind on the waves. They surfed until the sunlight turned golden, and when they walked back to the car, she felt exhausted and content in a way she hadn't felt since she was a child.

She changed out of her bikini in the car and pulled on a tunic dress. She'd forgotten to bring a comb, but hopefully her hair would dry in nice waves from the salt water. "Wow," Mike said as they got inside the car. "You really do look gorgeous."

They drove through town and then toward Lake Montauk, turning into a driveway that led to a low white-shingled building.

"Check out the line to get in," said Mike, pointing to the people waiting along the porch and down the steps onto the driveway. Luxury cars idled in the drive. "It's already douchey."

A valet dressed in surfing trunks and an aloha shirt came out to take their car. "Welcome to the Ripcurl Lounge," he said to Mike, handing him a ticket. "Aloha."

"Aloha," Mike said back to him. "If this place is lame, we're leaving," he said to her under his breath.

"Good plan," she said, and got out of the car.

They walked in front of the line to the door.

"Hey, we're friends with Leelee," Mike said, and the bouncer opened the door without a word.

"Aloha," he said once more, and Isabel couldn't help but giggle.

Inside, the decor was both retro and sleek: tables whittled from driftwood, pink love seats and couches with rattan frames, whitewashed brick walls, black-and-white photographs of surfers from the 1960s. The crowd looked to be in their late twenties and professional. These were people who worked in the city, made good money, and wanted to feel like they were at a club in the Meatpacking District when they came out here. It wasn't her scene. And she knew that it wasn't Mike's, either.

"Hey, you made it!" Leelee walked over to them dressed in a pair of teeny-tiny shorts and a white shirt knotted at the waist. Isabel watched her balance a tray of drinks on one hand as she kissed Mike on the cheek.

"Cool place here," Mike fibbed. He threw an arm around Isabel. "You remember Isabel."

"Oh, right," she said. Her smile was subtle to the point of nonexistent.

"Hi," Isabel said.

"Gordy and those guys are over there," Leelee said, pointing. "Make sure they don't get totally smashed, okay? I still want to have a job tomorrow."

Isabel looked over and saw Gordy holding court on two sofas with a few guys and girls. She'd never seen the girls before. They sat at the end, having their own conversation over what looked like strawberry daiquiris. They looked like they were in their early twenties. *Great*, she thought. *I'm the youngest person here, again.*

"And what can I get you guys to drink?" Leelee asked.

"I'll have a beer," Mike said. "Isabel, you want a beer?"

She nodded.

"Does she have ID?" Leelee asked, pointing at her.

Mike looked at Isabel, unsure how to respond.

"I don't," Isabel said.

"Then sorry," Leelee said flatly. "I can't. A bunch of other clubs have been busted for underage drinking."

There was an uncomfortable pause. Isabel wanted to ask Leelee if Mike would have been barred from having a drink here a few weeks ago, when he was still technically underage, but she let it go. "I'll just take water, then," she said.

"Coming right up," Leelee said with an arctic smile, and walked away.

Isabel gazed out at the crowd, too embarrassed to look Mike in the eye. "So, this place is okay," she said vaguely.

"We won't stay long," Mike said. "Sorry they're such hard-asses about the beer."

"That's okay."

"Let's go say hi to Gordy. We'll only stay for a bit."

They headed over to Gordy's table. From the number of beer bottles on the table, it looked like he and his friends had been celebrating for a while.

"Hey, Gordy, what's up?" Mike said as they approached.

"Castelloni!" Gordy cried out. "You made it! How's it hanging, guy?"

Isabel put on her best fake smile. Gordy could be a little lame.

"Everything's good, man. You remember Isabel, right?" Mike asked, putting his hand on her back.

"Oh, yeah, hey," Gordy said. "Sit down, you guys. Everyone, scoot over for Mike."

Mike squeezed in next to Gordy. Isabel sat down between Mike and the girls. The one on her right had bleach-blond hair that fell in winged pieces on either side of her face, like an updated Farrah Fawcett do, and she seemed to be the ringleader. The other two hung on to her every word. One of the girls, a skinny brunette, had a nose ring. The other girl had obviously dyed red hair and very green eye shadow. They all briefly looked at Isabel as she sat down, and kept talking.

"So, can you believe this place?" Gordy asked, turning to Mike. "Ten-dollar Coronas."

"Admit it, G," Mike said. "You love these kinds of places."

"Yeah, you got me there," Gordy said. "I really need to spend twenty bucks on a burger to feel like a man."

Leelee reappeared and placed something that looked like a Slurpee topped with an umbrella on the table in front of Mike. "Here's our house specialty. The Hot Lava. Compliments of Leelee." She winked.

"Thanks," Mike said.

"And for you?" Leelee said, placing a glass of clear fizzy liquid and ice on the table. "A Seven-Up."

"I didn't ask for this. I asked for water," Isabel said, feeling everyone's eyes on her.

"Not drinking tonight?" Gordy asked her.

"She can't," Leelee said sharply. "Underage." She looked back at Isabel. "Sorry about that. I'll bring you a water."

Isabel quietly seethed as Gordy started telling Mike about someone he'd run into from high school. That had been such a deliberate move, Isabel thought. Maybe Leelee really did like Mike. Well, she wasn't going to let her win. No way.

Suddenly, Farrah Fawcett leaned over and said, "Hey. How old are you?"

There was no use in lying. "Seventeen," Isabel said.

"And you and Mike met... *how*?" she asked.

"In the water. He was surfing in front of my club."

"Oh, wait, wait, we heard about you!" The brunette with the nose ring leaned closer. "You're from the city, right?"

"Yeah."

"But we didn't know you were in *high school*."

"Well, I am," Isabel said.

"Sorry, it's just... well, considering who Mike normally dates," said Farrah Fawcett. "He's always dated older people. His last girlfriend was, like, twenty-five."

Isabel felt her stomach plummet to the floor.

"Oh yeah, Nicollette," chimed in Nose Ring. "I think I just saw her in a Ralph Lauren ad."

"What?" Isabel asked.

"She was a model," said Farrah. "They dated a long time. Lots of drama."

"Yeah, I heard it was pretty steamy," said Nose Ring.

As the word *steamy* hung in the air, Leelee returned and placed a glass of water in front of her. "Anything else?" she asked in a bossy voice.

Isabel shook her head. Her heart was galloping in her chest.

Leelee stormed off.

"I'll be right back," Isabel said, getting up. As she waded into the crowd, she felt like she'd just been punched. All this time, she'd suspected that Mike had been comparing her to other girls who could stay out all night and order a beer at a bar. But to be compared to a girl who was paid to look beautiful and travel the world and get her picture put on ads in magazines, and who could provide him with a relationship that was *steamy*—she'd never felt so small before.

She found the ladies' room and locked herself in a stall. Outside, she heard girls chatting happily at the sinks about the guys they were with or the guys they were trying to be with. Girls who were older, who wouldn't understand or even relate to what she was going through. Girls who lived on their own. Girls for whom sex was just part of having a boyfriend. Maybe sex was actually less of a big thing than she'd thought. Maybe if she just had sex with Mike, she'd see that it wasn't worth all this worry and concern and feeling bad about herself. It was probably like getting your driver's license—something that felt like a big deal at first, but then would become as routine and ordinary as anything else.

She missed Rory. There was something about how level-headed she was, how immune she was to the highs and lows that Isabel had always known. Rory would help her feel better. What was she doing tonight? Anything? She couldn't remember. Now she wished she had invited her along. She reached into her purse and pulled out her phone, but the small upside-down cone at the top of the screen was gone. No service. She'd have to call her outside.

When the other girls left the sinks, she unlocked the stall and opened the door. In the mirror, she saw that her hair had dried into soft, tousled waves and her face had just the softest bit of color from the sun. But all she could see was that other girl Mike had dated—whoever she was, whatever she looked like—posed in a field, wearing a black ball gown and a pair of galoshes, looking gorgeous and unattainable and more beautiful than Isabel would ever be.

When she walked back into the lounge, Mike was talking to another waitress, who Isabel suspected was Leelee's friend. "Hey, babe," he said. "You okay?"

"I'm fine," she said. There was something about the way he was standing next to the waitress. So close. "I don't feel so well. I think I'd like to go."

Without waiting for him to respond, she walked out the doors, past the line that still waited along the porch and that the bouncers still attempted to control. The air was thick and humid, and as she skipped down the steps into the gathering dark, away from the club, she could hear a chorus of bullfrog calls from deep in the bushes.

"Isabel? What's wrong?" Mike asked, following her.

She turned around. "Why didn't you tell me about the ex-girlfriend?" she asked, barely able to look at him.

"What?" he said.

"The Ralph Lauren model. Who's twenty-five. Or was twenty-five. What is she, thirty now?"

"Why are you getting so mad? I don't ask about your old boyfriends."

"Why didn't you tell me about her?"

He stepped toward her. "Why is that so important?"

"Because I would want to know."

"Fine, yeah, I dated a girl who's a model and who's twenty-five. And yes, I've had some older girlfriends. Who the hell cares?"

"I do! I care!" she yelled. "If all you want to date are models, then what are you doing with me? What are you getting out of this?"

He backed away. "You're being a little bit crazy, okay?"

"I just need to know what you're doing with someone who's gonna get carded, and who can't drive, and who needs to be home by midnight. When you can obviously just go off with some model to Paris or whatever. Is this about seducing the rich girl from Lily Pond Lane? Is that what this is?"

He flinched, as if she'd held up her arm to punch him. From the look on his face, she knew that she'd said too much.

"Maybe we shouldn't do this anymore," he finally said.

"What?"

"I don't want to date someone who doesn't know why I'm with them," he said. "Or who thinks that all I want is someone who doesn't get carded." He turned and began to walk back toward the building.

"Hey, I'm sorry," she said, going after him. She reached out and grabbed his hand. "I'm just having a freak-out. Don't go, okay?"

He kept walking, refusing to look her in the eye. A breeze rustled the leaves.

She stepped in front of him. "Hey. I'm sorry. It's just...I'm not used to feeling like this."

He looked down at the gravel, and then finally she felt him squeeze her hand. Then he drew her into his arms and held her without a word.

She buried her face into his shoulder and then reached up to cradle the back of his head with her palm. "Let's go home," she said as meaningfully as she could. "Right now." She hoped that he knew what she meant.

"Are you sure?" he asked, his hand kneading her shoulder. "I don't want you to do anything that you're not sure about."

She raised her head. Those liquid brown eyes seemed to see the most hidden parts of her. And she realized that she was helpless against them. There was no use in fighting it anymore.

"I'm sure," she said. "Let's go."

CHAPTER FOURTEEN

Rory looked at the phone and then at the clock. It was pitch-black outside, and through the open window she heard the agitated pulse of crickets. She couldn't put it off any longer. Three weeks had passed, it was a holiday, and if she didn't do this tonight, then the silence between her and her mother would go from imagined to very, very real. As usual, she would have to be the one to make the first move. At home, this involved walking up to her mom's door, knocking three times, and apologizing through the door. But she couldn't do that now. She grabbed the cell phone lying nearby on the duvet and dialed. It rang several times. At least the landline was still on—that was a relief.

A man picked up. "Yeah?" he said, as video-game gunfire sounded in the background.

"Hi, Bryan!" she said, forcing herself to sound cheerful. "Is my mom there?"

"Hold on *one* second," he said. A particularly loud explosion sounded behind him. Then she heard the cordless phone drop to the carpet. "Lana?" he yelled. "Phone!"

There was a scrabbling sound, and finally she heard someone pick up the extension. "Hang it up!" her mom shouted in the background.

Bryan clicked off.

"Hello?" her mom said, her voice as smooth and warm as hot caramel.

"Hi, Mom. It's me."

"Rory!" her mom said. "I've been thinking about you. How are you, honey?"

Her mom's expansive mood could mean only two things: She'd had two glasses of Chardonnay, and Bryan had moved in.

"I'm fine," Rory said. "I just thought I'd call because it's been a while since we talked. Is everything okay?"

"Everything's just wonderful. It is. Bryan and I are just having so much fun together. Really," she said. "You would just love him. How's everything there?"

"Great. Fee says hi."

"That's nice," her mom said. "And honey, everything worked out with Bryan. He's just the best. He helps around the house, he fixed the toilet so it doesn't run all the time, and we're just having an *amaaaaazing* time."

"That's great," Rory said, inwardly cringing at her mom's teen-speak. "I'm really happy for you."

"You'll see when you get back," her mom said. "I think you're going to really enjoy having him around."

"So he's moved in," Rory said.

"Yeah, he was having some trouble with his roommates. But

it's all wonderful. And now we have to get going. Stacey's having a party down at the lake. What are you doing tonight?"

"Some of the other staff went to watch the fireworks, but I'm kind of tired tonight. I thought I'd just stay home and do some summer reading."

"Well, that's my daughter!" her mom said. "Staying home on the Fourth of July."

I guess it is, Rory thought.

"We'll talk soon, honey."

"Good-bye, Mom," Rory said. She hung up the phone and placed it on the nightstand, right on top of the wrinkled cover of *A Confederacy of Dunces*, which she was supposed to be reading for English. *How appropriate*, Rory thought. It was the perfect title for her mom and Bryan.

She sighed and put her head down on the soft white bed-spread. At least that was over. Now she could think about Connor.

She plucked at the edges of the bandage on her hand. This morning's dramatic incident with the crazy dog seemed like a year ago. Was it really possible that just a few hours earlier she'd sat next to him on the chaise by the pool as he bandaged her hand? Was it really possible that he'd held on to her hand for minutes on end? Was it really possible that he'd said he was wor-ried she might leave and go home?

She turned over on her back and, still smiling at the memory, looked up at the ceiling fan. But then she remembered the disap-proval on Steve's face. She knew that Steve wasn't trying to be a buzzkill. For him to give her a lecture like that, he had to at least think that he was saying the right thing. Connor Rule *was* off-limits. Even if he did feel the same way about her, which she wasn't sure about, it still couldn't happen between them. Dating Connor could only ever be a bad idea. And you always paid for bad ideas in the end. Look at her mom, she thought. She'd decided not to tie herself down and get married when she got pregnant, but to be a bohemian earth mother instead. Which was the first of many bad decisions for Lana McShane.

A yawn overtook her, and she pulled down the duvet. Just as she reached for her book, she heard the sound of a car coming up the drive. She looked at the clock. Eight thirty. Someone was home early—*very* early. She listened as the car made its long approach and then parked. The purr of the engine sounded familiar. With a pounding heart, she got up and went straight to the window and very carefully peeked through the curtains.

The silver Audi was there. She jumped back out of sight. There was the sound of footsteps. Connor. He was alone. And now the two of them were going to be alone in this house together.

She wanted to jump up and down from excitement, but she forced herself to stand still. As she listened, the back door opened. Footsteps came into the hall and continued on into the kitchen. She let out her breath. It was now or never, she thought, slipping her feet into her flip-flops. She had to let him know she was here. She'd just pretend she needed a snack from the fridge. And if he didn't want to hang out, then she'd make a discreet exit.

As she padded down the hall, she could hear him in the

kitchen, opening and closing cabinets and drawers, unwrapping plastic. When she got to the swinging door, she bravely pushed it open. "Hey," she said, walking into the kitchen. "Early night?"

Connor looked up from the mess of cold cuts that he'd placed on the counter. "Hey," he said, smiling in a way that made her belly flip-flop. "I didn't know you were home. You didn't go to Sag Harbor?"

"No, I just felt like staying in."

"Cool," he said, letting his smile linger. "Come on in. Can I make you a sandwich?"

"Oh. That's okay. I was just looking for one of the chocolate chip cookies." She felt like she was floating. She'd been wishing for this all day. Now it was actually happening.

"So how's the hand?"

"Good," she said, holding it up. "Bandaged by a master."

"Great. Does it hurt?"

Rory shook her head. "I think it was pretty small. What are you doing home? I thought there was a big party at the club."

"There was. But I left." He slapped some turkey on a slice of bread. "The Georgica Club really isn't my thing."

"Haven't you been going there your whole life?"

"There were a few years when we stopped going. We'd spend Fourth of July here on the beach. Have a bunch of people over and everyone would bring blankets. It was so much more fun," he mused. "Now it's this forced socializing. It all feels so uptight there. Or maybe I'm just not in the Fourth of July mood tonight."

She laughed. "I know what you mean. I just got off the phone with my mom. Five minutes talking to her and the last thing I feel like doing is celebrating anything."

"I hear that," he said.

"But you and your mom seem to get along so well," she said.

"Well, we already have one rebel in the family. What choice do I have?" His smile was rueful.

"So you're the good son. In capital letters."

"Kind of," he said. "It's just easier that way. What about you?"

"Well, my mom got back together with her boyfriend, so now she's no longer mad at me for coming here."

"Good for you," he said with a smile. "That probably took some guts."

"Yes and no," she said. "If I'd stayed in New Jersey this summer, I might have lost my mind. It was really just survival instinct kicking in." Just then, she heard a loud pop from outside, and then a distinctive crackle. "Are those the fireworks?"

Connor put down the knife. "They're starting. You want to go down to the beach and watch?"

She swallowed. This was more than she'd expected. "Sure. I'll get a sweater."

She ran down the hall into her room. Down on her knees, she hunted for her sneakers under the bed, finally found them, and crammed her feet into them. *Just stay calm*, she thought, lacing them up. *Don't be too excited. He's just being friendly.*

With a chunky sweater in her arms, she dashed back into the hall. Connor had a blanket in his hands. "You ready?" he asked.

Don't look at the blanket, Rory thought. *Just don't look at it.* "Sure," she said.

As they walked out to the patio, an exploding firework took the shape of a weeping willow and then slid down the sky. "Wow," she said. "It *is* a good view."

"It's so much better from the sand," he said. "Come on." He grabbed her hand and led her across the patio and down the creaking wooden planks.

When she reached the bottom, a loud sigh and whistle rang through the air. She looked up to see purple and gold rockets fly through the sky in all directions. Connor had been right. This was like having their own private fireworks display. They walked east down the beach, until there was nothing behind them but a large, grass-covered dune.

He lay the blanket down on the sand. "Go like this," he said, lying back on the blanket so that he looked up at the stars. She did the same thing. Their shoulders touched, but she tried not to think about that. Above them one explosion after another became a brilliant kaleidoscope of color.

"This is amazing," she murmured.

His shoulder pressed into hers.

Over and over, lights sizzled and flamed in the air, taking different shapes.

He's going to kiss me, she thought. *Before we go back in the house, he's going to kiss me.* It was almost too much to believe. She thought about Steve's concerned face, everything he'd said. Maybe she needed to be worried. Maybe this was all a bad idea.

But lying here, feeling the warmth of his body so close, she knew that this was exactly where she wanted to be.

They stayed there for what seemed like an hour, watching the lights burst into shape in the sky. When all that was left was the echo of explosions and the acrid smell of smoke drifting over the water, they sat up on the blanket. She wiped sand off her legs. She was suddenly so nervous that she was trembling.

"You cold?" he asked, and she felt him wrap an arm around her shoulders.

"A little."

She leaned closer to him, and he leaned closer to her, and in front of them the ocean was silver, churning softly under the moon, almost complicit in what she knew was about to happen. He tilted his face toward her, slowly, and she tilted hers toward him.

Let this happen, she thought. *Just let something happen for once.*

Slowly, she reached for his hand and twined her fingers with his. As their eyes closed, and their lips touched, a thousand objections passed through her head. But then they vanished into thin air, just like burned-out fireworks.

CHAPTER FIFTEEN

Isabel opened her eyes. Bright light shone around the edges of her blackout shades. She buried her head under her comforter, listening to the soft whir of the ceiling fan and the birds chirping in the elm trees outside. It was a summer Saturday morning like any other, and all was right with the world, except for the necklace of thoughts that flew into her sleepy brain and made her catch her breath: last night, Mike, *sex*.

She rolled over onto her side and put her knees to her chest. Physically, she felt exactly the same. All her limbs were still accounted for. She didn't have a fever or a sore throat. And yet, deep inside her, something felt altered. She pulled off the covers and sat up on one arm. Was this feeling bad or good? She didn't know. Not yet. She'd need to go over all the details of the night, later, when she was more alert. For now, all she could remember was that Mike had been so sweet and gentle with her, making sure that she felt okay at every step. "Just tell me if you want to stop," he'd said, more than once.

No, she'd shaken her head. She didn't want to stop, and even though it was scary to keep going, it was a relief to not have to stop. Then there had been the part that hurt, and that was, frankly, a little unpleasant, but all in all, it had been okay. More than okay— it had been wonderful. When it was over, he held her and played with her hair and told her that she was beautiful. And she'd breathed in his smell and closed her eyes and listened to the *ta-TUM ta-TUM* of his heart and eventually fallen asleep. Then she'd woken with a start, hours later. She'd patted him on the arm until he woke. "I have to go," she whispered. On the drive home they didn't speak, only held hands. When he turned into her driveway, his high beams shed a ghostly white light over the iron gates.

"You okay?" he asked.

"Yeah," she said.

"I wish you didn't have to go," he said.

"I know."

She'd leaned into him, and they'd kissed. Then she'd reluctantly pulled herself from his arms and gotten out of the car. She typed in the security code and walked through the opening gate. Dawn was already breaking, and bright pink and purple sky showed behind the branches of the trees. It was too late to knock on Rory's window. But to her massive relief, someone had left the back door open. She'd walked in, exchanged a nod with a very drowsy Trixie, crept up the stairs, and crawled into bed.

But now, as she lay under the covers, something about last night felt slightly off. She just couldn't name what it was. After they got home from the Ripcurl Lounge, everything had been perfect. Mike had lit a bunch of stubby candles that he'd found in the kitchen, and then put on soft music. He didn't break eye contact with her once the entire time. He'd been gentle and respectful. But there it was again, that gnawing feeling that something was missing. As she got out of bed and stepped into the shower, she realized what it was.

He didn't say he loved me.

She squeezed some shampoo onto her palm and lathered her hair. Her mind raced, begging her to hitch a ride on the merry-go-round. *Wasn't that what he* should *have said?* she thought. *Isn't that what someone else, like Aston March, would have said? Wasn't that what a guy who loved you said when you were being* that *close to each other?*

She shut off the water and grabbed the towel hanging outside the shower door. *Stop*, she thought. *Don't do this. You are* not *the girl who freaks out about guys. Ever.*

But it was too late. She'd opened the door to the questions, and now she was going to have to contend with a whole swarm of them in her brain.

She walked into her closet and switched on the light. Clothes had always been a good enough distraction before. She pulled on a pair of skinny jeans and a trapeze-style striped top. But still, there was the thought.

He didn't say he loved me.

She ran back out to where she'd dropped her bag on the bedroom floor and crouched down, rooting around inside it for her phone. *You're being ridiculous*, she thought. *You're Isabel Rule. Of course he loves you. So what if he didn't say it?*

She finally got the phone in her hands and clicked it awake. There was the text he'd sent while she was in the shower.

Woke up missing you. M.

It wasn't the *L* bomb, but it was enough. She pressed the phone to her chest with a sigh. Everything was going to be okay. Of course it was.

Rory sat on the edge of her bed fully dressed, staring straight ahead, and tapping her foot madly over her ankle. Last night had been a mistake. She knew that now. She'd known it almost from the moment she'd opened her eyes and smelled the coffee being brewed in the kitchen and heard the whip of the sprinklers on the lawn. Even though it had been, without a doubt, the most romantic experience of her life. After they'd said good night outside her door, she'd lain in bed and stared straight up at the ceiling without blinking for at least an hour, too giddy and excited to even think about sleeping. But still, what she'd done was probably against every single rule about being a good employee. Not that she was actually a real employee here, in the technical sense of the word, but she was close enough. It had been a mistake and a momentary lapse of good judgment, and she would have to tell him that it could never, ever happen again. She wasn't here to fall in love. She was Rory, the smart girl, the disciplined girl, the girl who wouldn't jeopardize a summer job with a tawdry, dead-end fling.

Because the truth was, this couldn't go anywhere anyway. He was Connor Rule—the golden-boy swimmer from St. Bernard's and USC, destined for privilege and his own hedge fund and a gorgeous, skinny, blue-blooded wife. She was Rory McShane from

212

Kittattiny High, destined for a long, arduous, uphill climb toward whatever it was she decided she wanted.

But, she thought, her foot going still, kissing him on the beach had been wonderful. His lips, his fingers... She could have stayed out there with him all night. When she'd finally pulled away from him and suggested they go inside before anyone came back to the house, it had felt like a monumental act of discipline.

"In a second," he'd said, reaching for her again.

"No, now," she said. She stood up on wobbly, half-asleep legs to help him shake the blanket. She wished she could give herself a shake, too. All they'd done was kiss, but sand was everywhere on her: in her hair, on the back of her neck, inside her shoes, and even in her sleeves. They walked back across the quiet beach, and at the bottom of the dunes, he pulled her to him again.

"I've been wanting to do this for so long," he said. "Ever since that day at the pool."

"When I killed your phone?"

"Yup," he said.

They kissed again, clinging to each other in the cool wind, and then he grasped her hand to lead her up the pathway over the dunes.

They entered the house, which was still empty, and Rory couldn't help but feel like she finally belonged here now. He followed her to her door.

"You are *not* coming in," she said.

He smiled and kissed her again. "Okay," he said, his hand lingering on her shoulder. "I'll be right upstairs. Thinking about you."

"G'night," she said, wriggling away from him.

He stared at her with the same longing look. "Good night," he said.

She went inside and shut the door. As she showered off the sand and got ready for bed, she went over everything that he'd said. To think that he'd wanted to kiss her that *first day* by the pool. It couldn't be real. She slipped into her pajamas and got into bed, feeling more blissed-out and elated than she ever had in her life.

Now, ten hours later, in the cold bright light of morning, she knew that it had been a mistake. If she saw him, and he seemed like he didn't want to pretend that it hadn't happened, she would just tell him that it couldn't happen again. It was always less painful to rip off a Band-Aid than slowly peel it.

In the hall, Trixie ran to greet her, her collar jingling. "Hi, sweetie," she said, scratching her head. "How's my little baby?"

She petted Trixie for a few minutes, conveniently stalling. But it was no use. Connor walked out of the kitchen, eating a blueberry muffin. One look at his face and she knew that ripping off this Band-Aid wasn't going to be easy.

"Hey," he said, smiling. "How'd you sleep?"

"Pretty good," she said quietly. "You?"

In one smooth movement, he grabbed her wrist and pulled her into the laundry room. Then he shut the door.

"Connor," she whispered, but she was cut off by his kiss. He pressed her against the door, and almost instantly, she relaxed into his arms, kissing him back, deeply, passionately. Then she pushed him away.

"I can't stop thinking about you," he whispered.

"Connor, we can't do this," she said. "Not here."

"Rory," he breathed.

"Connor," she said, unable to stop smiling as she opened the door. Breathless, she slipped out into the hall just as Isabel stomped down the back stairs. Connor stepped into the hall behind Rory.

"Hey," Isabel said. Her large blue eyes jumped from Rory to Connor and back to Rory. She didn't seem to suspect a thing. "What's up?"

"Hey," Rory said.

"Why aren't you at work?" Isabel asked him.

"I'm off," he said. "Day after Fourth of July."

"Cool," Isabel said distractedly. "Hey, can I talk to you for a minute?" she asked Rory. "In private?"

"Sure."

Now it was Isabel's turn to drag Rory by the wrist down the hall. Rory turned and glimpsed Connor watching her longingly as they walked into Rory's room. Isabel closed the door.

"What is it?" Rory asked.

Isabel sat on the edge of the bed and grabbed one of Rory's throw pillows. "I slept with him last night."

"Slept with who?" Rory asked, suddenly confused.

"Mike. Who else?"

"Oh." Rory blinked, back on track. She'd temporarily forgotten about other guys besides Connor. "That's great."

Isabel smoothed the pillow's lace hem with her fingers. "Do you think it was the right thing?" she asked.

"Sure. I mean, why wouldn't it be?"

Isabel traced a circle on the rug with her bare big toe. "I guess...yeah...I mean, right."

"Do *you* think it was the right thing?" Rory asked.

Isabel nodded. "Yeah. Of course."

"Then, great."

"It just feels...different now," Isabel said. "It's hard to explain. I mean, I know you have no idea."

Rory let that last bit slide.

"It's just...the mystery, the holding back, the not letting them know how you feel—that's all kind of done now." Isabel leaned against the dresser. "It's like I don't know how to play things anymore. You know what I mean?"

"But maybe that's the whole point," Rory said. "Maybe when you're really in love with someone, you shouldn't be playing things at all."

Isabel chewed her bottom lip. She didn't look convinced. "What'd you do last night?"

"Oh, not much." Rory picked up her hairbrush from the dresser and began to brush her hair. She could never lie right to someone's face. "I just stayed home. Read. Went to bed early."

Isabel raised her eyebrows. "Sounds kind of sad. Want to come to the Georgica for lunch?"

Rory stopped brushing her hair. "Really?" she asked skeptically.

"Yeah. I skipped out on the big fireworks party last night, and now I have to go and kiss a little butt. And I could definitely use some backup." Isabel went to the door. "I'll loan you a cute cover-up, if you want."

"I don't know if I can just take off like that."

"I'll clear it with Bianca," Isabel said. "She doesn't own you, for God's sakes. And thanks."

"For what?"

"I don't know. For listening."

She left the room, shaking out her blond hair, and Rory felt a wave of guilt. After what Isabel had just told her, it felt only right to tell her about Connor. But she couldn't. There were too many signs not to. During all the times that Isabel had racked her brain trying to think of a guy for Rory, Connor's name had never come up, not once. That had to mean something, and what it probably meant was STAY AWAY FROM MY BROTHER in big, blinking neon letters.

She needed someone to talk to about this. Someone who wouldn't beat around the bush, or spare Rory's feelings. Someone who would tell her, in no uncertain terms, what to do about this experience.

Steve.

She ran to the window. His black Jetta was parked next to the Prius. She went to the back door and pushed it open.

Steve walked the tennis court, picking up scattered tennis balls through the wire slats of a hopper. He looked lonely out there, and a little bit sad. Rory wondered if he liked this job.

"Hey, Steve!" she called. "Need some help?"

"Hey!" Steve waved her to come closer. "Nah, I got this. How was your Fourth?"

As she neared him she could smell the brand-new balls in their hopper. Fee had mentioned that the Rules got new tennis balls every week. "It was pretty good, actually. I stayed here."

"Yeah?" Steve said, still picking up balls with the hopper. His reflective sunglasses made it hard to know if he was onto her.

"Yeah. I watched the fireworks from the beach right here." She put her hands on her hips, steeling herself for Steve's disapproval. "And I made out with Connor Rule."

Steve put down the hopper. "Please tell me you're joking."

"I'm not. Unfortunately."

"Rory," he sighed, and took off his sunglasses. "I thought you were supposed to be smart." A faint smile curled around his lips.

"Is it really that bad?" she asked. "I like him. And I think he likes me. But if there's something you know about him that I don't—"

"Come here." Steve walked over to a nearby table and grabbed a small bottle of Evian from an ice bucket. He twisted off the cap and drank most of it in one long swallow. When he was finished he gestured for her to sit down in one of the patio chairs. "I don't know anything bad about the guy," he began, sitting down. "As far as I know, he's a perfectly good person. It's just that you're—"

"The help, I know," Rory said.

"Not just that," Steve said. "These people live on a different planet than you and me. They may seem perfectly nice, but they can be ruthless about things. And I've learned that the hard way."

"Why are you sounding so mysterious?" she asked. "I thought

you liked the Rules. You told me how down to earth they were. How cool and nice they were."

Steve ran a hand through his hair and sighed. "Last summer, I had this student," he said. "A woman. She was married to a much older guy, a guy who had a lot of money but not much else. There wasn't love there. That was clear. Now, I'd always been professional about my job, never got involved with someone I was teaching. And there'd been times that it could have happened. But I never acted on anything, ever. But there was something about this woman. She was just...amazing," he said, his eyes looking past Rory's shoulder. "We had such a good time. She was incredibly unhappy. Her husband was never around. He ignored her. I knew he was seeing other people on the side." He took another swig of his water.

"So you fell in love with her."

"Yeah," he said. "I did. Just fell absolutely in love with her. We were like kids. We were walking on air. I knew it was only a matter of time until we got caught, but I couldn't stop myself. It was like I was addicted." His face darkened with the memory. "And then, the husband saw us kissing one afternoon. We didn't even notice. He confronted me later in private. And instead of firing me, which I was prepared for, he was thrilled."

"Thrilled?" Rory asked.

"He felt so guilty about all his affairs, he wasn't even jealous at all. In fact, he offered to up my fee. To keep his wife happy and take care of his conscience."

"Ugh," she said. "That's disgusting."

"Yeah, I know," he said. "Needless to say, I didn't take him up on his offer. I wanted nothing to do with him ever again. And that made teaching her impossible. See, he'd known exactly what he was doing, offering me that money. He knew that it would end the relationship either way. If I took it, I would just be another pretty-boy tennis player sleeping with someone's wife like a kept man. And if I didn't take it, but kept seeing her with him knowing about it, then I'd be keeping a secret from her. Which I couldn't do. So I ended it. With some bullshit reason. I told her that I was in love with someone else. I could barely keep a straight face, but that's what I told her. I had no choice. So I broke her heart. And my own."

Rory watched Steve linger a moment longer in the memory and then shake himself free of it. "That's terrible," she said, "but what exactly does that have to do with me and Connor?"

"These people can play hardball, Rory," he said patiently. "Lucy and Larry—they're nice, *outwardly* nice—but if you cross them, they can find a way to get rid of you."

Just hearing him say those words made her shiver. "And what makes you think that I'd be crossing them?" she asked.

Steve ran a hand through his hair. "*I* think any guy would be lucky to have you. But it's not my opinion that matters here. It's Mrs. Rule's. And I think she's got a pretty good idea of what type of person her son is supposed to be with. And when these people *don't* get what they want..." His voice trailed off.

"So you're saying to end it," Rory said.

"That's what I'm saying," Steve said. "Look, I come in, I help them with their doubles game, they pay me well, and I go on my way. That's how I've lasted seven summers out here. I don't get involved with them. Or I try not to."

In the distance, Rory could see Mrs. Rule heading across the grass toward the tennis court. Her blond ponytail bobbed up and down as if she were a carefree young girl, not the matriarch of an intimidating family.

"But nothing's even really happened yet," she said.

"I know. That's why you need to stop it now."

"Okay," she said. Mrs. Rule was getting closer. "Thanks, Steve."

She went to the bathroom in the pavilion both to catch her breath and to avoid running into Mrs. Rule. She stood in the darkened bathroom, smelling the cedar-scented candle that was replaced every two weeks. He was right. She would have to end this as soon as possible. But then she remembered the way Connor had kissed her last night, how soft his lips were, how his hand had caressed her cheek over and over, how he'd told her just a few minutes ago that he hadn't been able to stop thinking about her.

Maybe she didn't have to make her mind up right away, she thought. Maybe she could wait a little bit longer.

CHAPTER SIXTEEN

The other times Rory had pulled into the Georgica driveway, the parking valets had treated her strictly as a chauffeur, but today, for some unknown reason, they actually allowed her to get out of the car. A parking valet pulled open the driver-side door, all smiles under his visor. "Welcome to the Georgica," he said in a cheery voice.

Rory grabbed the bag she'd packed with sunblock, her one-piece bathing suit, and her book and handed him the keys. "Did you tell them that I was coming?" she asked Isabel.

"Uh, *no*," she said. "Why would I have done that?"

"It's just every other time I've been here, it's like I've had the plague."

"Maybe it's what you're wearing," Isabel said, and Rory looked down. The cantaloupe-and-ivory batik-print sundress that she'd borrowed from Isabel wasn't her style at all, but it did make her look a little more Georgica-esque. "That looks pretty good on you," Isabel said. "I should take you into Calypso sometime."

Isabel led the way into the main building. Rory took in the

lobby's horribly dated gold-and-green-patterned wallpaper and formal wooden chairs. It was all such a surprise. She'd expected plush club chairs and white linen-covered sofas—furniture like the Rules had in their house. Not something out of the 1960s.

"Checking in a guest," Isabel said to the girl at the front desk. "Rory..." Isabel looked like she was at a loss.

"McShane," Rory supplied. "Do you not know my last name?"

"Whatever," Isabel said. "McShane," she repeated to the girl.

They walked toward the white-and-green-striped umbrellas and the clear blue rectangle of the pool. Isabel felt the gnawing in her belly get worse. Anxiety over Mike had become anxiety about Thayer and Darwin, neither of whom she'd seen since that day when she'd told them about Mike. She'd also ignored all their texts, including the ones they'd sent last night asking where she was during the fireworks. In all the years she'd known Thayer and Darwin, she'd never out-and-out ignored them for so long. She had a feeling that this wouldn't go unnoticed—or unpunished.

"Everyone eats lunch on the patio," Isabel explained. "You go into the cafeteria and order it, and then bring it to a table."

Rory looked at all the tables of people eating from plastic trays. Apparently the Georgica resembled a high school cafeteria in more ways than one. *And this is an exclusive club?* Rory thought.

"I usually sit with Thayer and Darwin," Isabel said. "They must be here already."

"Is that them?" Rory said, pointing toward a girl with reddish-gold hair and bony shoulders whom she recognized.

Isabel looked over. Sitting together were Thayer, Darwin, and nonmember Anna Lucia Kent, who was eagerly casing out the lunch scene that she'd heard so much about. Isabel felt a twinge of jealousy. She'd been replaced. They walked toward the girls. "Hey, guys," she said to the table. "What's up?"

"Hey," Thayer said, barely looking up from her salad.

Darwin gave a small wave.

"Hi, Isabel!" Anna Lucia gushed, oblivious to Thayer's and Darwin's lukewarm reactions. "That's such a pretty cover-up. Is it J. Crew?"

"Calypso," Isabel said. "This is my friend Rory, Anna. The rest of you met her a few weeks ago."

"Hey," Rory said. She stood behind the fourth chair, not sure whether she should sit down.

"Hey," murmured Thayer, who was still absorbed in her salad. Darwin gave another small wave.

"So, how was the party here last night?" Isabel bravely asked her friends.

"Amazing," said Thayer, her eyes lighting up with uncharacteristic enthusiasm. "Tons of cute guys. Weren't there so many cute guys, D?"

"Tons," Darwin agreed. "Like, I'd never seen so many before. Everyone brought their friends from college."

"That's great. Looks like we need another chair," said Isabel, looking over her shoulder. "Unless...we should just sit somewhere else."

Thayer and Darwin exchanged a glance as Anna Lucia tried

to smile. "Whatever," Thayer said coolly, and returned to her lunch.

Rory looked out at the pool, the beach, the umbrellas, anywhere but right in front of her. The awkwardness was so intense, she had to fight the urge to wander off toward the pool.

"Then I guess we'll just find another place to sit," Isabel said thickly. "Since it's obvious we're sort of interrupting you."

"See ya later," Thayer murmured.

"Yeah, you and your charity case," Darwin said.

"You guys are such jerks," Isabel muttered.

"Right, we're the ones being jerks," Thayer erupted. "You're the one who's given us the finger all summer, and *we're* the ones being jerks. You're such a hypocrite."

"She's not a hypocrite," Rory said.

Thayer looked surprised to see that Rory could speak. "Excuse me?" she said.

"Why should she want to hang out with you guys when you're so judgmental?" Rory said. "She told me what you said about Mike."

"What are you, her bridge-and-tunnel bodyguard?" Darwin asked.

"You know what?" Rory said. "At least she's breaking out of this ridiculous bubble you're all in here. Believe it or not, there's more to life than your beach club and your horses and your stupid Cobb salads."

"Rory, let's go," Isabel whispered.

"And you know what else?" Rory went on. "The only thing

that makes this place cool is that nobody can get in. And eating on plastic trays? The food court at Rockaway Mall is classier than this."

Everything had gone very quiet. Rory noticed that three women at the next table, all with blond hair piled in messy updos and chic sunglasses, were staring at her. As were Thayer and Darwin, except they seemed to be looking at something just behind her. She turned around.

Mrs. Rule stood right behind them, her blue eyes unusually bright. "Hello, girls," she said in a forced voice. "Isabel, so nice of you to join us."

"Hi," she said.

"And, hello, Rory," she added, in a tone that sent the hairs on Rory's arms standing on end. "What are you doing here?"

"We asked Bianca to give her a day off," Isabel said.

"Who's we?" she asked, glaring at Rory.

"Me and Connor."

"Well, I'm glad to see that you've already made an impression, Rory," she said brightly. "And that you're making some friends."

"Why don't you go order something to eat," Isabel said to Rory, pulling her mom aside. "Just sign for it under my name."

Rory watched them go, feeling icy quiet behind her from Thayer and Darwin. She headed to the cafeteria. Once she was safely inside the fluorescent-lit space, she stood over the stack of trays, too perplexed and in shock to actually pick one up. All she could think about was Mrs. Rule's face when she'd turned around. Her tight, fake smile and furious eyes.

"You okay?" someone asked.

She looked up and saw Connor sidle up beside her. "You look like you're gonna be sick."

She should have been thrilled to see him, but it only made her feel more anxious. "What are you doing here?"

"I figured if my sister was dragging you here on your one day off, the least I could do was show some solidarity. Here, take a tray. What do you want?"

"I can't eat," she said. "Is there somewhere we can talk?"

"Sure, yeah, the cabana." He put down the tray, and they walked back across the patio. Rory could feel several pairs of eyes boring into her back.

When they reached the cabana, Connor opened the creaky door, and she stepped into the dark, narrow room that smelled of suntan lotion. He switched on the light, and she blinked, letting her eyes adjust to the dim light.

"So, what happened?" he asked.

"Thayer and Darwin were being mean to Isabel, so I stood up for her. And said some possibly rude things. And your mom overheard."

Connor smiled. "What'd you say?" he asked.

"I said that the food court at the Rockaway Mall was classier than this place."

He burst into laughter.

"It's not funny," she protested.

"Yeah, it is," he said. "It's hilarious. That's what I like about you. You say what you think." He walked up to her and put his arms around her.

227

"Connor…" She forced herself to step out of his arms. "Look. Last night was really fun, and I had a blast, but it can't happen again."

A cloud seemed to pass over his face. "Why not?"

"Because it can't."

He still looked bewildered. "I don't get it."

"Well, for one thing, what are we supposed to do now? Sneak around for the rest of the summer?"

"No, we'll tell my family. We'll tell them right now if you want."

"And then what? You think they're gonna be happy?"

He hesitated for just a second. "Who cares what they think? I don't."

"Well, I do," Rory said. "Your mom already has her doubts about me. I can't imagine what she'd think if she knew that I was dating you. It would just be too weird. And I don't think I could handle it."

Connor's smile left his face. "So that's it? We're just not going to do this? We're not gonna at least try it out?"

"Let's just think of it as a really fun night and leave it at that. And I'm not looking for a boyfriend right now. Not this summer." It was a lie, but it slipped out of her mouth so easily that she almost believed it.

"Fine," he said. His voice sounded small. "If that's what you want."

"That's what I want," she said. "So…are we friends?"

He looked down at the ground and shook his head, as if he was completely bewildered. "Whatever, Rory." He walked out, and the door clanged shut on its hinges.

She stood in the pool of light, trying to absorb what had just happened. She knew that she was supposed to feel relieved, safe, and certain that she'd done the right thing. But she only felt lost. And the musty, coconut suntan-lotion smell in here was making her dizzy.

Isabel struggled to keep up with her mom as she walked up the winding path to the tennis courts. "She was just sticking up for me," she argued. "It's not that big of a deal."

"She bawled them out," her mom said. Her tennis skirt swung to the left and right as her tan legs carried her up the hill.

"It wasn't that bad. It's not like she cursed anyone out."

"Why is she even here?" her mother said over her shoulder. "If she's going to have a day off, that should come from me, not you and Connor."

"What's the difference? It's not like she has anything that important to do."

Her mom turned around. "Yes, she does. She's here to work. That was the agreement."

"Oh, come on," Isabel groaned. "It's not like she's from some Third World country."

"Exactly," her mother said, wiping her hairline with the back of her hand. "She has a mother. She has somewhere to live. She didn't need to stay with us. But I said she could, in exchange for a little help. And now, not only is she at our club, but she's insulting everyone here."

"She didn't insult anyone—"

"And why do you care so much about her all of a sudden?"

her mom countered. "You couldn't even stand to be in the same room with her."

"Because she's cool. Because she's my friend. She's a better friend than Thayer and Darwin are ever gonna be."

"That's wonderful, but she doesn't belong here if she's going to embarrass us," her mom said. "And if you've been egging her on, Isabel—if she's gotten this from you—"

"I haven't egged her on. Why do you talk to me like I'm contagious or something?"

Her mom turned back up the path. The bright sun on her white tennis dress made Isabel squint, even with her sunglasses on.

"Why are you always walking away from me?"

And then Isabel saw a man step out from behind the tennis courts. It was Mr. Knox. He was dressed for golf, not tennis, and his handsome face was pink from the sun. From the relief that swept over his face, he looked like he'd been waiting behind the tennis courts in the no-man's-land between the club and the dunes for quite a while. But Isabel couldn't figure out why, when the golf course was on the other side of the patio. Then her mother whirled around. "Isabel," she snapped. "We'll talk about this at home. All right?"

"What are you—"

Mr. Knox looked at her, shading his pink face.

"Not now!" her mother snapped.

Isabel turned around and headed back down the path, as cowed and as shamed as if she'd just walked in on her parents having sex. Her mom never yelled at her in front of people. She couldn't figure out why seeing Mr. Knox had made her so nervous. It was almost as if she'd just jumped out of her skin. And the way Mr. Knox had looked...like he'd felt almost guilty at being caught.

She found Rory sitting at one of the tables on the patio, reading *A Confederacy of Dunces*. She thought about taking a picture with her camera—it was a great visual—but thought better of it.

"Want to get out of here?" she said.

"Thought you'd never ask." Rory stood up and put her book in her bag.

Isabel watched Thayer, Darwin, and Anna Lucia Kent take their trays to the garbage and start the walk toward the beach. *Good-bye and good riddance*, she thought.

"So how bad is it?" Rory asked. "Does your mom want to boot me from the house?"

"She'll get over it," said Isabel. "And I don't really care what she thinks, anyway."

"I wish I could say the same thing," Rory said.

They walked out to the valet area, and Rory handed one of the guys her ticket.

"Thanks for sticking up for me earlier," Isabel said. "That was really cool of you."

"I shouldn't have lost it on your friends like that," Rory said.

"No, I'm glad you did," Isabel said. "I should have lost it like that a long time ago."

Rory watched the valet back the Prius out of the lot and drive it up in front of them. The valet stepped out of the car, and Isabel placed a dollar in his hand.

"Okay if I drive?" Isabel asked.

"Sure."

Rory got in the car, and Isabel clicked her seat belt. Rory thought about Connor's face just before he walked out of the cabana, and resisted the urge to look over her shoulder at the club disappearing in the distance. *You'll see him at home*, she told herself. *That wasn't good-bye.*

"Do you want to get some ice cream?" Isabel asked. "My treat."

"Sounds good," Rory said. When she felt tears coming into her eyes over Connor, she swallowed them gone.

CHAPTER SEVENTEEN

"I really love it here," Isabel said, lying in Mike's arms and watching the shadows made by the flickering candlelight. "It's great to have this place to ourselves like this."

Mike's stubbly cheek brushed against her bare shoulder. "Yeah, it's nice."

She scratched Mike's forearm with the tips of her fingernails. Three long days after their first time, they were finally together again. This time sex had been an altogether easier, and less awkward, experience. Again, Mike had been incredibly gentle with her, and again, he'd asked her multiple times if she was okay, if she'd wanted to stop. But now, lying in his arms, Isabel felt the same nagging feeling she'd had that morning in the shower. He still hadn't said he loved her. She'd waited for it to come out of his mouth, especially at a few crucial moments, but it hadn't. She pushed the thought away and snuggled closer into his shoulder. Bob Marley's soothing voice came from the iPod dock.

"How long are Esteban and Pete up in Maine?" she asked.

Mike turned down the volume on the iPod. "The whole week," he said.

"God, how amazing would it be if I could just pack a bag and come here and stay that whole time? Maybe I can." Five nights of falling asleep in Mike's arms and waking up next to him in the morning was an unbelievably tempting thought. "Maybe I should just try it," she said. "I could tell my parents that I'm staying with Thayer or something. I could go to work with you in the morning. Help out at the stand."

"Hmm-hmmm," he said, busy kissing her up and down her arm.

"Hey, why haven't I met your family?" she asked.

"I don't know," he said between kisses. "I haven't met your family."

"I know, but that's because mine's crazy."

"So's mine."

"No, really," she said. "I think I'd like to meet your parents. I'm really good with parents. They love me."

"I bet they do," he said.

"So... am I gonna meet them or not?" she asked.

He stopped kissing her. Quickly she turned to face him, but his gaze was on the wall behind her, studying something.

"Hey," she said. "Do you *not* want me to meet your parents?" She laughed a little to balance the question, which had just a touch too much seriousness to it.

"You'll meet them." He pulled away from her and sat up. "But I think I'm gonna go up to Maine and meet those guys for a bit. Just for a few days."

"You are?" she asked.

"Just sounds like fun to be at Peter's summer house. It's just for a few days," he said. "Then I'll be back."

"So, when will you be back, exactly?" She propped herself up on her elbow, aware that her heart was racing.

"Next week," he said.

"And you'll be leaving . . ."

"Probably the day after tomorrow."

"That's longer than a few days."

"It's, like, five days," he said, sitting back against the wall. "Is that too long?"

She looked down at the putty-colored bedsheet. Suddenly she was having trouble looking him in the eye. "No," she said.

"I'll be back before you know it," he said, stroking her hair. "I'd think you'd be getting sick of me by now."

"Yeah, right," she chuckled. "Sick of you." She circled his wrist with her fingers. "So I'll meet your family when you come back?"

"Definitely." He lifted her chin so that she could look him right in the eye. "I'm gonna be thinking about you the entire time. It's gonna be torture."

Then don't go, she wanted to say, but she didn't. Instead, she gave him what she hoped was one of her most seductive, enigmatic smiles over her shoulder. "Good," she said, and kissed him softly on the lips.

The next day, she woke with a heavy sense of dread in her chest. That morning in the car with Rory, she had to tell someone.

"He's leaving," she said. "Going on a trip to Maine. For no reason. Don't you think that's a little weird?" She drove onto the highway, which was actually moving for once, and adjusted her mirrors.

"Car-and-a-half distance between you," Rory reminded her. "I don't know if it's weird. Depends on what he's gonna be doing in Maine."

"Drinking beer? Hanging out? Nothing important. And I checked. Where he's going, there's not even any surfing. He surfs every single day. So, why's he going to a place where he can't surf?"

"Maybe it's just for the reasons he said," Rory said, leaning over to check Isabel's speed. "Maybe he just wants to hang out with his friends. Hey, that guy up ahead is slowing down," she said. "You might want to put on the brake."

"I don't know, there's something about this that is just strange," Isabel said, slowing down. "I mean, we just started having sex. Why does he want to go out of town *now*?"

"You'll see him next week," Rory said. "Invite him to your dad's birthday party. That way he can meet your folks without all the attention being placed on him."

"When is the party? The fifteenth?"

"I think so."

"It's so weird. I've never cared about meeting people's parents before. Oh, and speaking of that, don't worry. I talked to my mom. She's not mad at you about the other day. I promise."

"Great," Rory said.

"I'm serious," Isabel said, looking over at her. "She doesn't care."

Rory wondered if she should tell Isabel that she knew for a fact that Lucy Rule did care, at least enough to come by her room that evening after their trip to the club. But she knew that she couldn't say anything. Not out of any loyalty to Mrs. Rule, but out of her own pride.

She'd been getting ready for bed when she heard the sharp knock on the door. She'd hoped it was Connor, wanting more of an explanation for why she'd unceremoniously dumped him in the cabana. Instead, it had been Mrs. Rule standing on the doorstep and smiling in a way that made Rory's skin prickle with dread. "I know it's late," Mrs. Rule said sweetly. "Can I come in?"

"Sure," Rory said, grabbing a few pieces of clothing from the bed and hiding them behind her back.

"I just wanted to have a quick chat," she said. She closed the door behind her. In leggings and a long striped top, she looked like she could be Isabel's sister. "I hope you had a good day off today," she said with an inscrutable smile, reaching down to straighten the glass clock on the nightstand.

"I did."

"And I also understand that you had words with some of Isabel's friends at the Georgica," she said, still smiling. She yanked the bedspread down on one end, making the wrinkles in the fabric instantly vanish.

"Yes," Rory said.

"Rory, I understand that you may not be familiar with how

one should act at a country club," she said, perching on the edge of the bed, "but I hope you know that what I saw and heard was not appropriate. Especially for the Georgica. People are encouraged to be a little more...civil there, if you know what I mean."

"Okay," Rory said slowly.

"Frankly, I didn't take you for that type."

"Type?" Rory asked.

"The hard-edged type," Mrs. Rule said. "The girl who tells people off. That kind of sassy, in-your-face thing."

Rory looked at Mrs. Rule, trying to think of something to say to this.

Mrs. Rule stood up from the bed and ambled over to the dresser. "Well, you've certainly made yourself at home here," she said, rearranging the various starfish and sand-dollar accessories that Rory had pushed aside over the weeks. "It's a comfortable room, isn't it?"

"It is," Rory said.

"Well, I'm glad we had this talk," said Mrs. Rule, looking in the mirror and running a hand through her hair. "I suppose I should get to bed. We have a lot of planning to do for Mr. Rule's birthday party. And you are going to help out at that, of course?"

"Of course," Rory said.

"Good." Mrs. Rule gave her a beatific smile. "Have a good night." With another smile, she waved and closed the door.

Rory stood alone in the room, looking at the tchotchkes that Mrs. Rule had just rearranged on the dresser. The Rules would allow you inside their world, they'd put you up in their best room, they'd even invite you to play Ping-Pong, but if you stepped over the line, they'd remind you lickety-split just where you stood. Now she understood why Fee was living in a cramped basement room. There was no doubt that she'd done the right thing with Connor.

Connor. His name echoed inside her stomach, a one-two punch of regret and longing. For the past few nights she'd lain awake wondering what he would do if she just slipped up the stairs and knocked on his door and said she'd made a mistake—that she did want to be with him, that she hardly thought of anything else. Would he let her in? Would he smile with relief and tell her he felt the same way? Would he pull her to him and ask her to spend the night?

It was impossible to know, because in the days after Mrs. Rule's little chat, Connor seemed to have disappeared. His Audi was gone in the mornings when she walked out to the driveway, and he came home well after dinner, when she'd gone to her room. She tried to tell herself that his absence was simply about his busy schedule, but before the Fourth, he'd never been gone this much. Now it was obvious: he was avoiding her. He never walked out onto the beach in the mornings when she walked Trixie, and she never saw him doing laps in the pool. She never found him dozing on the couch in the TV room. *Just as well*, she told herself at night, lying in bed. *This relationship didn't have a snowball's chance in hell.*

But at least once a day, her mind would wander back to the Fourth of July, and she would feel a deep, gut-wrenching ache at the loss of something she'd wanted for so long.

"You did the right thing," Steve said the next time he and Rory were alone in the kitchen and she'd given him the update.

"But it's hellish," Rory said, hunching over her coffee at the table. "Sometimes it's all I can do to not go upstairs and knock on his door and tell him how much I miss him."

Steve nodded over his Gatorade. "Believe me, it's better this way."

"But why should I let Mrs. Rule be right?" Rory asked. "That was totally out of line, what she did. Coming to me in my room, telling me how I misbehaved at the club? Why didn't I say something to defend myself?"

"Because you're in their house," Steve said. "That's just the way it goes."

And then, one day, while she sat polishing all of Mrs. Rule's silver tureens and chafing dishes, she heard that Connor was gone.

"They'll just be five for breakfast for a little while," Rory overheard Bianca say to Erica.

"Why?" Rory asked.

"Because Connor's in New York," Bianca said with a raised eyebrow. "Do you need more information?"

She went back to the silver, trying not to breathe in the toxic smell of polish. New York. For the rest of the day, she couldn't think of anything else. She pictured a thousand beautiful girls gliding up and down Park Avenue, or wherever the Rules lived, in their sundresses and sandals, beckoning him with their eyes.

As temperatures soared, her mood worsened. A heat wave spread over the area, sending the daytime highs up past a hundred, and making afternoons almost unbearable. Rory sat day after day on the highway in the afternoon sun, feebly pressing the air-conditioning button, willing the Prius to somehow get colder as she drove to Southampton or Sag Harbor. In the late afternoons she'd eye the Rules' pool, desperate to take a dip but too intimidated to get in. Instead, she'd take Trixie down to the beach and walk into the surf up to her waist, then sink her shoulders under the surface. It was the perfect vantage point from which to stare at the spot on the sand where they'd watched the fireworks. *God, get over it*, she'd tell herself, just as a wave crashed over her head.

But she did see Mrs. Rule every day, and it was almost impossible to look her in the eye. Fee was starting to notice.

"Everythin' okay?" she'd ask Rory as soon as Mrs. Rule would leave the room. "Get up on the wrong side of the bed?"

"Oh, I'm fine," Rory would say, shaking it off. "Nothing at all. Just a little tired."

Fee didn't seem convinced, but she seemed to know that Rory didn't want to say any more.

Luckily, Bianca didn't seem to know about what had happened at the Georgica. Her comments about Rory's clothes, shoes, and hair continued unabated, but she didn't say anything about Rory being "sassy." Not telling Bianca about Rory's trip to the Georgica was the one small mercy Mrs. Rule had extended.

Without Mike in town, she saw less of Isabel, who'd stopped sneaking into her room at night. Isabel seemed to spend more and more days in her room, reading and listening to music that filtered through the ceiling. Except now the music had a distinctly sixties and seventies classic-rock flair: Beach Boys, Pink Floyd, Van Morrison, Led Zeppelin. And Bob Marley. Stuff

241

Mike liked, Rory assumed. One night "Waiting in Vain" played through the ceiling so many times that Rory almost went up there and told her to turn it down.

But she left Isabel alone. She had more uncomfortable things on her mind, like Mrs. Rule's talking-to. Whatever happened, she'd make sure that she didn't get another one.

The day before Mr. Rule's party, Isabel marched up to her in the driveway as she unloaded some groceries and announced, "You have to come see this."

"Huh?" Rory said as she grabbed a runaway Meyer lemon from the floor of the trunk and put it back in the bag.

"Right now. Come here." Isabel grabbed one of the grocery bags and carried it to the back of the house. Rory followed. This had to be important if Isabel was pitching in with household chores.

After they'd unloaded the bags, Rory followed Isabel out of the kitchen, through the hot, still dining room, and into her dad's office.

"What are you doing in here?" Rory asked.

"Just looking through photos. I was trying to remember this dress I used to wear in seventh grade. And look what I found," she said, gesturing to a stack of dust-covered leather photo albums on her dad's desk. She picked up the one on the top and opened to a page of photos. "These are my parents with the Knoxes. That couple that just moved back here." She lowered her voice. "The guy I saw with my mom the other day. Look."

She handed the heavy album to Rory. The photos were of the two couples sitting at a street café in Paris. And on a cruise ship.

And standing in a harbor with an ancient-looking town built into craggy hills behind them.

"They were best friends," Isabel said. "They went everywhere together. Vacations, cruises—look at all this stuff. This is all from the year before I was born."

"So?" Rory asked.

"That night you spilled the sauce on me," Isabel said, "there was this guy over for dinner. He's a little bit psychic, and he told me that there were secrets in this house. That my parents had a secret."

"Okay," Rory said.

"And the other day at the Georgica, I saw Mr. Knox hanging around the courts looking like he was waiting to talk to someone. And then my mom basically yelled at me to get lost. It didn't really add up until I saw these photos. If they were such good friends back then, then why aren't they anymore? And why would my mom freak out at being seen talking to him?"

Rory shut the albums. "I don't know."

"What if there's something between my mom and Mr. Knox?"

"Do you mean an affair?" Rory asked with more skepticism than she'd intended.

"I don't know." Isabel shrugged, reopening the album. "It's crazy to think about, but it *could* have happened." She gazed at the photos. "My mom's always next to him in every picture," she said, pointing to a shot of Lucy Rule sitting next to the handsome, blue-eyed man at a café table. "Look at how close they used to be."

"I think I'm gonna head back to the kitchen," Rory said. "This room makes me nervous."

"Hold on," Isabel said, opening drawers. "Maybe there's

something else in here." The drawers screeched and whined as she pulled them open.

Rory dipped her head out of the room and did a quick recon of the hall. So far, the house was still quiet.

"Huh," Isabel said, unfolding a letter from her dad's desk drawer.

Rory watched Isabel's lips move as she read the piece of paper. "What is it?"

"It's about the new property," she said, looking up with concern.

Rory walked over to Isabel's side and looked at the typewritten letter in her hand. She could only make out an address in the first line—127 Town Line Road—before Isabel pulled the letter away.

"It's that farmer in Sagaponack," she said. "Mr. Robert McNulty. He's pulling out of the real estate deal. He says that he knows my dad has plans to build an 'extravagantly large mansion that is in breach of our original contract,'" she read. "How would he know that?" Isabel put the letter back in the drawer and pushed it shut.

"Look, I don't know what to tell you about your parents," Rory said. "Maybe what you saw the other day was something totally innocent. Maybe it had nothing to do with what you think."

"Maybe," Isabel said. "But just…don't avoid me, okay?"

"What?"

"I can tell, you're avoiding me."

"I'm not. I've just had lots of stuff to do."

"You sure?" Isabel asked, pushing some hair over her shoulder.

"Yeah. Definitely."

"Okay, good. Because this has been just such a weird couple of weeks and Mike's still gone—he's supposed to come back today—and well...I need a friend right now."

Tell her about Connor, Rory thought. *Just tell her. You'll feel so much better if you're honest.* "Sorry, I guess I've just been busy."

"You want to go get in the pool?" she asked. "I can loan you a suit."

"I have a suit."

"Ugh, that orange one-piece," Isabel said. "That doesn't count."

They left the room, and Rory realized that she instantly felt better. Mrs. Rule could keep her away from Connor, but she couldn't keep her from being friends with her daughter.

CHAPTER EIGHTEEN

Isabel opened her eyes and reached for the tiny electric fan on the bedside table, tilting it toward them. Sweat trickled down the side of her face and along the insides of her arms, and made Mike's sheets stick to her skin. It had to be almost a hundred degrees here in his room, but she couldn't bring herself to move. For a solid week, the entire time Mike had been in Maine, she'd thought about being just in this spot, and she was going to stay here as long as she could.

Mike dozed next to her, his head on her shoulder, his arm thrown casually across her back. She laid her head back down on the pillow. Their date the night before had been as fun as she'd hoped it would be: dinner on the back patio at Buford's, then hanging out on his deck under the stars with him and his roommates. But this afternoon had been the real romantic reunion. He'd picked her up at three o'clock and held her hand all the way to Montauk. When they got to his house, his room was sweltering, but she didn't care. She pulled off his shirt, then her cotton dress. It was becoming easier to be with him without talking.

Except now, as she was lying here next to him, there was

something that she wanted to say. She reached for his hand and caressed it. The fan whirred quietly.

"I love you," she said.

Behind her, there was just silence. She held her breath. Not the reaction she'd been hoping for.

"Are you awake?" she asked.

"Yeah."

"Did you hear what I said?"

"Yes." He kissed the back of her head. "I was just thinking about it."

She stared at the pillow.

"I love you, too," he finally said.

She turned around to face him. The trace of a knowing grin was still on his face, but there was something newly vulnerable in his eyes. "You do?"

He smiled at her. "Don't act so surprised."

"I'm not. But . . . you do?"

"Yeah," he said, staring into her eyes. "I think that's why I had to go up to Maine and chill out for a minute. So I could kind of think about it. Let it marinate. You know, figure it out."

"You had to figure it out?" she asked.

"You know what I mean," he said. "I just needed to take a beat. I don't say 'I love you' all the time. I don't know about you."

"I never say it," she said.

They lay in silence for a while. She was happy and relieved, but she couldn't get past the feeling that the exchange had rolled out a little differently than she'd wished. "And I still want to meet your family," she added.

247

"You will," he said. He kissed the tips of her fingers.

"We're having this party for my dad's birthday tonight," she said. "Maybe it would be a good way for you to meet my parents. It's supercasual. And lots of people will be there. You won't be on the spot or anything."

He held her fingers away from his lips. "Tonight?"

"Yeah. Tonight. Can you come?"

He considered this for a moment. She couldn't help but stare at his pouty lips. "As long as I don't have to put on a tie," he finally said.

"You won't."

"You promise?"

"I promise."

"Okay, then," he said, whipping off the sheet and exposing his slim, naked body. "I'll go just like this."

Isabel laughed. "Lookin' goooood," she said, giggling, as he pulled her under him.

"Rory!" An urgent knock on her bedroom door made her jump as she pulled her dress over her head.

"Yes?" She ran to the door, lifting her hair off of her neck.

Fee walked in with a focused look in her eyes. "Mrs. Rule wants this room clean for the party tonight," she said, rearranging the pillows on Rory's bed.

"Why? Are they doing the party in here?"

"No, but people like to walk around a house and go into the rooms at parties like this."

"They do?" Rory asked.

"It's hard to explain." Fee sighed. "Here, I'll help you." She walked over to the dresser to clear off the surface. "And don't you look pretty," she added, glancing at Rory's dress. "Is that new?"

"I just bought it today," she said. "Not that I can afford it." Rory looked down at her dress. Even on sale, it still cost more than anything she'd ever owned. On her way to pick up the birthday cake for Mr. Rule, she'd walked past Calypso and felt herself unable to resist going inside. And there it was, the tie-dyed silk dress with crochet trim and cap sleeves, marked down 30 percent but still far out of her price range. She tried it on, and it had looked surprisingly pretty on her—beachy with just the right amount of preppy thrown in. And Connor was coming back tonight for the party. She wanted to look nice for him, just in case it still mattered to him what she looked like.

"Well, you look beautiful," Fee said, grabbing an SAT prep book off the dresser. "Connor isn't going to know what hit him."

"Excuse me?"

Fee smiled as she dusted off the desk with a rag. "Oh, honey, do you think I'm blind? I have eyes. I see what's going on. You've been as cheery as a French movie since he's been gone. Don't worry, he'll be coming back tonight. He's driving his father out."

"What do you think about me and Connor?" Rory asked. "Can you see us together?"

"I've seen you together since you got to this house," Fee said.

"Then why didn't you say something?"

"I'm not a meddler," Fee said, opening Rory's top dresser drawer and dropping in all her books, pens, and notebooks among her underwear and socks. "There. That's good enough for now."

"Fee?" Rory looked down at the rug, too flustered to meet her aunt's gaze. "Something happened with him already. Something good, and sweet, and amazing. And then I messed it all up."

Fee stopped dusting the bookshelves and turned around. "What do you mean?"

"We...kissed. On the Fourth. And then I got scared. I guess I figured nothing could really happen, and it can't. Mrs. Rule would never approve of it. Not in a million years. And I just didn't want to get hurt. So I pushed him away. Told him that I didn't want anything to happen between us. Because it was sort of the truth."

Fee folded her arms and sighed. "But not all of the truth. You have to tell him how you feel."

Rory leaned against the dresser. "What about Mrs. Rule?"

"Let me tell you something about Mrs. Rule," Fee said. "She might act like butter doesn't melt in her mouth, but believe me, she's not above breaking the rules from time to time to get what she wants."

"What does that mean?" Rory asked.

Fee shook her head. "Nothing. Just don't you worry about her. And they could all do a *lot* worse than you, my dear. If they don't see that right away, they'll see that in time." She put her hands on her hips and surveyed the room. "All right. This place looks presentable. Guess I should run back and see if Bianca needs anything else."

"Thanks," Rory said, touching her aunt's arm. "And please don't tell anyone. Isabel doesn't know. I haven't said anything to her."

"I won't," Fee said, pretending to close a zipper across her lips.

"But just remember: You never lose points in life by telling people how you feel."

Fee walked out of the room and closed the door. Rory's mom may have been the sister who'd had all the men, she thought. But it was her aunt Fee who knew the most about love.

"Mom?" Isabel knocked on the door of her mother's bathroom. "Can I talk to you?" She pushed open the door and stepped into a cloud of sickly sweet perfume.

Her mother leaned over the sink, rubbing foundation into her skin with short, sharp strokes of her bare fingers. Her eyes traveled over Isabel's dress. "Is that new?" she asked.

"Sort of. I got it last summer." She lifted the neckline of her dress, which kept slipping forward down her chest. She'd lost weight over the past few weeks. "I just wanted you to know that I have a friend coming tonight," she said.

"Oh? Did you make up with Thayer and Darwin?" her mom asked over her shoulder, brushing powder over her nose.

"No," Isabel said, forcing herself to stick to her spiel. "His name is Mike and he's from the North Fork and he works at his dad's vegetable stand in the summers and he goes to Stony Brook," she said, rushing through it. "And we've been seeing each other for a few weeks, and he's my boyfriend, and I really need you to be nice to him."

Lucy put down the brush. "Where'd you meet him?" she asked after a few moments.

"On the beach. He was the one who pulled me out of the water that day."

251

Her mother rummaged through her makeup tray. "Well, that's very interesting news." She glanced at her daughter as she plucked an eye shadow out of her bag. "I guess I should have known something like this was coming. Is this somebody Rory knows?"

"No. Why would you think that?"

"Because I think it's interesting that this girl comes to our house and now you're suddenly dating a kid from the North Fork."

Isabel bristled. "She hasn't infected me with some kind of blue-collar disease, if that's what you're thinking."

"Isabel, don't start," her mom sighed, turning back to the mirror to apply some shadow. "I have enough on my mind."

"I'm sure you do."

Her mom's hand was still over her eyelid. *What secrets are you hiding?* Isabel thought.

"Anyway, I just wanted to tell you that he's coming, and I love him, and he loves me, and I need you to deal with it. Nicely."

Her mom threw the makeup brush in her bag. "So you love him," her mother said. "I hope you know what you're getting into."

"What does that mean?" Isabel asked.

"Nothing," her mother said tonelessly, taking out a lipstick. "I can't wait to meet him."

Rory found Bianca in the kitchen, hovering outside the swirl of busy cater-waiters and cooks, looking a little unsure of what to do with herself. She'd pulled her silver hair half up and back from her face, and she seemed to have taken even more care with her makeup.

"Is there anything I can do?" Rory asked.

"*There* you are," she said, her eyes lighting up at the prospect of someone to boss around. "Take this and light all the votives outside, including the ones in the paper bags around the pool," she said, handing her a gas lighter. "Then I want you to scatter these floating candles across the surface of the pool. Like lily pads." She gave her a clear bowl filled with small, flower-shaped candles. "And I see you actually went shopping." She looked Rory up and down approvingly, until she noticed her chunky platform slides. "Though not for shoes," she said, sniffing, before stepping away.

"Of course," Rory said aloud. She walked out of the kitchen with the bowl and the lighter and stepped through the back door.

Outside, the back patio and pool area had been transformed. Round tables with white linen tablecloths and white folding chairs lined the flagstones in front of the lap pool. Banquet tables near the back of the house held an array of hors d'oeuvres that could have fed a small town: meats, cheeses, crudités, and baskets of fruit spilled attractively onto their sides. Rory stared at all the food and then the two bars, each equipped with two white-jacketed bartenders who stood behind an arsenal of vodka, Cristal, and red and white wine. *This must have cost a fortune*, Rory thought. *All this because Lucy Rule felt like entertaining.* If Mr. Rule hated birthday parties as much as everyone had said, and their marriage was already in trouble, then this didn't seem like money well spent.

She'd lit the hurricane lamps in the center of each of the round tables and was starting on the votives around the pool when she saw Steve make his way across the patio toward her. It was almost startling to see him dressed in a sports jacket and jeans.

"You need some help with that?" he asked, crouching next to her as she reached into a paper bag to light a votive.

"No, I think I got it, but thanks."

"You look very pretty, Rory. That's a beautiful dress."

"I splurged on it with all the money I'm not making."

Steve laughed. "Cool. How's everything going with you know, what we talked about?"

Rory clicked the gas lighter and lit another wick. "Well, I did what you said I should do. I ended it with him."

"You did?" He sounded disappointed.

"Yeah. But now I kind of wish I hadn't. I made him think that I didn't care about him. I lied to him."

Steve let out a long exhale. "Yeah. I hear you on that."

"I'm just going to tell him how I feel about him," Rory said. "I mean, what do I have to lose? Really?"

Steve nodded. "Sounds like a plan, then. And hey, I'm sorry if I steered you wrong on that."

"That's okay. I know you were trying to help."

The back door flew open, and Isabel walked out in a stunning, strapless lavender dress that swept the floor. Each of the bartenders turned to stare at her. Isabel sighted Rory and Steve and began to glide over to them on her heels.

"Isabel still doesn't know," Rory said. "Very important."

"Got it," Steve said, and with a quick wave to Isabel headed in the opposite direction. Isabel joined Rory at the edge of the pool and crouched down next to her.

"I can't believe they're making you work at this," she said.

"I just have to light these."

Isabel swirled her hand in the water and Rory realized that she looked like she was about to cry.

"What happened?" she asked.

"I did something kind of insane today," Isabel said. "I told Mike I loved him."

"You did?" Rory asked. "That's great! Good for you!"

Isabel glanced at Rory with a pained expression. "I kind of want to throw up."

"Why?"

"Because I said it first." She took her hand out of the water and shook it. "And then he said it, but it took a few seconds, and it was just a little weird because I'd said it first. And now I can't stop thinking about it. Do you think that's bad?"

Rory pushed one of the candles out onto the surface of the pool. The lit wick fluttered as it moved but stayed lit. "You love him, right? So you just have to be honest with people. You never lose points by saying how you feel."

"Except when you say it first," Isabel said.

"But really, who cares who said it first? He said it back to you, right?"

Isabel nodded. "Well, he's supposedly coming tonight."

255

"He is?" Rory asked.

Isabel gave Rory a suspicious look. "Why do you say it like that?"

"Nothing, no reason," said Rory. "I'm sure he's going to come and everything is going to be fine—it really will."

Isabel sighed and stood up. "I'm gonna go get a drink."

Rory finished lighting the candles and began carefully placing the rest of the floaters, one by one, on the surface of the pool. A month ago, she would have never guessed that Isabel could feel this vulnerable. The day that she'd dropped Connor's cell phone in the water seemed so long ago now. She couldn't wait to make everything right again with him. As soon as he got here, she'd take him aside and tell him how she felt. *So I messed up. I freaked out. I really like you. And I don't want to cut this off just because of what I think might happen.* Like Fee had said, all she could do was be honest.

Guests started to appear on the patio. The women wore sleeveless dresses and shawls that cradled their bare shoulders. The men wore striped button-downs tucked into stone-colored slacks. Rory sent the last candle floating across the surface of the pool and saw Mrs. Rule emerge from the house in a shimmery, beaded off-white dress. She looked like she wanted every pair of eyes on her, so Rory turned away toward the water. The ocean looked as bright and silvery as that night two weeks ago. Any moment he would be here. And if she was going to do this right, she would need to have Isabel's permission. It was time to tell her.

Isabel ambled back over to her from the bar, sipping a glass of what looked like ice water. Or at least Rory hoped it was.

"One of those bartenders is supercute," Isabel said. "Though he might be a little old for you."

"So there's something that I really need to tell you," Rory said. "Something that's been sort of on my mind."

From behind her, Rory could hear the noise of the party suddenly soar upward and get louder.

Isabel turned around. "Oh, look. My dad's here."

Rory looked over and saw the lean, tall figure of Mr. Rule standing outside the sliding glass doors, his arms raised in a gesture of surprise and defeat.

"At least he doesn't look too pissed off," Isabel said.

Rory watched Mr. Rule greet his guests with hugs and handshakes, and waited for Connor to walk out behind him. And then someone who matched his tall, slim build walked out of the sliding glass doors and down the steps. Connor looked incredibly handsome in a dark sports jacket and blue button-down. She started to walk toward him, drawn toward him like a magnet, and then saw someone tagging along behind him. Someone also tall and slim, but with long, dark hair. Someone who was wearing a dress.

"Ugh, *Julia*," Isabel groaned, as if Rory knew exactly who this was. "Unbelievable. I guess they got back together."

"Back together?" Rory asked.

Rory watched Connor turn around and extend a hand to the girl behind him, and she accepted it gracefully, as if they'd been together a lifetime.

"Yeah, that's his ex-girlfriend," said Isabel. "He dumped her last year. She was so not good to him. I can't believe he got back together with her. What's he thinking?"

257

Rory watched them walking hand in hand right toward them. So he was trying to make her jealous. It was working. "I guess we should say hi," she said.

"Yeah, I guess," Isabel said, sounding extremely annoyed. "She's kind of insufferable. Just warning you."

Rory let Isabel take the lead as they approached. She kept her eyes on Julia, not just because she was excruciatingly pretty, with doll-like dark eyes, poker-straight brown hair, and the longest neck she'd ever seen, but because she couldn't bear to make eye contact with Connor. *Why are you even surprised?* she thought. *Did you think that he was going to wait around for you to make up your mind?*

"Hey!" Isabel said as she kissed Julia on the cheek. "Long time no see. I didn't know you'd be coming to this."

"Neither did I," Julia cried, overjoyed. "It just sort of happened!"

"Awesome," Isabel murmured.

Julia looked up at Connor adoringly. "We ran into each other a few days ago at this party, and I told him how much I missed him, and then he said how much he missed *me*"—Rory watched her nuzzle her cheek against his arm—"and then we went to see the Gotye show, and now we're back together. And he doesn't even like Gotye. I mean, isn't that cute?"

"Yeah, it's adorable," Isabel said.

Connor glanced at Rory. He appeared to have lost the ability to talk.

"Well, that's great," Isabel said, resisting a smirk. "This is Rory, by the way."

258

"Hi!" Julia chirped, taking Rory's hand. "It's so nice to meet you."

"Hi," Rory said.

"Rory is staying with us for the summer," Connor finally said.

"Oh, really? Are you guys friends?" Julia asked, looking at her and Isabel.

"No, I'm the housekeeper's niece," Rory said.

"Oh!" Julia chirped again, a little too loudly. "That's great!"

"Yeah, it's...great." With a look at Connor that she hoped was equal parts reproachful and shaming, she said, "I'm going to get a soda. Excuse me."

On her way to the bar, she reminded herself to calm down. Connor hadn't done anything wrong. She was the one who had pushed him away and pretended to be cool. She almost deserved this in a way. But to get back together with an ex-girlfriend and then bring her to the house for a family party seemed a *wee* bit vindictive.

At the bar, she ordered a ginger ale and tried to think of somewhere to hide.

The bartender handed her the fizzing glass. "Here you go," he said.

"Thanks," she said. She stayed with her back to the party, unable to turn around, until she sensed a familiar presence standing next to her.

"Hey," he said.

She turned to see Connor beside her, pretending to watch the crowd.

"How's it going?" he asked.

"I'm fine." She looked up at Connor as she sipped her drink. "How was New York?"

"Good," he said. "You know. It was New York."

"I'm sure it was."

"How were things here? Did I miss anything?"

"Nope, not really." She took another sip. She really wanted him to go away.

"So the deal with Julia is that we went out for almost a year, and we sort of ran into each other—"

"I already heard the story," she said, stepping away from him. "And you don't owe me an explanation."

At last he looked her in the eye. "Rory. Can we just talk about this?"

"What's there to talk about? We're not together. You can be with whomever you want."

Just then she felt someone tap her on the shoulder, and when she saw that it was Bianca, she was actually relieved.

"We need you to move the presents people have brought into the laundry room," Bianca ordered. "Mrs. Rule doesn't like how messy they look in the foyer."

"Fine."

"*Now*," Bianca stressed before moving away into the party.

Rory watched her go, wondering if she should just follow her and end this painfully awkward conversation with him once and for all.

"Rory, you were the one who said you just wanted to be friends—"

"I know," she said, smiling. "Have a good time."

He looked wounded, but she didn't let that stop her from walking away from him. At least she still had her pride. Isabel would have been proud of her.

"So anyway, that's pretty much why I'm going to pledge Delta Delta Delta," Julia said, wrapping up her ten-minute monologue on the intricacies of rushing at Duke. "I think it's probably the best fit."

Isabel kept her eyes on the living room sliding door. It was nine o'clock. Mike still wasn't here.

"Do you think you're gonna rush when you go to college?" Julia asked.

Isabel still kept her eyes on the door, lost in thought.

"Isabel? Is everything okay?"

"Oh, yeah," she said, finally hearing Julia's question. "Um, would you excuse me?"

Isabel stepped past her, slipping through the crowd on the patio with a minimum of waves and hellos. Inside the house, she went to the front stairs, in case Mike might be in the foyer, but the only people she saw were Mr. and Mrs. Kendall, ambling around and muttering something gossipy about the Rules' decorating taste.

She took the stairs two at a time, gripping the banister, dread starting to build in her gut. She ran down the hall. When she walked into her room, her phone was right where she'd left it, faceup on her bed. And a text was on the screen.

Hey Beautiful. Can't make it tonight but let's def hang this
week.

She read it over. And over. Of course, it could have meant any number of things—he'd gotten sick, there was a family emergency, he'd had a fight with one of his roommates. But deep inside, she knew that none of these were probably true. He was blowing her off.

She put down the phone. It was just a dumb party, she told herself. It really didn't matter whether he was here. And maybe it was just as well that she didn't bring him into the arena of crazy that was her family.

But just a few hours ago he'd said that he loved her. And if you loved someone, then you did things for that person if you knew they were important. Didn't you?

She closed the bedroom door and lay down on her bed. She tried to tell herself that everything was still okay, that this didn't signal anything. But there was that feeling once again, of something missing. And maybe something had been, from the very beginning.

CHAPTER NINETEEN

"Okay, the first thing to know is that you always get on a horse from the left," Isabel said, leading the majestic white mare out of the stable. "Then you just put your boot in the left stirrup, grab the saddle, and pull yourself up. It's pretty easy. Like this."

Rory watched Isabel demonstrate by placing her toe in the stirrup and stepping up gracefully right into the saddle. Mascara, the horse, didn't blink.

"See?" Isabel said, as if it were the simplest thing in the world.

Rory sighed. She couldn't believe she'd let Isabel talk her into a semiprivate riding lesson at Two Trees, but after four days of watching Connor and Julia hanging out at home in cuddly bliss, she'd decided she needed to escape. Everywhere she went, it seemed, there was Julia: sunning herself on the patio, watching TV in the library, playing tennis with Steve on the court. She'd made herself instantly at home overnight, and Mrs. Rule appeared to be thrilled. Just that morning at the breakfast table, while Rory delivered the mail, she'd overheard Mrs. Rule ask Julia if she wanted to go with the family to Nick and Toni's the following night.

"Of course!" Julia said in her Chipmunks-on-helium voice. "I love it there!"

Connor still hadn't been able to look Rory in the eye since the party. The few times she'd seen him in the kitchen, he'd given her a brief hello and nothing more. He spent most of the day teaching at the yacht club, coming home only for dinner. At least he and Julia weren't sharing a room. That would have been the final straw.

"See how easy that is?" Isabel asked, snapping on her chin strap under her helmet.

"No," Rory said.

"Come on. Don't be scared. Flame is really sweet."

They watched as a petite, freckled woman named Felicia led a chestnut-colored horse out into the ring. At the sight of Rory, he flared his nostrils and whinnied. "I think he knows I can't do this," she said.

"You'll be fine," Isabel said. "Just get on. From the left."

The instructor held out the stirrup, and Rory placed her toe on the metal.

"Great. Now just swing your right leg over."

Rory grabbed the saddle to pull herself up and sank right back to the ground.

"Felicia, can you give her a boost?" Isabel asked.

Felicia walked around behind Rory and put her hands on her waist.

"Okay, on the count of three," Felicia said. "One, two, three..."

Rory grabbed the front of the saddle, stepped up, and with a huge push from Felicia got her other leg up and over. Flame whinnied in protest.

"Great," Isabel said. "How does it feel?"

"Wonderful," Rory muttered as Flame began to pace in circles. "Hey. Chill out," she told him. Flame picked up speed. "Isabel, uh, where is he going?"

"Just yank on the reins and make him stop," Isabel said.

"Stop!" Rory said, pulling the reins as hard as she could.

Flame ignored her and began to walk straight back to the stable, as if he knew that this was all a waste of time.

"You know, this might not be such a great idea," Rory said over her shoulder.

"If you can teach me how to drive a car, I can teach you how to ride a horse," Isabel replied, holding her reins like a pro.

"A car can't throw you to the ground," Rory said, watching Flame busy himself with eating some grass by the fence. "Or ignore you."

"It's just a beginner lesson. And I wish we could get started. What's keeping her?"

"Sorry, I'm coming," a tinkly voice said.

Julia emerged from the stable atop a sleek black horse, wearing an outfit of gloves, jodhpurs, and riding jacket that would have put the US Olympic equestrian team to shame.

"Oh, it feels so good to be doing this again," Julia cooed, patting her horse's shiny neck. "Hey, Rory. Looking good so far."

"Thanks," she said. Naturally Julia had decided to come with them, as soon as she found out where they were going. Not even Isabel could come up with a way to tell her not to come. On the way here Julia had talked nonstop about all the trophies she'd won for her riding skills up in Westchester. Rory wasn't sure, but she could sense Isabel getting annoyed with her, too.

"So, since Rory's never done this before, why don't we start with some basic walking and then move into posting?" Isabel offered. "That cool?"

"Sounds great to me," Julia said.

Felicia clapped her hands and stalked into the center of the ring. "Okay, girls, let's start walking."

Isabel and Julia expertly steered their horses into the ring. Rory pulled on the reins, hoping that Flame might lose interest in the grass, but he didn't budge.

"Rory!" the instructor called. "Just press into his sides with your heels a little. That'll get him moving."

She pressed into Flame's sides, and he jerked his head up.

"Now click your tongue a little," she said.

Rory clicked her tongue. Like a shot, Flame trotted straight into the ring and right up behind Isabel's horse. "Ow, ow, ow," Rory said as she bounced in the saddle.

Behind her, she heard Julia's saccharine laugh. "Ooh, that looks painful," she joked.

Rory quietly seethed.

"All right, let's try the post trot!" yelled the instructor. "You want to start with your butt slightly raised out of the saddle, with your hands and ankles down."

Isabel raised herself out of the saddle. Rory did her best to mimic her.

"Rory, not so high with the butt!" the instructor yelled.

Behind her, she could hear Julia's laugh once more.

"Okay, now you're going to rise up when the horse takes a step with his front right leg," Felicia yelled. "You ready? Press your heels in to get him to trot."

In front of Rory, Isabel's horse began to trot, and Isabel rose up and down in the saddle with perfect timing and grace.

Rory tried to follow along but rose up on the wrong leg. "Ow, ow, ow," she muttered again.

"It's up on the *right* leg," Julia said behind her. "Like this." Rory saw Julia come up on her left, passing her in the ring. "See?" she said. "Like this."

Rory watched Julia sail in front of her, her perfect butt rising up and down.

"Okay, Rory, let's bring Flame back to a walk," said Felicia. "Pull back on the reins."

She tugged on the reins and Flame came to an abrupt halt, almost sending her into his mane.

"This is a little tricky," Felicia said, trudging over across the dirt. "But I'm sure you can get the hang of it. You want to rise up on the front right leg and sit down with the front left leg. Do you get it?"

"I think so," Rory said.

"Okay, let's try it again. Get in position. Like you're about to ski down a mountain."

Rory tried to mimic that pose, even though she had no idea how to ski down a mountain, either.

"Now, press your heels in," Felicia ordered.

Rory pressed in her heels and clicked her tongue. Nothing

happened. Then Julia put her fingers to her mouth and let out a high-pitched whistle.

That was all Flame needed to hear. He burst forward into a gallop that sent Rory out of her seat and clinging to his mane as he rounded the curve of the ring, past Felicia, past Isabel, and past Julia, who watched her pass with their mouths agape, looking frightened and also in awe.

"Pull back on the reins!" the instructor yelled. "Pull back!"

Rory tried to pull, but Flame was going too fast. All she could hear was the pounding of his hoofs on the dirt. *Just hold on*, she thought, staring at the peeling white rail and grabbing on to Flame's mane. *You cannot fall in front of this girl.*

"Stop!" Felicia ran in front of them, waving her arms like she was on fire. Flame stopped, just a few feet from Felicia's arms. Rory slid back into the saddle. Her hands still gripped the mane.

"You okay?" Felicia said, coming over and taking the reins.

"I think I'm done," Rory said, carefully lowering herself to the ground.

Isabel jumped off her horse and ran over to her. "You okay?"

"I think so."

Julia ambled over on her horse. "Good job, Rory," she said. "You did just the right thing. You held on, and you didn't panic."

"She wouldn't have had to if you hadn't whistled like that," Isabel snapped. "What were you thinking?"

"I was just trying to help," Julia said defensively. "Her horse wasn't moving."

Rory reached the ground and swore to herself that she would never leave it for a saddle again.

"You whistled," Isabel said. "It got spooked."

"That had nothing to do with me," Julia argued.

"It's really okay," Rory said, taking her first awkward steps. Her legs felt bowed out, like Popeye's.

"I think I'm done, too," Isabel said, walking over to get her horse.

"That's it? We're not going to have the lesson?" Julia asked.

Isabel glared at Julia. "No, we're going home."

Isabel led her horse, Mascara, back inside the dim stable and into her stall as Rory continued trying to walk normally. She was going to be sore tomorrow—extremely sore.

Julia dismounted and walked over to Rory. "I hope you know that I was just trying to help," she said, looking like she might burst into tears.

"Sure," Rory said. "I mean, it's not a big deal."

Isabel rolled her eyes behind Julia's back. Rory could tell that Julia felt bad, but she'd clearly enjoyed making Rory feel stupid during the lesson. She wondered if Connor knew that Julia wasn't exactly a nice person. She didn't seem like his type at all.

The ride home was quiet and tense. This time, Julia didn't talk.

"I want to stop at the Red Horse for kale juice," Isabel announced.

"You drink that stuff?" Julia asked.

"Yes, and I like it," Isabel said, in a way that ended the conversation.

At the Red Horse Market, which was a smaller version of Citarella, Rory joined Isabel on the hunt for her kale juice as Julia lingered over the blueberries.

"God, she is so annoying," Isabel said. "I knew we shouldn't have let her come. That was so uncool what she did to you."

"It's not really her fault," Rory said.

"Of course it's her fault," Isabel replied. "And she can't even admit it. It's like she wanted that to happen." She stopped in front of a selection of green juices and grabbed a few bottles. "I don't know why my brother went back to her. She treated him so badly the first time."

"What do you mean?" Rory said, trying not to sound too interested.

"I just think she's fake. She's not in love with him. She doesn't know anything about him as a person. She just likes what he comes from. That he has money, that people know who he is." She grabbed a bottle of cold kombucha tea. "I just want him to meet someone who deserves him."

Rory was gripped with the wild urge to tell Isabel everything. There was no reason not to anymore. She knew that she had nothing to lose. And Isabel would at least be on her side instead of Julia's.

But the ring of a cell phone sent Isabel searching for her phone.

"Is it Mike?" Rory asked as Isabel pulled it out.

"No, it wasn't," Isabel sighed, and bit her lip. She put her phone back in her bag. "I can't believe he's doing this. First he blows off the party and now he can't even call to explain himself."

"Maybe something came up."

"For *four days*? Four days of something coming up? He obviously just wanted to sleep with me and end it." Isabel felt tears come to her eyes and willed them away. "God, I'm so stupid. But then why tell me he loved me? And why hang out with me for two days after he got back from Maine? I don't get it." She shook her head. "God, I sound pathetic. Like one of those girls I always made fun of."

Rory patted her friend on the back. She didn't want to say that she'd had a bad feeling about Mike from the beginning, ever since that first time she saw him, when he walked across the gravel drive like a threatening storm. "I'm sure there's an explanation," she said.

"I should just call him, shouldn't I?" she said. "Or just show up at his house. Right?"

"I don't think—"

"Forget it, forget it," Isabel muttered.

They walked back up the juice aisle to the cash registers. Isabel pushed the tears back again. Whatever happened, she would not, *not* cry about this guy, especially not in a public place. She'd told herself this hundreds of times in the past few days, but it didn't stop the tears from coming. And all the questions: Where was he? What had happened? Why hadn't he written her back? Could it have been what she texted after the party? She couldn't have been more relaxed if she'd tried.

Hey, no worries! Party was fun. Is everything ok?? Xoxo I.

But she'd heard nothing. Zip. Not a peep.

"Isabel?"

She looked up and saw Mr. Knox standing in front of her. He looked just as excited to see her as he had at the Georgica that first day, and Isabel got the sense he would have tried to hug her if he hadn't been holding a five-pound bag of ice in his arms.

"Oh, hi," Isabel said. She wiped one of her eyes with the back of her hand, just in case she still looked teary.

"You seem like you're a little preoccupied," he said with a kind smile. "Are you all right?"

"I'm fine. Oh, this is my friend Rory."

"Hello," he said, nodding at Rory.

"This is Mr. Knox," Isabel said to Rory. "He's friends with my parents."

"How was your dad's birthday party? We were so sorry we couldn't make it," he said. "I hope he enjoyed it."

"I think he did."

"Dad?" A gangly blond girl with enormous blue eyes trudged over to them with a basket on her arm. "I got all the stuff Mom wanted."

"Holly, can you say hi to Isabel?" Mr. Knox asked with an odd smile on his face.

"Hi," Holly said shyly.

Isabel stared at her. It was almost like looking into a mirror. Holly's hair was slightly darker than hers, but it had the same

272

wavy texture. She had the same heart shaped face, with the same hint of a dimple in her right cheek. And she had the same large blue eyes, almost white in their blueness. This girl she'd never met before looked more like her than her own sister did. "Hi, Holly. Well, it's nice to see you guys," she said.

"Same here," Mr. Knox said. "We better go. We're having company this weekend and Michelle needed some emergency items." He patted the bag of ice. "You take care, Isabel. It was great to see you."

Mr. Knox and his daughter walked off toward a far register. Isabel saw that she and Holly had the same stride—shoulders back, slow, long steps. Suddenly she couldn't breathe again.

"God, that's weird," Isabel said.

"What?" Rory asked.

"That girl." Isabel turned to Rory. "We look like we could be sisters. We look more like sisters than I do with Sloane."

Rory didn't say anything, and Isabel wondered for a moment if she was being crazy. Then Julia reappeared with a basket on her arm. "Hey, you guys," she said. "Does anyone know what kind of sports drink Connor likes?"

"You're his soul mate," Isabel said, too irritated with Julia to care. "Don't you already know?" Then she stalked off toward the cash registers.

CHAPTER TWENTY

"You've done this before," said Bianca, gesturing to the platters of hanger steak in red wine sauce, bowls of broccoli and garlic, and dishes of corn on the cob that Erica had prepared and placed on the marble-topped island. "Everyone serves themselves from the platters. Just make sure that you're on everyone's left. And *don't* spill," she warned.

"Right," Rory said, leaning against the counter to stretch. This morning's ride had completely pulled her hamstring.

"I still don't understand why they can't come in here and serve themselves," Fee said from the table, where she folded freshly washed table linens.

"Mrs. Rule wanted to be served at the table tonight," Bianca said abruptly as she fingered a chain of rose quartz around her neck. "Did you want me to stop her?"

"It's fine," Rory said. "I'll bring out the steak first."

"I'll help you," Fee said. She gave Rory a sympathetic glance as she opened the door to the dining room. She'd been giving Rory a lot of those lately, ever since Connor had shown up with

Julia that night several days ago. "Go get 'em," she whispered as Rory walked into the dining room.

Rory smiled to herself. Only Fee seemed to grasp that acting like a servant tonight was the last thing she felt like doing.

She walked into the room and headed straight for Mrs. Rule at the head of the table. As Rory crouched down, almost crying out from muscle soreness, Isabel gave her a somber look. They hadn't talked any more about what had happened at Red Horse Market, but they hadn't had to—Rory knew that it had been on Isabel's mind all day.

She leaned down next to Mrs. Rule and offered her the platter so she could serve herself with the tongs. The Rules seemed to be having a heated conversation. "But he doesn't have any proof!" Mrs. Rule exclaimed. "How can he say that you're in breach of contract when we haven't started building yet?"

"He says that he knows our plans," Mr. Rule said, buttering a roll. "No idea how he knows, but he knows."

Rory stood up, moaning silently from the pain in her legs, and hobbled over to the next person at the table.

"Steak?" she whispered as she crouched.

Connor looked questioningly into her eyes, as if she'd asked him something very different. He picked up the tongs and slowly served himself from the platter.

"So he's backing out or he's threatening to sue?"

"It's all a little unclear," Mr. Rule said. "Let's change the subject."

Connor put down the tongs and looked again into Rory's eyes. "Thank you," he murmured.

"You're welcome," she said as briskly as possible, and then

moved on to Julia, who made sure to take the smallest, leanest piece of steak on the plate.

"I have something to say," Julia said, putting the tongs back on the platter without making eye contact with Rory. "Connor and I have been talking about next year. About me leaving Duke for USC. I've already done the application online," she said proudly. "And I think I have a really good shot at transferring."

"Wait," Isabel said. "You're gonna transfer to USC? For *Connor?*"

Rory stood up so quickly that the tongs almost slid off the platter and right onto the floor.

"Well, yeah," Julia said, sounding a little sore. "It's not that big a deal."

"Yes, it is," Isabel said. "It's going across the country."

Rory allowed herself a momentary glance at Connor. He seemed to have gone slightly pale.

"I didn't know you'd done the application," he said quickly, his eyes on Julia.

"I guess I forgot to tell you," Julia said, taking another sip of water. "It all seems pretty straightforward. And my grades at Duke have been really good. It shouldn't be a problem."

"Well, I think that's a great idea," Mrs. Rule said. "Connor would love the company."

Rory left the room as soon as she could. She smacked the platter down on the counter with a loud thud.

"What's wrong with you?" Erica asked her, as she spooned chocolate gelato into individual cups.

276

She clutched the edge of the counter. She couldn't do this. Not tonight. "I don't feel very well," she said. "I think I'll just go lie down."

"I'll bring out the dessert. When Bianca comes back in, I'll tell her."

"Thanks, Erica," she murmured. "And I just want you to know, you're doing an amazing job here."

Erica's stricken expression only deepened. "Do you know something I don't?" she asked.

Rory shook her head. "No. Just wanted to give you a compliment." She walked out into the hall. Only in this house would a compliment be seen as something suspicious.

She was so tired and sore that her legs felt as if they might buckle at any minute. She closed her door and lay down on the bed. She could still feel Flame underneath her, galloping around the ring in endless circles. That's exactly what she was doing about Connor, she realized. Going in endless circles, torturing herself, when it was never, ever going to happen between them. Not when Julia was going to be transferring to his school, and Rory was the girl serving them their hanger steak. She lay there for what felt like an hour, until there was a knock on the door.

"Yes?" she asked, sitting up.

To her shock, Connor walked into the room. "Erica said you weren't feeling well," he said hastily. "Are you okay?"

His face was so full of concern and kindness that she knew exactly what she had to do. "Connor, I'm sorry."

"For what?" he asked.

"For all that stuff I said in the cabana. That I didn't care about you, that I didn't want a serious relationship, that it was just fun. I didn't mean it. I didn't mean it at all. I was just scared of what your family would think. And what you would do. That you'd be really into this for a few weeks and then when you saw how much they disapproved, you'd decide you didn't want me anymore."

His face was so inscrutable and so emotionless that she instantly regretted what she'd said. "Rory," he said slowly, his eyes on the floor. "I just want you to—"

"Connor? What are you doing in here?" Julia strode in. She looked from Connor to Rory and back at Connor again.

"Erica said Rory wasn't feeling well," he said. "So I just came to check on her."

"Oh, you're not feeling well?" Julia sat next to Rory on the bed and took her hand. "That's awful. What's wrong?"

Rory tried to think of something. "Nothing. I guess my stomach hurts."

"Oh, poor thing," Julia said, nodding. "Is it, you know, *the runs*?" she whispered, loudly enough for Connor to hear.

"No, I don't think so," Rory said firmly.

There was another knock on the door, and Mrs. Rule walked in. "Rory, are you all right?" she asked.

"I'm fine," she sighed.

"It's her stomach," Julia said helpfully. "She might have diarrhea."

"Ohhhh," Mrs. Rule sighed. "Do you have any Kaopectate?"

"I don't think so," Rory said.

"Then maybe you might want to run over to the Rite Aid in

278

Bridgehampton?" Mrs. Rule proposed. "We really could use some in the house."

"Wait," Connor said. "You're going to make her go to the Rite Aid when she's sick?"

"Well, it's not like she needs to go to the hospital," said Mrs. Rule in a pouty voice. "I'm sure she can drive. Rory, can you drive?"

"Leave her alone," Connor said.

"What's wrong with you?" Mrs. Rule asked sharply.

"I'm fine," Rory said, getting to her feet. "I'm happy to go." She'd never seen Connor and his mother disagree about anything before.

"See? She's fine," Mrs. Rule said to Connor. "Rory, while you're there, if you could also pick up some Ricolas for me? I have such an itchy throat at night."

Julia got up from the bed and tugged Connor's arm. "Come on," she said. "Let's watch something in the screening room."

"I'll be there in a second," he said.

"Come, Julia, have some gelato," Mrs. Rule said, steering her out of the room. A few moments later, they were gone.

"I'm sorry about that," Connor said when they were alone again. "Let me go instead."

"It's really okay," she said, crossing the room to get her purse off the dresser. *This is just what I was talking about*, she wanted to say. *We would never work out here.*

"Then in that case, let me finish what I was saying," she heard him say.

She looked at him in the mirror above the dresser.

"What is it you want?" he asked.

279

She knew the smart thing to say, the safe thing to say. But she knew that this was her only moment to tell him the truth. She turned around to face him. "I don't care if your mom sends me to Rite Aid to get her cough drops in the middle of the night," she said. "I don't care if I have to serve you guys at every single meal. I don't care if I'm barred from the Georgica Club for life. It's all worth it. If I can be with you."

She saw something pass over his face but steeled herself to continue.

"And I know that you're back with Julia and that she's going to transfer to your school, and you guys are perfect together, and your mom is in love with her," she said, trying to keep her voice steady. "And I know that I'm a complete mess when it comes to guys and I always have been."

She walked up to him and stood right in front of him.

"But I just want to be with you."

He stared at her for a long minute. From the look on his face, she could tell that he didn't have anything to say. Her words hadn't stirred anything in him, apparently. She wanted to cry.

"So...I guess I should get going," she said, feeling slightly pathetic.

"Yeah," he said.

She waited to see if there was anything he had left to say, but he still only looked at her with a hard stare.

"Okay. See you later, then." She grabbed her purse and headed toward the back door.

She walked to the Prius, wondering how long she could possibly stay out, when she heard footsteps behind her. She wheeled around, hoping to see Connor. But it was Isabel, looking wild and out of breath. Her raffia clutch was in her hand. "Where are you going?" she asked.

"Bridgehampton."

"Will you take me to Montauk?"

"Right now?" Rory asked.

Isabel stepped closer. In the moonlight, Rory could see the worry on her face. "I just heard from him. Finally. And his text was so weird. I think he's going to break up with me."

"Then why do you want to go see him?" Rory asked.

"Because I have to. Just take me there, okay?"

"Where'd you tell your mom you were going?"

"I said that I was going with you to the store and that maybe we'd stop to get some candy at Dylan's on the way home."

"But what happens when I come back by myself?" Rory asked.

"Rory, I don't give a shit," Isabel said. "I can't eat, I can't sleep...just take me there, okay? I need to be put out of my misery."

So do I, Rory thought as they got in the car.

CHAPTER TWENTY-ONE

With every bump the Prius took on the dark, pothole-ridden road toward Mike's house, Isabel felt her nerves fray even more.

"So what did the text say?" Rory asked.

"*'Hey, sorry I've been MIA,'*" she read from her phone. "*'Things have been hectic. I'll call you tomorrow. Mike.'*"

Rory slowed down around a curve. "That doesn't necessarily mean that he's going to break up with you."

Isabel looked at her. "So that's supposed to be good, then?"

"Yeah, I see your point," Rory said, going over another deep pothole.

"Maybe you're right. Maybe something bad happened with his family. Whom I still haven't met, by the way." She snorted. "Whom I'm sure I'll never meet. Here it is. It's right after that mailbox."

Rory turned into a driveway and parked behind Mike's Xterra. "*This* is his house?" she asked.

"Yeah," Isabel said, gazing out at the ramshackle building.

"Looks like he's home." Light shone behind the ripped screens on the windows. Suddenly, she didn't want to go inside.

"If he's there, do you want me to wait for you?"

"No, that's okay," Isabel said. "If he is gonna break up with me, the least he can do is drive me home." She took a deep breath. The crazy strand of Christmas lights still ran along the porch, and the Adirondack chairs still stood watch next to the door, but they didn't look welcoming anymore. She forced herself to get out.

"Good luck," Rory said.

Good luck, Isabel thought. Had anyone ever said that to her about a guy before? "Wait until someone answers the door."

"Of course," Rory replied.

She closed the car door. Slowly, she walked up the bare, packed dirt of the yard. She climbed the sagging steps to the front door, then rang the bell.

"Who is it?" Mike yelled through the door.

"Me," she said in a hoarse whisper.

The screen door opened, and Mike stood in the doorway. He wore only a pair of Levi's, which hung loose around his narrow hips. His hair was wet. He'd never looked handsomer.

"Hey," he said. "What are you doing here?"

She turned and waved to Rory that she could leave, even though she wanted nothing more than for her to stay in the driveway. Isabel watched the twin headlights of the Prius reverse and disappear into the night.

"I just wanted to talk to you," she said. "Can I come in?"

283

He stepped aside so that she could enter. Inside, she could hear Pete and Esteban in the living room watching TV. "Let's go to my room," he said, going to the hall.

Her heart thudded. Normally, he would have pulled her into the house with both hands and made out with her right in the foyer, then dragged her down the hall to the bedroom. But now he opened his bedroom door and gestured for her to walk ahead of him as if they were strangers, and when she went to sit against the pillows on his bed he sat on the arm of his sofa, across the room.

"So what's been going on with you?" she asked, trying to be as calm as possible. "You kind of disappeared."

"Yeah, I'm sorry about that," he said, looking down at the ground. "Things have been really busy." He picked up a T-shirt lying in a ball on the floor and pulled it on.

"Yeah. I hear that," she said. Maybe if she acted like this was all totally normal, things would get back to normal. "Stuff has been really weird for me at home. Remember that guy that my mom's been hanging out with? Well, things have gotten even weirder—"

He sat on the sofa hunched over like an old man, staring at the dusty floor. She realized that he wasn't listening.

"What's wrong?" she asked. "You look terrible."

"I just don't think we should see each other anymore," he said quietly.

She'd been expecting it, but the words still exploded like a bomb inside her chest.

"I just can't handle anything serious right now," he went on. "I should have told you that. I let this go on way too long." He looked up at her, and she could see that his eyes were dead. "I'm sorry."

She tried to process his words. Her skin hurt, like she'd been sprayed with broken glass. "I don't think I've put any pressure on you to do anything—and the party, I didn't even care about that—"

"It's none of that," he said. "It's me. It isn't you."

"But you said that you loved me."

"Yeah," he said, knitting his brows as he mulled that over. "I know. I shouldn't have said that."

She looked down at a cluster of dust bunnies on the floor. She'd played this nightmare scenario in her head a hundred times, but now that it was actually happening, she had no idea what to do or say. "Is this about your ex-girlfriend? The model?"

"No. It's just me. It's my problem."

"Then how can you go from being totally into something to being totally *not* into something?"

"Isabel, don't make this worse than it is," he said. "I'm sorry. I'm really sorry."

"Unless you were *never* into it," she said. "Unless you were just making all that up."

He sighed, and his shoulders sank. His silence was enough of an answer.

"Just take me home. Right now." She stood up and walked on rubbery legs to the door. "Please? Let's just go. Now."

"Isabel, I'm sorry," he said. He placed a hand on her shoulder. She waited until it fell away, useless. Then she heard him put on his flip-flops and grab his car keys. The tears were itching to come out, but there was no way that this boy was going to see her cry. Ever.

Rory drove through the slowly moving gates and back down the Rules' gravel drive. She'd taken her time driving to Rite Aid and browsing the aisles, just in case she got an emergency text from Isabel. But almost an hour had passed since she'd dropped Isabel off, and so far she hadn't heard a word. She hoped Isabel was okay. Something told her that Isabel's instincts were right, and that Mike was about to end things. Though maybe the two of them were having wild makeup sex right now, the kind that she would never actually relate to or experience.

She parked the car and grabbed the plastic bag with the drugstore items. On her way out of the car, she noticed that Connor's Audi was gone. *Whatever*, she thought. Nothing he did or didn't do mattered to her anymore.

She walked into the empty kitchen and deposited the bag of Ricolas on the counter. Her stomach ached with hunger, but she couldn't bring herself to open the refrigerator. She'd practically thrown herself at Connor, and it had been all for nothing. Tears came, and she blinked them away. Some fresh air would make her feel better. She went back to her room and grabbed a sweater.

She let herself out through the sliding glass door onto the patio. The moon was just a thin glowing crescent in the sky, and the Little Dipper glittered brightly. The night was clear and warm, almost too warm for a sweater. She tied it around her waist just in case and headed toward the path through the dunes.

Down on the beach, she slipped off her flats, left them near the path, and started to walk through ankle-high sand. It was low tide, and the exposed wet sand looked silver in the moonlight. As she walked, she thought about the waves and the sand and the wind. Nature didn't care about money or breakups or love. The water and the waves and the tides were so much bigger than anything that went on in one of these beachside mansions. And this wasn't her life anyway. She was going to leave here in a month, and this would all be just a faint memory. Her small-town life and small-town expectations were a blessing. She could see that now.

And of course, she didn't have to wait a month. She could leave now. She looked up at the sky, crowded with stars, and knew that this was what she wanted to do. Going home a few weeks early wouldn't kill her. It would probably be for the best, anyway. Sticking around here after pouring out her heart to Connor seemed unbearable. And this family didn't need her. Isabel needed her, but she would understand one day, when Rory told her everything.

She edged closer and closer to the water until it kissed her toes. At least she'd told him how she felt, she thought. She could go home knowing that. And then she heard a voice, muffled by the wind, call out her name.

She wasn't sure whether she'd imagined it or not. Then she heard it again.

"Rory?"

She turned. In the dim light she could make out the figure of someone on the sand. Alone.

"Connor?"

"Hey. I thought you might be out here." He stepped closer to her, and she could see the features of his face.

"What's going on?" she asked, trying to ignore the thrill that went through her.

"I just wanted to tell you something," he said. "I put Julia on the jitney. She's on her way back to the city."

"Now?"

"Yeah. Just now."

She waited for him to go on. "Why right now?"

"After you left, we had a fight. We both decided that it was better she leave. Well, let's just say that I decided a little bit quicker than she did."

"But why?"

"It was pathetic how that started up again, actually," Connor said. "And being with her again, it was pretty obvious we'd grown apart. For good. And of course, you had a lot to do with that, too."

A gust of wind blew, but she barely felt it. "I did?"

"I didn't believe you that day in the cabana. But I forced myself to. By the time I went to New York, I'd convinced myself I didn't have a chance with you anymore," he said.

Rory swallowed.

"When I ran into Julia, I was feeling lonely and weak... *real* weak. But when I came back here, I knew that I'd made a mistake." He smiled. "But then I couldn't get rid of her. She's pretty fond of the luxe lifestyle. If you couldn't tell."

Rory smiled. "So . . . what kicked off the fight just now?"

"She said I wasn't being supportive about her going to USC. And when I told her that I didn't think it was a good idea, all my doubts about her kind of came out. I was finally honest with her. It wasn't pretty. And we both decided it was better she leave."

She took two more steps to him, until she was close enough to touch him. "Are you okay?" she asked.

He pulled her close to him. His arms wrapped around her waist, and before she knew it, she'd put her arms around his neck.

"I'm more than okay," he said. "We can tell everyone, we can keep it to ourselves, whatever you want. But you have to promise me something."

"What?"

"That you have to trust me. Because I just want to be with you."

"Why?" she asked. "Why do you want to be with me? I know I shouldn't have to ask, but I think I need to hear it."

"Because you're strong, Rory. Do you know how amazing that is? Do you know how much it makes me want to be with you?"

"Not really," she said, "but I'm getting a good idea."

"You're so strong. You're your own person. You're—"

"Okay, that's enough," Rory said.

He laughed. "Can I kiss you now?"

"Yes," she said. "You can kiss me."

He leaned down and pressed his lips against hers, and she felt herself melt into his arms. Icy seawater rushed over her feet, but she didn't feel a thing.

Mike brought the car to a stop in front of the iron gates. Isabel kept her gaze fixed on the windshield. They had barely spoken since they'd left his room. The lump that had been growing in the back of her throat was so painful now that she doubted she could say anything to him. But to get out of the car meant that things between them were finally, absolutely over. And it still didn't feel over.

"So this it?" she made herself say. "We're saying good-bye now?"

"Don't make this harder than it has to be," he said.

"What did I do?" she asked, feeling the tears slide into her eyes. "Just tell me what I did."

"You didn't do anything," he said coldly. "That's what I'm trying to tell you. It has nothing to do with you."

She opened her mouth to speak, but nothing came out. "Well, I guess that's it, then," she said. "Good-bye."

"Isabel—"

"What?"

He sighed and leaned his head back against the car seat. "Just...I don't want you to hate me."

"Too late," she said. She got out of the car and slammed the door.

He drove off before she'd even snuck through the hedge. As soon as she'd crawled through and was safely on her property, she began to run. She sprinted up the lawn, faster and faster, the knot at the back of her throat starting to burn. She needed to find Rory. Rory would help her get through this.

The back door was open. She slipped inside the house. Trixie raised her head from her bed to investigate and then went promptly back to sleep. Isabel went to Rory's closed door and knocked. There was no answer. She knocked again and then pushed the door open. Rory's room was empty. Her bed was made. Her purse was slung over the chair. But Rory wasn't here.

Isabel searched the rest of the house downstairs—the kitchen, the library, even the screening room. She started to get sleepy and thought of going back up to her room. But she couldn't risk missing Rory before she went to bed. She had to talk to her.

She went back to Rory's room and pulled back the duvet on her bed. She would wait here for her, she thought as she curled up in her bed. The knot in her throat continued to burn, but she wouldn't cry. Not yet.

Rory, she was sure, would know what to do.

CHAPTER TWENTY-TWO

In the half darkness she saw a hand by her face on the pillow, and beyond that a nightstand she didn't recognize, topped with an iPod dock and a pile of John le Carré books. Rory waited a moment and then felt someone beside her shift position. A large, warm body lying right behind her. *Connor*, she remembered. They'd fallen asleep on his bed, in each other's arms, still in their clothes. They'd come up from the beach and snuck up to his room and lain on his bed kissing for hours, until well past two in the morning. And now it was . . . what time was it? She sat up on one arm and peered at the phosphorescent clock face on the nightstand. 7:10 AM. She needed to go back to her room right this second.

She turned and looked at Connor's peaceful sleeping face. Even unconscious, he was still beautiful. She leaned down and kissed him on the forehead, and his eyes blinked open. "Hey," he said drowsily.

"Hey," she whispered. "It's seven. I better get back."

"Okay." He reached up and touched her face. "I'll see you later," he said, cradling her cheek.

She slipped on her sandy Keds and went to the door. Luckily, the house was still quiet. She tiptoed into the hall, past Isabel's closed door, and went down the stairs. Trixie was already up and alert, and Rory let her out into the backyard for a few moments to pee. The sun shone brilliantly outside, and birds chirped noisily in the trees. Last night still felt like a dream. When she woke up a little bit more, she'd be able to really enjoy it. She brought Trixie back inside and then opened her door. What she saw made her freeze.

Isabel lay curled up on her bed, sleeping peacefully, almost like a modern-day Goldilocks. Something terrible must have happened with Mike. Rory felt a pang of sympathy for her. "Hey," she said, softly touching Isabel's shoulder. "Isabel. Wake up."

Isabel opened her eyes. Then she lifted her head and gave Rory a groggy but accusatory look. "Where were you?" she rasped. "I waited for you."

Rory tried to think of the right way to say this. But there was no right way. "I was in Connor's room. I fell asleep there. By accident."

"*Connor's* room?" Isabel asked, rubbing her eyes. "What were you doing there?"

Rory sat down on the bed. "Julia went home. And...we're sort of together now. We were kissing in his room, and we fell asleep."

293

Isabel stared at Rory. "What?" She sat up. "*What?*"

"Connor and I are going out," she said. "I'm sorry, I should have told you that this might happen. But it just didn't look like anything was going to happen again—"

"*Again?*" Isabel asked. "So you guys have hooked up *before?*"

"Just once. On the Fourth of July. And then he got back together with Julia and I just figured it wasn't even worth saying anything to you when nothing was ever going to happen again—"

"So you kept this from me," Isabel interrupted. Her face was starting to flush. "For weeks. Right?"

"Y-yes," Rory stammered. "But I wanted to tell you. So many times."

"So, after all the lectures I got about keeping Mike away from my family, and about sneaking into your room, and hiding him away from people, you've been having this secret love affair with my brother, basically right under my nose. Right?"

Rory fidgeted. "I wouldn't exactly call it a love affair," she said.

Isabel threw off the duvet and got to her feet. "I can't believe that I thought you were my friend."

"But I am your friend," Rory said. "Nothing has changed."

"Oh yeah, it has," Isabel said. "Everything has changed."

"Why are you so mad?" Rory asked. "It's not like I did this to hurt your feelings or something."

"Is this why we're friends?" Isabel asked. "So you could get to my brother?"

"Of course not," Rory said. "And I'm sorry I didn't say anything. But why are you so mad?"

"I really needed to talk to you last night," Isabel said. "And you weren't there for me. Because you were having sex with my brother." She put on her shoes. "Ugh. It's so disgusting I can't even think about it."

"We weren't having sex. Not even close."

"Thank god," Isabel muttered.

"You know, I actually thought you might be happy for me. Or at least, supportive."

"Well, I needed *you* to be supportive last night." She blinked, and Rory could see the tears in her eyes. "Mike dumped me."

"Oh god, I'm so sorry," Rory said. "I'm so sorry."

"For no reason. Just doesn't want to see me anymore. Won't tell me why, won't tell me anything. And I came back here, needing to talk to you. But I guess you had more important things to do." Isabel threw open the door.

"Isabel, please don't be mad."

"Oh, please," Isabel snapped. "Just stay away from me, okay?"

Rory watched her slam the door, so hard the copy of *A Confederacy of Dunces* slipped off the nightstand and fell to the ground.

AUGUST

CHAPTER TWENTY-THREE

"So did you guys hear the big news?" Thayer murmured as she squeezed a fat slice of lemon into her iced tea. "Tatiana and Link Gould are getting a divorce."

"No way," Darwin said, pulling her hair into a ponytail. "Because he's cheating on her?"

"No, because she's cheating on *him*," Thayer said with as much gleeful emotion as her monotone could handle. "He caught her in bed with an Argentinean polo player. Isn't that awesome? And terrible, at the same time?"

"Wow," Darwin said. "What's she going to do now? Who's going to want her?"

"Yeah, totally," Isabel said listlessly. She looked up from her Cobb salad and saw Thayer and Darwin eye her with faint suspicion and then nod in agreement. She'd passed inspection.

Ever since she'd started eating lunch again with Thayer and Darwin, she'd found that all she needed to do was just agree with whatever stupid thing came out of their mouths and they'd leave her alone. Of course, she'd had to do a little bowing and scraping in the beginning. She'd gone up to their table that first day with her tray, said simply "We broke up," and then sat down and spilled a few pertinent details. Mostly that Mike was a "total jerk" and that they'd had a "massive fight" where she'd finally realized that he was "totally from another planet" and that she was "better off without him." At first, Thayer and Darwin listened in cold, skeptical silence, and then when they were convinced that Isabel really might have been genuinely hurt, they grudgingly asked questions. After that came the smug assurances that they'd seen this coming all along. A guy from the North Fork? A surfer? "Please," Thayer had said. "Of course he was bad news."

When she told them about Rory and Connor, however, they were actually incensed.

"How could she do that to you?" Darwin demanded.

"Did you catch them together?" Thayer wanted to know.

"Do you think she's a gold digger?" Darwin asked.

She managed to wave off their indignation with a shrug and an "I really don't want to talk about it." And just like that, she was back in the circle, sitting with them, gossiping and picking at her salad—to any casual observer, still the alpha princess of the Georgica. But there was little comfort for her in appearances anymore.

"So Anna Lucia saw your brother and that girl walking out of the movie theater last night. *Holding hands.*"

"That's nice," Isabel said, poking at a lettuce leaf.

"What do your parents think of it?" Darwin asked.

Isabel gave it another shrug. "They're not thrilled. I stay out of it."

"There's just something so gross about that," Darwin said, wrinkling her nose. "One of your friends, going after your brother? I mean, I think Connor is really cute, but I would never, ever do that. That's something you just don't do."

Isabel eyed Darwin closely. "You think Connor's hot?"

"Well, you know what I'm saying," Darwin hedged. "You must have felt so betrayed. I mean, the way she chewed us out you'd think she was your bodyguard or something."

"Yeah, she was obviously doing that out of guilt," Thayer said. "Now you might want to think about getting back together with Aston. He asked about you the other day."

"Oh?" Isabel asked, pretending to sound interested.

"Go back to him, Isabel," Darwin said. "He's just so much more your type."

Isabel put down her fork. She had no idea what her type was anymore. "I don't think so," she said.

"But why not?" Thayer asked. "You're just so stubborn. Let him take you out and treat you like a princess again. Sounds like you could use that."

"Whenever you really fall in love with someone, it's never really worth it," Darwin opined. "That's what my mom always says. You can't ever let yourself get too into a guy. She says that the guy always has to be more into you than you're into him."

"That is such bullshit."

Isabel watched Thayer and Darwin exchange a glance.

"Look at Tatiana," she went on. "I mean, what *didn't* she do to hold on to Link? What game *didn't* she play with him? And it *still* didn't work. That's not a real relationship. You shouldn't have to play games with someone who really loves you."

There was an uncomfortable silence, and then Darwin giggled. "Wow. You're like a walking self-help book," she said.

"Maybe I am, but I want to love someone as much as they love me."

Her friends stared at her, clearly unsure of what to say in response to something so insane.

Isabel put down her fork. "Whatever," she said. "I should probably go. I have my driving test out in Riverhead."

"Who's taking you?" Thayer asked.

Isabel realized that she had no idea. Up until now she'd always assumed that Rory would drive her. "I'm not sure."

"Don't look at me," said Thayer, pulling her wide-brimmed hat further over her eyes. "I am not fighting that traffic."

"Me, neither." Darwin laughed. "And Riverhead kind of depresses me."

Isabel stood up and grabbed her bag. "Well, I guess I'll just have to walk, then," she said.

Darwin giggled. "Don't be mad, Iz."

"Whatever. See you guys later," Isabel said, and turned around.

"Good luck!" Thayer called out, in a way that made Isabel's skin crawl.

Isabel trudged up the hill to the main house, back to where she'd left her bike locked to the rack. Out of pure habit, she pulled her phone out of her bag. No text from Mike. It had been ten days now. It was time to face that this relationship was totally and completely over. And she would never know why. The staggering injustice of this was almost worse than the loss of him. How was she supposed to move on from being dumped when she would never know why it had happened in the first place?

Or maybe there is no reason, she thought. *Maybe people's feelings just change, and there is nothing you can do about it.* She walked into the cool, dim lobby and sat down on one of the chintz-covered love seats. Maybe she could still text him. True, it was a desperate move, and something that only the most pathetic, clueless, and non-mysterious girls resorted to in times like this. But she needed to know why he'd done it. Who cared what it looked like? What else did she have to lose at this point?

Quickly, she typed out the text.

Hey. Think we need to talk. Call me.

She pressed send before she could chicken out. The bubble turned green on the screen, marking it as final and irrevocable. She forced herself to put the phone away and stared at the swirl of pattern on the rug. Now she knew what Aston March had felt that night a year ago on Madeleine Fuller's lawn, and what all the other guys she'd left so coldly had felt: the devastation, the helplessness, the blindsidedness. She'd pitied them at the time, and now she understood.

The sound of high-pitched laughter pulled her out of her thoughts, and she looked up to see Holly Knox and two other girls breeze through the main doors, oblivious to the rest of the world as they giggled and talked. Isabel stared at Holly as she walked by. Yes, the similarity between them was uncanny.

Mr. Knox followed the girls into the lobby, dressed for golf. "Isabel," he said. "How are you? Beautiful day, isn't it?"

His kindness was so touching that for a moment she thought she might actually break down and cry. "Yeah. It's beautiful." She stood up and walked over to him, then stopped, suddenly feeling too vulnerable to say anything more.

"You okay?" he asked, regarding her with concern.

"I have a driving test in Riverhead. And I need a ride. Can you take me?"

Mr. Knox scratched the side of his head. It was a gamble, but something told her that this man was kind enough to actually consider doing this.

Finally, he dug into his back pocket and produced a ticket stub. "Give this to the valet while I go tell the girls," he said, placing the stub in her palm.

"Thank you," she said, afraid she might cry. "Thank you so much."

"You're very welcome," he said almost formally, and then hurried through the lobby.

Rory sat with Connor on the bench in front of Starbucks, sipping an iced latte and watching the cars inch up and down Main Street. Throngs of people strolled along the sidewalks, looking in the windows of Tiffany and Ralph Lauren. Suddenly, a white stretch limo moved past them in the traffic, as slow and ponderous as a whale.

"It really does get so much more crowded in August," Rory said.

"And it's only gonna get worse," Connor said. "Just wait 'til Labor Day. You don't even want to come near town."

Rory took another sip of her cool drink as Connor put his arm around her. Feeling his touch still sent a thrill through her. "I think we need to talk about some stuff," she said.

"Isabel," Connor said.

"She still isn't talking to me," Rory said, playing with her rope bracelet. "I don't know what to do."

"I told you that they'd just need a little more time," Connor said. "And you know I've told my mom that it makes me really uncomfortable that you're still running around doing errands for them."

"I don't even mind that," Rory said. "I just wish Isabel would talk to me. She won't even look at me if I pass her. And your mom won't, either. She's never even acknowledged that we're going out."

"I told you, don't worry about her," Connor said, squeezing her shoulder. "I wish she weren't such a snob. My dad is fine with it."

"That's good," Rory said. "I'm just bummed about Isabel. The one person who could really vouch for us sort of hates me. But it was sort of my fault. I know I should have told her before."

"We have to stick it out," Connor said. "That's the only way. We're not doing anything wrong, Rory."

He looked over at her, and Rory brushed away the lock of hair that always fell over his forehead. *He's my boyfriend*, she thought. *And if this is what I have to put up with to be with him, then fine.* Still, the sacrifice she'd made for this relationship made her wonder sometimes.

"This'll blow over, I promise," Connor said. "Just don't worry."

Rory leaned her head on his shoulder as a meager breeze cooled her hot skin. "I just wish you didn't have to go away tonight."

"It's just for one night," he said. "And Block Island really isn't that far away."

"It's a ferry ride," Rory said. "You're going over water. I can't even drive there if I need to."

"Just hang out with Fee," Connor said. "And I'll be home before you know it."

He leaned down and kissed her. She snuggled further into his arms, which always surprised her with how safe they made her feel.

"You better get on your way," she said. "I'll miss you."

"I'll miss you more," he said, and kissed her again.

CHAPTER TWENTY-FOUR

Rory banged open the back door of the house, trying to get all the groceries and the dry cleaning into the hall in one trip. After saying good-bye to Connor in town, she'd done a run to Citarella and the East Hampton IGA, and then she'd dropped by Sweetwater's to pick up Mrs. Rule's cleaned clothes, even though she knew she didn't need to get them until tomorrow. It couldn't hurt to do a little bit extra these days, considering the state of things in this house at the moment. One more awkward look from Mrs. Rule and Bianca and she thought that she might finally sneak off to the train station and just go home. She schlepped the bags and the plastic-covered clothes down the hall, watching Trixie bob and weave around her feet. As soon as she dropped this all off in the kitchen, she'd take her out for a run.

She pushed through the kitchen door with the bags and was already at the counter when she noticed Mrs. Rule sitting alone in front of her laptop at the butcher-block table. Her fingers stopped moving as soon as Rory entered.

"Sorry," Rory said. "I'll just put these away real quick."

Mrs. Rule barely looked up from the screen. Rory heaved the bags onto the counter. She needed to get this over with in a hurry.

"And this is your dry cleaning," she said, holding up the hangers. "Would you like me to take it upstairs?"

"No, that's all right. You can just leave it on the chair there," Mrs. Rule said. To Rory's relief, she went back to typing.

Rory opened cabinets and drawers and the refrigerator, putting away the jars of fig chutney and truffle oil and the paper-wrapped free-range organic chicken breasts.

With a sharp snap, Mrs. Rule closed her laptop. "Rory, can I speak to you a moment?" she asked.

Rory stopped what she was doing and slowly turned around. Mrs. Rule brushed away some dust from the table and then examined the tips of her fingers. "Have you had a nice summer here?" she asked with a smile.

"Yes," Rory said. "I've had a great summer."

"Good," Mrs. Rule said, resting her chin on her intertwined fingers. "I'm glad. I'm glad you had a wonderful summer, Rory. It's been good for us to have you, too." She smiled again—that same warm, welcoming smile she'd flashed that first day. "But your mother must miss you terribly," she said. "Along with your friends. And I think it's time that you started making plans to go back to them. After all, it's August now." She paused. "What do you think?"

Rory glanced at the center island and its bowl filled with peaches and plums. "Um, I hadn't really thought of it yet."

"I just think that summers are so . . . important for families," Mrs. Rule went on, stretching out her fingers and examining her nails. "And I just feel terrible depriving your mother of you, in these last few precious weeks before school starts. Do you know what I mean?"

The hair on Rory's arms rose up. "Uh-huh," she said, unable to look away from Mrs. Rule's smile.

"So, I've gone ahead and let your mother know that you'll be coming home tomorrow. And don't you worry about train and bus fare. It's all taken care of."

"You've let her know that?" Rory asked.

"Mmm-hmm," said Mrs. Rule. "I just wrote her an e-mail. Fee gave me her address. I just think it's better for you to be back with your own friends and family, Rory. And you've been working so hard here. You really do need some time to relax."

"This is about Connor, right?" Rory said. "You don't want me dating your son. That's what this is about."

"Oh, now, come on, Rory," she said, smiling, "do you really think I'm *that* vindictive? I'm just looking out for you. We are so appreciative of your help, but we really don't need an errand girl anymore. I want you to have some fun this summer. You shouldn't be worried about my dry cleaning."

Something about the emptiness of the kitchen struck Rory suddenly. "Where's Erica?" she asked.

"Erica's gone," said Mrs. Rule. "Things weren't working out with her," she said. She straightened a jar on the table. "Luckily, chefs are easy to replace."

Rory took a deep breath. "Just so you know, I understand that this is weird for you," she said. "Me and your son. But Connor and I have feelings for each other, and that's why we decided

309

to come out in the open with it when we did. It's not like we're having a secret relationship."

"Well, I have it on good authority that Bianca already found you with a boy in your room this summer," Mrs. Rule said. "And while I wouldn't exactly pin you as the type for that kind of thing, I'm sure you can see how that's *not* the kind of girl I'd like my son to be dating."

Rory began to object and then remembered she couldn't. She couldn't sell Isabel out, not even now. "Something tells me that that isn't the reason you disapprove," Rory said. "Let's just be clear about that. And I think Connor can make his own decisions about the people in his life."

"Possibly, but he is very susceptible to other people's opinions," Mrs. Rule went on. "Especially mine. Anyway, I'm sure that after a few days, he'll understand that this is for the best."

"You can't do this," she said. "You can't kick me out of here without talking to Connor. He's on his way to Block Island now."

"Oh, is he?" Mrs. Rule asked. "I guess I forgot. And cell service is so spotty on the ferry." Mrs. Rule smiled sympathetically. "But don't worry. You've had a wonderful six weeks here, Rory. And can you imagine how awkward it would be, to say the least, if you decided *not* to leave?" Mrs. Rule's eyes were ice-blue as she stared at Rory, unblinking.

"Fine," Rory said. "I'll leave tomorrow."

"*Morning*," Mrs. Rule clarified. "I have you on an eight-thirty jitney. If that works."

"But he won't be back until the late afternoon. I think I'd rather say good-bye to him in person. If *that* works."

"We'll have to play that by ear, won't we?" Mrs. Rule said, barely able to conceal her delight. "Oh, and something else I forgot to mention. I know that we never talked about salary while you were here, but considering how much you've done for us, I've decided that I could rethink all of that. So what would you say to about twenty-five hundred dollars for the whole summer?"

Rory let this sink in. "So you want to pay me to leave," she said evenly.

"I'm paying you for a job well done," Mrs. Rule said. "And I'm sure your mother, when she reads the e-mail, will agree. Naturally I mentioned something about it to her. Just so that she wouldn't think your time here would be completely wasted. Think about it." She checked her watch. "Oh, it's time for my massage. Excuse me." She stood up and slowly walked out toward the dining room.

Rory went straight out to the car. She pulled out her phone with shaky hands and called Connor. It went to voice mail. She stood looking out at the patio and the line of the ocean beyond as the wind fluttered the tips of her hair. She could just leave right now and not even wait for the jitney tomorrow morning. Just drive herself to the jitney and hope that Fee could handle packing up her things. Or she could go back inside and find Fee and tell her, in humiliating detail, what had just happened with Mrs. Rule. Or she could go to the Georgica and try to find Isabel. Only Isabel stood a chance of talking some sense into her mom.

She got back into the car and turned on the engine. The people at the Georgica probably wouldn't let her in, but she was going to have to try.

CHAPTER TWENTY-FIVE

It was almost four o'clock when Mr. Knox turned off the highway at Ocean Road and hooked a left for the shortcut east, going fast enough so that Isabel's temporary driver's license fluttered beside her on the seat. She'd passed—just barely—but passed, nonetheless.

"How do you think you'll celebrate?" Mr. Knox asked. "Do your parents have something planned?"

"Not really," she said. "I don't think they even know that I had the test today."

But Rory knew, she thought. Rory would have remembered, though she probably wouldn't really care at this point.

"I know you go to school in Santa Barbara, but you should come down to LA and spend some time with us," he said. "We'd love to have you."

"That'd be great," she said. "And thank you so much for today. You saved my life."

"It was no bother," he said. "Holly and Krista probably don't even know that I've been gone. And congratulations. This is a big moment. I'm proud of you."

He sounded so much like her father, she thought as his words hung in the air. Actually, she thought, he sounded so much better than her father. Her own father would never have said anything that heartfelt to her. She watched as he fiddled with the satellite radio.

"Why do Holly and I look so much alike?" she asked suddenly.

Mr. Knox glanced over at her. "What?"

"I mean, we look exactly alike," she said. "Like we could be sisters. Haven't you noticed that?"

Mr. Knox drove quietly for a few moments and then pulled over to the side of the road. "I'm not sure how to say this, Isabel," he said, blinking steadily. "But I suppose it's not your fault that your parents haven't told you yet."

"Haven't told me what yet?" she asked. She felt the weird urge to laugh.

"That you're my daughter," he said.

Isabel laughed out loud and then covered her mouth. "What?" she asked.

Mr. Knox's expression was painfully serious. "Back when your parents and I were friendly," he continued, "your mom and I fell in love. At least, it was love for me. But for your mother...It wasn't quite the same thing." He looked out the windshield and shook his head. "I wasn't very successful, and we were both married, and it was just too difficult for us to be together. Your mother did the best thing by you. She really did."

Isabel leaned back against the seat "Please get back on the road," she said. "I need you to be driving right now."

"Uh, sure," he said, and pulled back onto the road.

After a few moments, she said, "Is that why you came back? For my mom?"

"No," he said. "I came back for you."

Isabel stared at him.

"All these years, I've never stopped thinking about you. How you were getting on. Wondering how you've been. I'm sorry that this is how you're finding out."

She watched him ease his way into traffic. A fury that she'd never felt before rose up in her chest, and she had the crazy urge to open the car door and run down the highway, as far away from this place as she could get. And then she felt a balm settle over her, as if someone had just wrapped her up in a thick, warm towel after a dip in the pool. *So this is why,* she thought. *This is why everything has always felt so weird.*

Mr. Knox looked over at her again. "Are you okay?"

"I think so," she said. "My mom could have said something."

"Take it easy on her. She's not nearly as strong as she pretends to be."

"Does my dad know?" It felt odd to say *my dad,* but she didn't know what else to say.

"He does," Mr. Knox said. "Needless to say, he doesn't like me a whole lot."

Or me, Isabel thought. "So that day at the club, when I saw you hanging out by the tennis courts—"

314

"I was trying to speak to your mother alone," he said. "About you. About how I can be in your life."

Isabel tapped her fingers on the car door. "But don't you already have two daughters?" she asked.

"I have three daughters," he corrected her.

They crept forward in the traffic. Isabel picked up the driver's license and held it between her fingers. Right now, it was the only thing in her life that was certain. "So you're a big Hollywood producer now, huh?" she asked, hoping to change the subject.

"I don't know about big, but yes, I've had a couple of successes."

"That's cool." Isabel played with her charm bracelet. "Sometimes I think about being an actress."

Mr. Knox glanced at her. "It's a lot of hard work. A lot of rejection."

"I'm getting used to that," she muttered.

They were coming up on a farm stand by the side of the road. Parked in the lot by the side of the tent was a dark red, weather-beaten Xterra.

"Hey, can you stop here, please?" she asked suddenly.

"Here?"

"Yes."

Mr. Knox pulled into the parking lot. Isabel looked at the car. From the scratches on the back and the black bumper sticker that read AIR AND SPEED SURF SHOP, MONTAUK, NY, she knew that it was his. She'd finally found Mike's family's farm stand.

"Can you wait here for a sec?" she asked.

"Sure," Mr. Knox said. He seemed relieved to have a moment to himself.

She got out of the car.

The stand was actually a large tent that hung over tables displaying crates of heirloom tomatoes, strawberries, peaches, ears of white and yellow corn, and potatoes. Everywhere, people hustled past with brown paper bags, eagerly stuffing them with produce.

She walked up to a woman standing behind one of the tables. She was in her twenties, with dark hair, and she appeared to be helping the actual person in charge, who was an older, skinnier woman who weighed people's bags on a scale and then tallied up their amount with frightening efficiency.

"Excuse me, is Mike Castelloni here?" she asked.

The dark-haired woman looked her up and down. "Just a minute," she said gruffly, and disappeared through a gap in the tent's walls.

Isabel looked around. It was dusty here, and hot, and she realized how thirsty she was. She needed a drink. She walked over to ask someone if there was any water when she saw the wooden sign at the entrance to the tent. MCNULTY'S GREEN MARKET. *McNulty*, she thought. It was a familiar name, though she couldn't place it.

And then an image popped into her brain: of her and Rory standing in her dad's study that hot afternoon, and the feel of the letter between her fingers, the onionskin texture of the paper. The letter written to her dad threatening to sue. From Robert McNulty. The farmer who owned the property her dad had just bought. The farmer who owned this stand. The one where Mike worked with his family.

His family.

She had the feeling that someone was watching her, and as she glanced over her shoulder, she saw Mike walking toward her. Even with a crate of potatoes in his arms, he had the same lazy, sensual gait. As pieces of him came into view—his large brown eyes; his full lips; his narrow, muscular torso, clothed in a plain white undershirt—it was hard not to feel herself fall under the same spell that she had every time he'd driven into the parking lot at Main Beach.

He put the crate on one of the tables and ambled over to her. "Hey," he said, brushing some hair off his forehead. "What are you doing here?"

"I saw your car from the road. Is this your family's stand?"

"Yeah, why?" he said.

"McNulty's your dad?"

"He's my uncle." He looked at her warily, and now she knew.

"So your uncle is the guy who is in this big dispute with my dad?"

He looked down at the ground and then over his shoulder. "Let's go talk over here," he said, nodding toward the parking lot.

She followed him to the lot. "Why didn't you tell me?" she demanded.

"Isabel, just calm down—"

"Don't tell me to calm down!" she yelled. "You break up with me with no explanation, no answer...and now you have this weird connection to my dad?"

317

Mike looked off into the distance and sighed.

"Does this have something to do with why you broke up with me?" she asked.

He pawed at a few stones of gravel with his flip-flop. "It kind of does, yeah," he said.

She folded her arms. *Calm down*, she told herself. *Just breathe.*

"When I figured out who you were, I remembered that my uncle had sold some property to someone named Larry Rule, and it turned out to be your dad," he said. "And I guess there'd been some back-and-forth, some problems with him, some stuff they weren't sure about, and my family wanted me to see if I could get any info."

She took a step back. "Info? On my family?"

Mike threw up his hands. "Yeah."

"So this is why you dated me? To get *info*?"

"No. I was into you. From the beginning. That day on the beach. I thought you were the most beautiful girl I'd ever seen. But when I told my family who I was dating...I mean, what was I supposed to do? This land has been in my mom's family for two hundred and fifty years. They've never sold to anyone. And they had a bad feeling about your dad. And when you said that he was gonna build a huge house on the property, I had to tell them."

"So that's how they knew that," she mused.

"Just hear me out, okay? I didn't know what to do. I really started to care about you, Isabel. The night we slept together for the first time, I knew that I couldn't keep lying to you. That's why I went to Maine. I needed to get away. And when I came back, I told my family that I wasn't going to be telling them anything any longer. But then you invited me to your dad's party, and I knew that I couldn't go. And I knew you'd be upset. And that night I realized I'd just gone too far with it, you know? I couldn't tell you the truth, because I was sure I'd lose you. And I couldn't stay with you and hope that my family would leave me alone. So I did the only thing I could do. I ended it." He finally looked her in the eye. "And I know that you probably don't believe this, and I know that you probably think I'm just saying this right now, but I just want you to know that I did love you. I *do* love you. Still."

Despite her anger and disgust, the urge to throw her arms around him and tell him that she loved him was almost overpowering. But as he ran a hand through his hair and looked at her sideways, fidgeting a little in that sexy way of his, something occurred to her. All the inscrutable mystery and deep pools of passion and barely expressed desire that she'd thought lay within him weren't there at all. All this time, he hadn't been hiding a smoldering well of feeling. He'd just been hiding a secret. Maybe Mike had fallen in love with her, like he said. But he hadn't fallen in love with her enough to tell her the truth. And that was all she needed to know.

He reached out to touch her forearm. "Isabel, I'm sorry," he said. "I love you."

She stepped back. "Don't. It's over."

"But I just told you—"

"You lied to me. I gave you everything, and you lied to me."

He didn't appear to fully understand her words. "But I just told you why I had to."

She felt tears push up from the back of her throat. "I have to go."

"Where are you going?"

"I'm not mad. I get it. But it's just over."

"Isabel—"

She stepped farther away from him and shook her head. "I have to go. Take care of yourself, all right? Have a good rest of the summer." She turned and walked toward the car before he could say anything. She'd walked away from guys before when she'd ended things, and normally she never felt much, except the need to get as far away as possible. Now, as she trudged across the gravel, feeling his eyes on her, she wasn't in the same hurry to be rid of him. She knew that she would always be attracted to him. She would probably always miss him. But she knew that she had no choice this time. All the times before, she could have stayed with the guy if she'd really wanted. But this time, Mike hadn't given her a choice. She couldn't stay. She had to walk away.

When she got to the Knoxes' car, she turned around. "Oh, and thank you," she called out.

"For what?" he asked.

For making me stronger, she wanted to say. But instead, she just shrugged.

"For all of it," she said, and got into the car.

CHAPTER TWENTY-SIX

When Isabel walked into her kitchen, thirsty from the bike ride home from the Georgica, she looked at the woman chopping tomatoes and basil at the center island and asked, "So I guess you're the new chef?"

The woman was tall with blunt-cut red hair to her shoulders, and she walked to Isabel with a slightly quivering, outstretched hand. "I'm Marisa. I just got here."

"Isabel," she replied, shaking the woman's hand. "Welcome."

"Thanks," Marisa said. She glanced at the kitchen cabinets with faint trepidation. "Do you happen to know where I can find the salt?"

"Oh, right in here," Isabel said, opening one of the cabinets. "And we've got all kinds of salt: pink, black, gray, sea...Take your pick."

"Wonderful," Marisa said, clearly grateful for the help.

"Anything else you need, just ask," she said. "And just a word of advice—don't let Bianca rattle you. She just needs to be the boss. Deal with it, and you'll be okay."

A smiled curled around Marisa's lips. "Okay, good to know."

Isabel grabbed a bottle of water from the refrigerator and walked down the hall to Rory's closed door. She took a sip of water and prepared herself. She had no idea what she was going to say, only that she needed to say something.

Gently, she knocked and then opened the door. She looked at the empty, neat room. It was almost six o'clock.

"I think she went out."

Isabel turned around. Lucy Rule walked toward the room in her white silk bathrobe, her blond hair freshly blown out by Frederika and gleaming on her shoulders. "Where have you been?"

"I passed my driver's test," she said.

"Oh, honey, that's wonderful," her mom said, touching her arm. "Congratulations. I'll have to tell Melissa to make something special tomorrow night."

"It's *Marisa*," Isabel said. "So Erica is gone?"

"Your father couldn't stand the food," her mother said, breezing into Rory's room. "Look at the way she makes this bed," she muttered, straightening one of the pillows.

"We really shouldn't be in here," Isabel said.

"Why not?" Mrs. Rule asked, walking into the bathroom. "It is my house."

"Because it's Rory's room."

Mrs. Rule walked out with a stack of towels and a small hair dryer. "It's *my* room."

"What are you doing?" Isabel asked.

"I'm just taking these to be washed," she said. "She won't need them anymore."

"Why not?"

"Because she's leaving," Mrs. Rule said flatly. "Tomorrow morning. We just had a talk about it, and we both agreed that it was time."

"What?" Isabel followed her mother out into the hall. "You both *agreed*?"

"Well, she's been here almost two months. How much longer do you want her here?"

"But...but she's supposed to be with us all summer," Isabel said.

"I thought you were furious with her. Keeping her feelings for Connor from you like that? When you were supposedly such good friends?" Her mom went into the laundry room. "I knew that girl was trouble at the Georgica that day. And now I really know it."

"So she just decided to leave?" Isabel asked, blocking the door.

"Well, when I mentioned the money, I think she warmed up to it."

"The *money*?" Isabel asked. "What are you talking about?"

"I offered to pay her. For the summer. Just as some compensation. I thought you'd be happy to hear that."

"But it was money to leave," Isabel said. "And Connor's not even here. How could you do that?"

"Don't be so dramatic. She's had a wonderful time. And she got what she wanted here. Believe me." She slipped past Isabel and walked into the hall. "We're having some people over for dinner tonight, so would you please put on something nice?"

Isabel charged after her. "I can't believe you would stoop to that. That is *so* disgusting."

"I'm disgusting?"

"Yes. You put on this act like you're so democratic and you're so giving, when really you can't stand being around people who aren't good enough for you. And you can't stand that someone in this family might be happy. For a second."

"What are you talking about?"

"My whole life, you and Dad have been miserable. Do you know how hard that is to watch? All the time? Seeing you guys put on these fake smiles for your friends and then the minute you're alone be at each other's throats? Do you think that's fun for us to watch?"

Her mother's jaw tensed. "What about you? Do you think it's easy for us to have you as a daughter?"

"When you say *us*, who do you mean?"

"Excuse me?"

"Who's my father—really? Dad or Mr. Knox?"

Her mom looked astonished.

"I saw Holly," she said. "She looks just like me. Same hair, same eyes, same walk. And I spoke to Mr. Knox. He told me that he's my dad. He told me, Mom."

Mrs. Rule smoothed a curl out of her face. "Isabel—"

"Just admit it."

Her mother looked down and slowly nodded.

"How could you keep that from me, my whole life?" she exploded. "How could you do something so psycho?"

"What was I supposed to do?" her mom asked. "Tell you that your real father lives three thousand miles away and hasn't seen you since you were born? A man I haven't seen in fifteen years? Was that what I was supposed to do?"

"Yes! You should have told me!"

Isabel ran to the back stairs and took them two at a time. She got to her room and slammed the door, but her mom rushed in, right on her heels.

"Okay, hear me out, all right?" her mom yelled. "You don't know anything of what happened."

"How could I?" Isabel yelled.

"I was very, very young when I got married," her mom said, "and soon after Gregory was born, I knew that your father and I were a mistake. But there I was, a young mother, living on Park Avenue, married to a handsome man who *wasn't* just living off of my money, like the rest of my friends' husbands were. So I stayed. And then I met Peter. The four of us went on trips, we went to Le Cirque, we had parties. But there was always something there between Peter and me. He understood me in a way that your father never had. And then one night—"

Isabel held up her hand. "Please. Don't even say it."

"I loved him so much. There was nothing I could do about it. And when I found out I was pregnant with you, I almost ran away with him."

Isabel wanted to fling herself on her bed and bury her head in the pillows. But she stood her ground. "Go on," she said stoically.

"But I couldn't do it," her mom said. "I just couldn't bring myself to do it. The kids were just too young. And your father would have taken everything. We had no prenup, nothing."

"What about Dad?" she asked dully, not looking at her mother. "Did he know?"

"Not at first. It took a little while. But then, eventually, he asked me. He could tell that you didn't look anything like him."

"No wonder," Isabel said, thinking about her dad.

"By then, Peter and Michelle had moved to Los Angeles. He'd had to move, to save his marriage. His wife caught on, eventually. He knew about you, though. I made sure to tell him before he left."

"So this is why Dad has no idea how to talk to me," Isabel said.

"I think you've had a good father, Isabel. I do." Her mother came to stand beside the bed. "He loves you."

"No, he doesn't. He treats me like I'm a freak."

"It's *me* he doesn't love," her mother said. "And I suppose I can't exactly blame him for that." Isabel felt her mom cautiously begin to stroke her hair.

"I just wish you'd told me," Isabel said. "It just feels really selfish of you both not to tell me this."

"I know," her mom said. "I'm sorry. I really did want to tell you."

Isabel sat up and wiped away the tears that had begun to stream down her face. "Then I want you to do something for me. I want you to stop being so hard on Rory and Connor."

"What does that have to do with anything?" her mom asked.

"Rory makes him happy. I think she's the first girl who ever really has. So don't kick her out. At least don't kick her out just because you don't like her."

Her mom tightened the sash of her robe. "Do you know that Bianca caught her with a boy in her room the first week she was here?"

"That was a boy *I* was trying to sneak in. Rory had nothing to do with it."

Her mom blinked.

"That was *my* boyfriend. Or, my *ex*-boyfriend. I snuck him in and didn't know it was Rory's room. Rory had no idea what that was all about. And then she covered for me. She took the blame. When it wasn't even her fault. What person does that if they're not kind of awesome?"

Mrs. Rule thought about this. "Well, maybe I have been a little hasty."

"And Mom, even if she did sneak a boy into her room, what does that make her? A slut? Please. I've done so much worse. And so have you."

"Isabel," her mom said, pointing a finger. "I'd like everything I told you to stay between us for the time being. The others will find out later, when they have to. When I've decided what to do. Can I count on you to keep your mouth shut?"

"On one condition," Isabel said. "That Rory can come back."

"Fine," her mom said after a moment. "She can come back. She can stay. And what's going on with that boy?"

"Nothing," Isabel said. "It's over. Way over."

Her mom put her hand to her chest. "Oh, thank god," she said. "Sorry. I just…Well, you can't blame me for being a little concerned. I mean, a surfer, from the North Fork, who lives in Montauk…"

Isabel sighed. "I'm going to be just fine. No matter what. You know that, right?"

Her mother nodded. "I know."

"I never want you to keep anything like that from me again. Okay? Life is hard enough."

"Okay," her mom said. She reached out to hug Isabel, who submitted to it quietly, passively, hardly moving.

Felipe had been right that evening at the beginning of the summer, she thought. This house held more secrets than she'd ever guessed. All this time, she'd felt like she was the thing that didn't belong here. She'd felt that she was the freak, the screwup, the smear on the family name. But the seeds had already been planted for trouble before she'd even been born. She hadn't done anything wrong. Her parents had.

Isabel broke away from her mom's hug and got up from the bed. "I'm gonna go find Rory. And for the rest of the summer, she doesn't work for us anymore. She's a guest, just like anyone else. Agreed?"

Her mom slowly nodded. "I'll have Fee put the guest towels back in her room."

Isabel sighed as she walked to the door. Her mom had just confessed her deepest, darkest secret, but she'd always prefer to stay on the surface of things.

CHAPTER TWENTY-SEVEN

Rory sat double-parked on Main Street, watching for any police cars in the rearview mirror as she spoke on her cell. "I want a seat on the first one out," she said. "Whatever is the next jitney. From East Hampton to midtown Manhattan."

"All-righty," came the breezy, corporate-trained female voice on the other end. "Okay, there's a jitney leaving from East Hampton in fifteen minutes, at six thirty, with one seat left. Shall I book it?"

Rory took a deep breath. She could just park the Prius in the parking lot and send a text to Fee to pick up the car later. "Yes, please."

"One-way?"

"Yes."

Rory drummed her fingers on the steering wheel as the clerk put her on hold. She was doing the right thing. After she drove around the back roads of East Hampton for an hour, her gut had finally beaten her heart into submission. The creepiness of Mrs. Rule's voice still clung to her like a bad cologne. *They don't want you here anymore,* she thought. *Connor will understand. He'll come see you. But you have to leave. Now.*

"Okay," said the jitney clerk as she clicked back on the line. "You're all set. The stop is across from the Palm restaurant on Main Street."

"I know, I'm looking right at it," Rory said.

"Be there in the next ten minutes to be sure you get on board," the clerk said.

"Great. Thank you." Rory clicked off, relieved. Now for the hard part. She had to write Connor a text. Isabel clearly didn't care if she stayed or went. But Connor would be upset. She had no idea what to say. She began to type:

Hey, can't get you on cell. Your mom has asked me to leave.
I think it's best that I go ASAP. Call me when you get back.

She deliberated over the next line.

I love you.

Yes, she would say it first. Even Isabel had broken that particular rule, and she'd survived it. Rory had meant to tell her how proud she was of her for that, and for the way she'd risked being open with Mike from the start, but it was too late. She should have told her about Connor. Her hesitation to tell her was exactly the reason why she should have. They weren't ever going to be friends, especially now. It was amazing how accurate first impressions remained, even after you got to know someone.

She hit send on the text and then dropped her phone in her bag and turned off the ringer. Otherwise she'd be subconsciously waiting for a call that wouldn't come for hours anyway. Then she backed the Prius up into the public parking lot. She got out and left the keys behind the back wheel. It was East Hampton, she thought. Nobody was going to steal a Prius.

A crowd had already started to form in front of the green curb that was the East Hampton jitney stop, and attractive people loitered attractively with their designer duffel bags, their cell phones pressed to their ears. She thought of the people she'd seen streaming off the train the first day. It would be good to get home, she realized. There she wouldn't have to worry about what kind of sandals she had on or how she wore her hair. She could finally be herself.

She was about to dig around in her bag for her book when she saw a black Porsche convertible glide down the street. It was going east, but as soon as it passed Rory, it stopped, veered into an illegal U-turn, and careened to a stop in front of the crowd. Isabel pulled off her aviators and waved at her from behind the wheel. "Hey! Where the hell are you going?"

The jitney-goers looked at Rory with annoyed curiosity.

Rory walked over to the car and crouched down to see Isabel behind the wheel, grinning madly.

"What are you doing?" Rory asked.

"I passed the test," Isabel said. "I got my license. What are you doing?"

"I'm leaving," she said. "Your mom asked me to."

"Get in the car," Isabel said abruptly. "She changed her mind."

"What do you mean?"

"She doesn't want you to go," Isabel said. "I just spoke to her. Get your ass in the car."

"I just bought a fifty-dollar ticket home," Rory said.

"So I'll reimburse you," Isabel said. "Get in the goddamn car!"

Not sure what else to do, Rory opened the car door and got inside.

Isabel pulled back into traffic. "You can't leave my brother like this," she said. "It'll kill him. And then he'll kill me."

"So now you care about what happens with me and your brother?" Rory asked. "And slow down."

"I'm sorry I acted like such a bitch to you," Isabel said. "I think I was just jumping to the worst conclusions. That you were using me to get to Connor."

"You know that's ridiculous," Rory said. "Right? Totally ridiculous."

"Well, then, why didn't you tell me about him?" Isabel asked.

"Because I wasn't sure you'd think I'd be good enough for him."

Isabel pulled over to the side of the road, in front of the cemetery. "Hey, listen to me," Isabel said, taking Rory's hand. "You're the best thing that's ever happened in my dumb brother's life. I'm sorry if I didn't make you feel that way."

"It's okay," Rory said.

"No, I'm serious. And you're the best thing that's happened

to me. The best friend I've ever had. And you deserved more from me than the cold shoulder all this time."

Rory smiled.

"I'm sorry, Ror." Isabel leaned over and hugged her.

Rory felt Isabel squeeze her ribs. "That's okay."

"So are we friends again?" Isabel's eyes were bright and happy, but slightly moist from tears.

"Sure," Rory said.

"Good." Isabel pulled back onto the road. "Oh, and one more thing. Mr. Knox is my real dad."

"Are you kidding?" Rory asked.

"He told me today. He's the one who took me to my test. It explains a lot. But I can't tell anyone. My mom made me promise not to say anything."

"Jesus," Rory said. "Are you okay?"

"I think I will be," Isabel said. "One day. It's probably going to take me the next year to even process it all. But at least I understand so many things now. So many more things make sense." She turned onto Lily Pond Lane and sped down the center of the empty street. "Damn, this car feels good to drive," she said.

"Just don't get us killed, okay?" Rory asked, as kindly as she could.

LABOR DAY WEEKEND

They sat on the blanket in almost the exact same spot where they'd watched the fireworks almost two months before, and this time, Connor sat behind her with his arms around her as she looked out at the water. The sun had set behind them, and the sky was a perfect blend of gray, gold, and pink.

"How're you doing?" Connor asked in her ear. "Everything good?"

"I can't believe this is my last night," she said. "It's too weird."

"It's your last night before we go back to the city," he said. "If you play your cards right, I might even be able to let you sleep in my room tomorrow."

She leaned her head against his shoulder. "California's so far away."

"I've already got you a ticket," he said. "You'll be there at the end of September."

"I can't wait," she said.

"Um, excuse me!" Isabel said, trudging over to them across the sand, an open bottle of Cristal dangling from her hand and a large paper bag in the other. "No making out in front of me, okay?"

Rory and Connor laughed as she flopped down on the blanket next to them. "I had no idea you were so uptight," Rory said.

Connor opened the paper bag and took out the items that Marisa had packed for their dinner picnic. "Yum. Fried chicken. Potato salad. Coleslaw. This is awesome."

"Hey, let's make a toast first," Isabel said, pulling out the champagne flutes that she'd snuck into the bag. She poured them each a glass of champagne and handed Rory and Connor their glasses.

"What are we toasting?" Rory asked.

"To Connor," said Isabel, "for finally quitting the swim team."

She held up her flute as Connor rolled his eyes.

"Dad will probably never get over it," he said.

"Congratulations," Isabel said. "And to me, for learning how to drive."

"And not getting a speeding ticket yet," Rory wisecracked.

"I second that," said Connor.

"And to Rory McShane," Isabel said. "Amazing driver. Wonderful friend. Terrible temper."

Rory laughed.

"This summer would not have been the same without you. And I'm sure my brother feels the same way," Isabel said with a grin.

"Maybe just a little bit," Connor said, kissing Rory on the side of her face.

"But seriously, I don't know what I'm going to do without you this year. Who's going to yell at me to slow down? Who's going to listen to me talk about guys? Who's not going to judge me when I do stupid stuff?"

"And to you guys," Rory said, holding up her glass. "I came here not knowing anyone or anything. And now I have two new best friends." She felt herself getting a little teary. "Who are both going off to California and deserting me."

Connor squeezed her. "You'll be there so soon."

"And then you're coming to visit me, right?" Isabel said.

"Absolutely," Rory said.

"So I got you a little something," Isabel said. "Just a little something so that you'll never forget us." She reached down into the paper bag and pulled out a small box. She handed it to Rory. "Go on. Open it."

"You sure you want me to do it here?" Rory asked.

"Uh-huh," Isabel said. "Go for it."

Rory opened the box to see a gold charm bracelet lying inside. She pulled it out and let it dangle from her hand. Two charms— an *I* and an *R*—shone in the light.

"As much as I love your rope bracelets," Isabel said, "I thought this might be an improvement."

"It's gorgeous," Rory said, slipping it on.

"And I got myself the same one." Isabel held up her wrist so Rory could see the gold *R*.

"I've had the most incredible summer," Rory said. "Thank you for having me, you guys. I'll never forget being here."

"Then you'll just have to come back," said Isabel. "Next summer."

Rory looked at Connor. "Really?"

"Definitely," he said.

Rory nodded. "Okay, then."

"You swear it?" Isabel asked.

Rory smiled. "I swear."

ACKNOWLEDGMENTS

Enormous thanks go to Becka Oliver once again for her supreme guidance, support, and friendship. My editor, Elizabeth Bewley, believed in this book from the start, gave me incisive notes all along the way, and seemed to know these characters better than I did at certain points. Thank you, Elizabeth. Cindy Eagan's wholehearted enthusiasm and good humor kept me on course, as always. Tracy Shaw, cover whiz, designed a beautiful image yet again. And big thanks to Christine Ma, copy editor extraordinaire, for getting me clear on exactly what (and where) I was talking about in the Hamptons.

Henry and Peggy Schleiff provided warm hospitality, and a lot of laughs, out in Water Mill. Blake Davis and Mariah Mitchell Davis answered my e-mailed questions within minutes. Cassidy Catanzaro responded to every text about Stillwater and Sussex County with amazing detail. Sarah Mlynowski and Courtney Sheinmel welcomed me into the hallowed halls of their writing lounge, not to mention the Twitterhood of the Butt-Lifting Pajants.

And to my family...Mom and Dad, thank you for being so wonderfully supportive of me while I worked on this book in the early stages. And JJ, thank you for everything. You are the best reader, best friend, and best sister anyone could ask for.

BEACHES. BONFIRES. BOYS.
IT'S SUMMERTIME IN THE HAMPTONS.

JOANNA PHILBIN

SINCE
last
Summer

a novel

Turn the page for a sneak peek of *Since Last Summer*,
the companion novel to *Rules of Summer*.

AVAILABLE JUNE 2014

CHAPTER ONE

She almost missed the sign, but Rory McShane made the turn at the very last second, guiding her uncle's sputtering Honda onto the smooth blacktop of Lily Pond Lane. The street was just as quiet and still as she remembered it. The midday sun filtered in through the canopy of tree branches overhead. A jogger ran gracefully on the other side of the street. She turned down the radio and lifted her hands from the steering wheel. Her palms were slick with sweat.

Relax, she thought. *Everything is going to be great.*

But there was no getting around it: Eleven weeks was a very long time. A record for them, in fact. They'd talked on the phone almost every day, and Skyped and texted and IM'd countless times, but she and Connor Rule hadn't been face-to-face since her last trip to LA in March, and from the moment she'd crossed out of New Jersey, doubts had begun to overwhelm her. What if they didn't know what to say to each other? What if things were awkward? What if she got to the house and realized that she was actually still the errand girl?

That's not *going to happen*, she reminded herself. For ten months, she and Connor Rule had managed to be in a happy, healthy, drama-free relationship, all while living on opposite sides of the country. Eleven weeks apart wasn't going to change anything. All those years of being single had screwed up her hold on reality, she thought. They'd been looking forward to this all year. East Hampton was where they'd met and fallen in love, after all. Everything was going to be just fine.

She turned into the break in the hedges and pulled up in front of the iron gates. After she typed the code Connor had given her into the silver intercom box, the gates swung open. She pressed the gas, rounded the turn, and began driving down the gravel path, past the Rules' immense front lawn.

The house, perched on a slight hill above the lawn, was still intimidating from a distance. But as she got closer and the faded silvery-gray shingles and bright white paint of the windows came into view, she remembered how familiar the Rules' mansion had become to her last summer. She pulled up to the bank of garages. She left her purse on the passenger seat and got out of the car. The sea air was bracing. In the distance, she could hear the roll of waves and the squawk of seagulls. The breeze whipped up her dark curls, unsticking them from the nape of her neck. She was finally here.

You're still coming out for the summer, right?? Isabel had texted Rory a few months ago. *Yes? I hope? My bro hasn't done anything to piss you off?*

Wouldn't matter if he had, Rory had texted back. *You're the one who invited me, remember?*

She walked around to the trunk of the car and unlocked it. She heard the back door of the house open with a creak.

"Finally," a voice said. "I almost sent a helicopter to come get you."

Connor stepped out of the house and walked through the rose garden, sunlight glinting off his blond hair.

"I didn't want to speed," she said, her heart pounding rapidly.

"I would have paid the ticket," he said, coming toward her.

She walked into his arms and tilted up her head to kiss him. As their lips touched, a jolt of electricity bounced around her rib cage, shot through her stomach, and made the backs of her knees loose and light. Instant bliss.

"So that was a long time," he said, looking down at her when they were done.

"Eleven weeks," she said. "And three days."

"And every one of them sucked," he said with a smile.

"Tell me about it." She leaned in to kiss him one more time.

Despite her nerves, it felt good to be back on familiar ground. The first time she'd visited Connor at USC had been a little bit of a shock. Up until then, she'd only known him as Connor Rule, Isabel's sweet, self-effacing, gorgeous brother. But at USC, he was CONNOR RULE. They couldn't walk around for five minutes before some guy passed and gave him a silent bro-shake, or some girl smiled shyly and said "Hey, Connor" under her breath. His years on the swim team had made him a bit of a celebrity. And his friendliness and golden-boy looks didn't hurt, either. Even his professors seemed to adore him. "Mr. Rule, would you like to comment on this?" was a common question whenever Rory sat in on one of his classes.

Around his friends, Connor was even more in demand. And his friends were, well, interesting. The girls were all skinny and tan and wore blousy silk tops with extrawide armholes so that people could see their lacy bras underneath. The guys drove sleek black BMWs with tinted windows and flashed gold credit cards at the campus snack bar. Sitting with them at a meal could send her self-esteem into a tailspin, as they discussed their White House internships or their summer jobs at Goldman Sachs or their plans to teach English in Uganda. *What is he doing with me?* she'd asked herself, more than a few times. *Me, a high school senior who doesn't even have her own car?*

Fortunately, Connor didn't seem to be thinking that. He always introduced her as his "ultra-high-achieving girlfriend" who made him "feel like a slacker." When she'd gotten in to Stanford early, he bragged about it to everyone they came across. But it was never enough to put her at ease. Going home to New Jersey was always a relief. Back in Stillwater, she could still be Connor's girlfriend without having to fit into his college world. It was kind of the ideal situation, when she thought about it.

"It's good to see you," she said, pressing her face against his neck and breathing in his smell of soap, laundry detergent, and shaving foam.

"How'd the speech go?" he asked. "Did you do that line at the end about the promise of a new generation?"

"No. It was corny."

"Come on! That was the best part!" he said.

"*You* thought it was the best part," she said. "Everyone else told me to cut it."

"Okay, fine, I'll take your word for it. I wish you'd let me come."

"To sit in my school gym with my mom and her tattooed boyfriend?" She took his hand. "I don't think so. It was just a graduation."

"And you were *just* the valedictorian," he said with a smile. He kissed her again.

"So," she asked when they'd finished kissing, "how does it feel to be home?"

"Oh, you know," he said, looking at the house over his shoulder. "This place never changes." He stepped in front of her and grabbed her suitcase out of the trunk. "Come on," he said. "Let's go inside."

After hoisting her duffel over her shoulder, she followed Connor over the paving stones and through the rose garden, with its abundant red, pink, and fuchsia blooms. She lifted her wrist to look at the gold charm bracelet, the one Isabel had given her at the end of last summer. The *I* and *R* charms shone in the sun. "Isabel isn't here yet, is she?" Rory asked.

"Nah, she's coming tomorrow with Fee," Connor said over his shoulder. "She's flying back from California today."

Inside the house, a ball of barking white fluff charged toward her down the hall.

"Trixie!" Rory said.

Trixie circled Rory's legs, trying to stand on her tiny back feet.

"Hi, sweetie pie! I've missed you!" Rory put down her bag and crouched to pet Trixie on the head.

The dog responded with a few sharp, happy barks. When Rory stood back up, Trixie trotted behind them down the hall.

"I think she wants you to take her to the beach," he said.

"Only if Bianca isn't here."

"I told you," he said over his shoulder. "My mom fired her."

"I know. But you didn't tell me why." Bianca, Mrs. Rule's house manager, had been horrible to Rory last summer, but Rory had assumed Mrs. Rule was happy with how she ran things.

"No clue," Connor said. "I try not to get involved with any of that domestic stuff." He stopped in front of the door to her old room. "Okay. The sleeping arrangements. You can have your old room again. *Or*"—he gave her a sly look—"you can be in my room."

"Are you kidding? What about your mom?"

Connor shrugged. "She likes you now."

"I'll just be in here again, if that's okay," she said, opening the door.

She walked into the cream-and-blue-colored guest room and looked around with a smile. She'd longed for the quiet luxury of this room so many times over the past year. The king bed with its downy soft mattress, the comfy club chairs, the elegant writing desk, the nautical map of Long Island hanging over the headboard—it all looked exactly the same. The only changes were the more current hardcover novels stacked on the night-stands and a vase of white-and-pink peonies on the desk.

"It's so pretty in here," Rory said. "And I love peonies." She dropped her bag on the rug and walked over to the flowers. Trixie was circling her feet, eager to be petted. "They're beautiful," she said, bending down. "But not as beautiful as this little dog right here."

"*You're* beautiful," Connor said, crouching behind her and kissing her on the neck.

She turned toward him and kissed him on the lips. He pressed her close to him and slowly pulled her down to the floor.

"Wait," she murmured. "Are we alone?"

"Pretty much," he replied, still kissing her.

The sound of approaching footsteps down the hall made them both shoot to their feet.

"Rory, is that you?" said a familiar voice. "May I come in?"

"Uh, sure, Mom," Connor muttered, and Mrs. Rule strode into the room.

Once again Rory was struck by how such a tiny, slim woman could exert the presence of a person twice her size. Especially because Mrs. Rule seemed to have gotten even tinier and slimmer since last summer. Her roomy boatneck sweater hinted at a significantly narrower chest, and her skinny jeans showed off legs that looked like toothpicks. Rory wondered if she'd been sick. But Mrs. Rule's hair was fuller and lusher than ever. It fell in loose, beachy waves past her shoulders.

"Rory," she said, coming straight toward her. "You're here." She grasped Rory's hand and leaned in to give her an air-kiss on the cheek. "You didn't need to bring your own car. We could have found one for you here. I think the Mercedes is probably free—"

"Oh, that's okay," Rory said. "I didn't mind driving. And thanks for having me again. It's really good to be back."

Mrs. Rule smiled. "Well, we're all very happy you chose to come back. Especially Connor." She looked approvingly at her son. "Steve didn't come back. He's decided to teach tennis down in Palm Beach. As if anyone would want to be *there* for the summer." Mrs. Rule gave a dismissive shrug. "And if there's anything you need—more hangers, a shoe tree—just let me know." Mrs. Rule's gaze lingered on Rory's duffel bag on the floor. "When do you start your job?"

"You mean my internship? I start Monday."

"What is it called?" Mrs. Rule asked. "The East End Festival?"

"That's right," Rory said. "It's sort of a film festival slash music festival. Like South by Southwest."

"South by South...what?" Mrs. Rule asked.

"Hey, Mom," Connor broke in. "Rory also got into Princeton. But she decided on Stanford."

"Really?" Mrs. Rule took a slight step backward. "That's wonderful."

"Thank you," said Rory.

"Stanford is an excellent school," said Mrs. Rule. "But I know the tuition is pretty steep."

"They gave me a really nice package," Rory said.

"Rory was class valedictorian," Connor added.

"Oh," said Mrs. Rule. Her steel-blue eyes seemed to peer right into Rory's soul. "How nice."

She knows, Rory thought. *She knows that I know.*

The secret about Mrs. Rule and Isabel's real father had gnawed at Rory all year. It felt a little unethical—and icky—to know something so shocking about Connor's family that even he didn't know. How did you tell your boyfriend that his mom had been in love with another man eighteen years ago and that his younger sister was actually his half sister? Was that even something you *did* tell your boyfriend? The easy solution had been to push it to the back of her mind and spend the school year making sure it stayed there. After all, she reasoned, it wasn't her place to say anything. Especially since Isabel had sworn her to secrecy. But now, being back under the Rules' roof, it seemed inevitable that Connor would find out. And when he did, Rory was going to have to pretend she didn't know. Just thinking about that gave her a stomachache.

Mrs. Rule continued to give Rory a penetrating stare for a few more seconds, and then she turned to Connor.

"So, we're having some people over for dinner tonight," she said. "I hope you two can join us? Sloane and Gregory will be there, too."

Phew, Rory thought. She was in the clear.

"Sure," Connor said.

"Do you need any help?" Rory asked before she could stop herself. "I mean, not with serving or anything but—"

Mrs. Rule smiled and gave Rory's arm a little pat. "Don't be silly. You're our guest now. You relax and have fun." She turned back to Connor. "How about some Ping-Pong before dinner? Six thirty?"

"Great," Connor said.

"Wonderful." She turned to Rory. "Once you're all unpacked, you should go down to the pool. It's a lovely day. Best not to let it go to waste." Mrs. Rule eyed Rory's bag one more time. "Come on, Trixie. Let's go."

Trixie gave Rory one last hungry glance and then followed Mrs. Rule out of the room.

"That was the longest conversation I've had with your mom since last summer," Rory said.

"What about Christmas?" Connor asked.

"Asking me to pass the sweet potatoes doesn't count," she said. She reached into her suitcase and pulled out a small wrapped box. "So I know I'm a little bit late with this, but I wanted to give it to you in person."

"Ror," Connor said gently. "I told you no birthday gifts."

"But you got *me* something in March," she said.

"That's different. You're my girlfriend." He kissed her again on the cheek.

"Oh, just take it," she said, handing him the present.

She held her breath as he ripped open the paper and then opened the small box. "Wow." He removed the silver Swiss Army knife and held it up to the light. "This is cool."

"Here, look," she said with relief, turning it so he could see the inscription on the underside. RM+CR.

"Very old school," he teased. "I like it."

"Do you really?"

"No. I *love* it." He kissed her. "I'm coming up north every single weekend next year."

"Oh, really," she said. "Is that a threat?"

"It's a fact," he said, wrapping his arms around her. "I may even have to get a little place up there. Palo Alto, here I come."

His lips met hers again, and this time Rory felt a surge of need for him. Normally she had to be around Connor for at least a couple of days before she could be this unselfconscious. Now she didn't care. She ran her hands over his shoulders and down his back. He pulled away from her and turned to close the open door.

"But what if your mom comes back?" Rory asked.

"You're a guest here," he said, shutting the door with a grin. "You're going to have to get used to having a little privacy."

The door shut with a click.

Isabel drummed her nails on the arm rest and stared out the plastic window at the empty blue sky. Somewhere below the cloud cover was the Sierra Nevada mountain range. Isabel grabbed hold of her white wine and took another long sip. The only good thing right now about going home was flying first class, even if the seats on this plane weren't as big and roomy as she would have liked.

"Do you mind?" asked the man next to her. He was a businessman in his forties. Up until this moment he had been hard at work, pounding the keys of a tiny laptop. The screen was filled with numbers.

"Sorry," she said.

He eyed her wine.

"I'm a nervous flier," she explained. "I'm twenty-one," she added.

The man shrugged and went back to pounding his keyboard.

Isabel turned back to the window and constructed another sentence in the e-mail she planned to write to Mr. Knox. *Flight was uneventful. Got kind of buzzed on plane. Thought a lot about what you said at dinner. Determined to be positive.*

Maybe it was a lame idea to write so soon, and about such

trivial stuff. But Mr. Knox—Peter, he always kept telling her to call him Peter—had insisted.

"I know you're going to be far away from now on, but I still want to be in touch," he had said to her the night before in the crowded Beverly Hills restaurant. "Send me an e-mail when you get home. Let me know how it's going."

"I can tell you right now how it's going," Isabel said, poking at her penne pomodoro. "Terribly. You sure there's no way I can just stay with you for the summer?"

Peter gave her a pained smile. "I would love that, but Michelle wouldn't be comfortable, and Holly and Krista, well..."

"That's okay," Isabel broke in. "I get it. Your family doesn't know—my family doesn't know."

"I'm just waiting for your parents to take the lead with this, Isabel," he said, giving her a gentle smile. "Out of respect for your mom."

A waiter came by to clear their plates.

"So, what do you have planned for the summer?" he asked, changing the subject. "Anything fun?"

"Rory will be there," Isabel answered. "But she's dating Connor, so..."

"So what?" Mr. Knox asked, sipping from his glass of red wine.

"So I don't know. It's different. I mean, we're still friends totally separate from that. And I'm happy for them. I really am. But when your friend is dating your brother..." She let her voice trail off. She was pretty sure Mr. Knox wouldn't know what she was talking about if she'd finished the sentence. "Anyway, I have no interest in hanging out at the Georgica. So I'm not sure. I think I'll try to go into the city as much as possible. Get ready for NYU in the fall."

"That's exactly right. It's your last summer before college. Have fun. Do something you'll never forget. If I could tell you how many times I wish I'd had more fun when I was your age—"

"Dessert?" the waiter asked. His face was Hollywood actor–handsome, with the requisite chiseled features and light blue eyes, but there was a streak of edge to him. A definite bad boy. Last year he would have been exactly Isabel's type: hot, older, dangerous.

"Sure," said Mr. Knox. "What do you recommend?"

"Well, the tiramisu is very good."

"I'll have some," Isabel said, smiling at him.

"Wonderful," the waiter said, grinning at her. He took their menus away and gave her a pointed, but discreet, smile.

"If I can ask you one favor," Mr. Knox said, folding his hands on the table, the candlelight flickering across his face. "Go easy on your mom this summer."

Isabel snorted.

"I know how much she loves you."

"Please," Isabel muttered. "If she loved me, she would have told me the truth herself. And she'd let my brother and sister in on this. Instead of making me the lucky one."

"We all come to things in our own time," Mr. Knox said as he leaned back in his chair and patted his stomach. "Be patient with her. And if you have to, vent to me. I won't say a word."

"Thanks for being so cool this year," Isabel said. "Coming

up to school to visit me, taking me out to dinner down here, the e-mails…It's all been really nice of you."

"I'm your father," he said. "Better late than never, right?" He stood up. "I'll be right back." He left to go to the men's room, and a moment later the waiter returned with the tiramisu.

"Here you go," he said. "Will there be anything else?"

"I think just the check," she said.

The waiter cocked his head and smiled at her. "I get off in an hour if you want to hang out," he said. "We could go get a drink."

It was tempting. The past nine months had been extremely quiet. All by choice, of course. Nobody at school had seemed that appealing. And her last relationship had been a disaster.

But as she looked at this guy now, something told her to stay away from him. *Too dangerous. And too good-looking.* If she'd learned anything last summer, it was to stay away from both of those things. "Maybe some other time," she said.

The waiter had seemed surprised. "Enjoy," he'd said, giving her a smile that promised a rain check on his invitation, if she wanted it.

"Excuse me?" she said to the flight attendant walking by with bottles of wine. "I'll have another, please," she said, holding up her cup.

The attendant tipped more white wine into it.

Beside her, the businessman subtly shook his head with disapproval.

"If you were going home to my house for the summer," Isabel said, "you'd get hammered, too."

B0B644

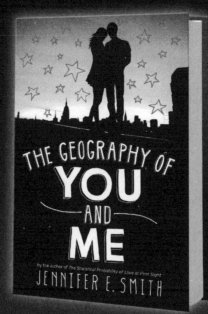